As Sonia worked on Alastair's account books, she felt ill. For she found huge debts amounting to hundreds of thousands of pounds. Some belonged to his father, some were Alastair's—gambling debts, mortgages, and jewels sent to a Mrs. Daphne Porter. Also, the rent of an apartment for Mrs. Porter!

She was dazed, bewildered. It was true then. He had married her for her money.

Suddenly a sound at the door interrupted her. Alastair had come in and was striding toward her, his tanned face dark with anger.

"What are you doing? What have you found there?" Blood had come up into his face and his blue eyes were dark with fury.

She took a deep furious breath. "You asked me to pay your bills for you—the rent for Mrs. Porter's flat is two months behind!"

"I didn't mean for you to see these, Sonia, really—"

"No? It was a secret? The fact that you were so deeply in debt, you had to marry a Jewess for her money?"

The words were out between them, the hateful words that could not be recalled. . . .

Star
Sapphire

REBECCA DANTON

FAWCETT CREST • NEW YORK

STAR SAPPHIRE

Published by Fawcett Crest Books, a unit of CBS Publications,
the Consumer Publishing Division of CBS Inc.

Copyright © 1979 by Rebecca Danton

ISBN: 0-449-23901-2

Printed in the United States of America

10 9 8 7 6 5 4 3 2 1

Chapter
1

•••••••••••••••••••••••••••••••

SONIA gazed in excited wonder, close to tears, at the magnificent chandeliers in the ballroom, lighting the polished floor, glinting off the paneled mirrors on the walls, glistening on the jewels and waving fans of the elaborately gowned ladies and gentlemen. Often, passing in her carriage, returning from a concert or a play, as she heard the music, saw the torches blazing, she had wondered how these houses looked inside. Now she was here, actually inside the home of a duke, a guest at his ball.

Her uncle's head bent toward her affectionately, his gray beard quivering. "Do you like it, my dear? Is it not grand? Is the drink to your liking?"

"Oh, Uncle Meyer," she breathed. "It is the most splendid place in the world!"

He smiled a little sadly, his dimming eyes shrewd. "No, not the most splendid, but it is very grand. The Prince of Wales himself comes here at times."

"Oh, really? The prince himself?" Her gray eyes sparkled

with unusual merriment and pleasure. She was stirred to such excitement, and indeed had been since the invitations had arrived. She fairly trembled inside, and she could not drink the cold punch. She was afraid she would be sick.

The music lilted, she watched the couples form into patterns, bow gracefully, move to the country dances. She noted the splendid ladies, the fine gentlemen. They stared curiously at her, some boldly. She wondered how she looked to them.

Outwardly, she must look much as they did. She had worn a simple white silk brocade of her own design, and with it the set of diamonds and sapphires on the silver filigree chain which she had completed recently. In her small ears were sapphire studs, and on one finger an immense sapphire ring. The white and silver set off her dark curly hair and luminous gray eyes. Leah, her abigail, had set her hair in a high pile with long curls to her neck. Some stray tendrils drifted about her ears, and she brushed them back nervously.

A gentleman came up, bowed to them, spoke in lisping French. Meyer Goldfine bowed to him, introduced him to Sonia.

"Monsieur Frery," he said, "my niece, Miss Sonia Goldfine."

The Frenchman bowed deeply, bent over her hand. She was afraid he would kiss it and braced herself. She did not care much for him, he wore such shocking bright colors and his perfume was strong and disagreeable. To her relief, her uncle was brusque with him—polite, but turning him off.

Another man came up, a dark-haired Englishman. He looked nicer. Sonia stiffened, wondering, shy, as he looked her over. He turned to her uncle, spoke politely.

Uncle Meyer was all smiles, clasping Sonia's arm firmly. He liked this man, she thought. She could always tell by his manner, for however polite he was, she sensed his manners and moods. She had lived with him and his two sons since the early death of her father many years ago, when she was eleven. Uncle Meyer had taken her—and her problems and tribulations—to his heart. He had been a father to her: a guardian, a mentor.

"Sonia, my dear," he said, "may I introduce Sir Frederick Toland? Sir Frederick, my dear niece, Miss Goldfine."

The man bowed. He was short, intense-looking, serious. She rather liked him. He did not look her up and down, merely gazed right into her face, murmured politely at the introduction. He remained to talk.

"A splendid occasion," said Sir Frederick, glancing into the distance as the couples danced and bowed.

"Very splendid," said Uncle Meyer amiably, one hand behind his back, one hand on Sonia's arm. "Ah—I believe the Prince of Wales sometimes attends."

"Ah—yes. But not tonight, I believe. He is out of London."

"Indeed?" said Uncle Meyer, as though not fully aware of it. He knew, because he had spoken of it at luncheon today. "Well, well, a fine company. Beautiful music."

"Very fine music. Ah—I wonder if I might ask your niece to honor me with a dance. Another set will be forming shortly."

He spoke so stiffly. Was he shy? Sonia wondered, as her uncle beamed, nodded his approal, and put Sonia's hand on Sir Frederick's arm. They waited for the music to cease, then Sir Frederick led her over to several other couples. They bowed to her, he introduced her amiably and correctly. The names were lost in the music.

He danced with her, silently, seriously, leading her through the maze quite correctly. It seemed a very long dance to her; she had rarely danced, though she knew how. Her cousins had taught her, and she had sometimes danced in their home to the music of violins. This was different. People were staring at her, whispering, their heads together, fans waving. She was relieved when he returned her properly to her uncle, bowed, thanked her for the dance, and vanished in the crowd.

But she breathed more easily. She had actually danced a set in the home of a duke! She was not a complete failure—a gentleman had asked her to dance, and she had acquitted herself with dignity. Now she dared to look at the spectators. She was not the only object of their curiosity. They nodded to others, whispered, giggled behind their fans. The gentlemen strolled about, eyed the young ladies, drank their punch and something stronger, and showed their fine legs in the tight pantaloons.

Sonia was twenty-three, but she had never been presented at Court. A Jewish girl could not expect this. Jewish merchants were accepted reluctantly at dinners, they headed charitable societies, they were bankers and brokers, they were in trade and did well. But their women were kept at home, in their own society. Now she wondered why Uncle Meyer had broken his own unspoken rule and taken her to the home of a duke. He seemed excited also, under his usual mild, amiable manner.

They did not eat. They had dined before coming, and had arrived a little late. Sonia did not observe strictly the rules of diet, but her uncle did, and she respected his observance. Her father had not done so, nor her mother, there in far-off Vienna, where they had lived so happily in her early years—until—

She shut off sad thoughts firmly. She had a stern rule for herself. Forget the bitter past, live for the present, do one's duty, and have charity for those less fortunate. They had served her well, those precepts.

On her uncle's arm, she strolled about the room during the supper hour. She caught whispers, and hoped he did not.

"Jewish!" uttered one hoarse voice from an immense female in purple satin, with plumes waving from her head like a handsome horse. "Know them—merchant—bankers—rich—look at those jewels! In trade. Disgusting, that we must associate with them wherever we go!"

Sonia did not flush. She turned a little pale and clutched her uncle's arm protectively. Perhaps he had not heard, his hearing was dimming with his eyesight.

"They would never have been received in my day!" said a shrill feminine voice near the first woman. "Never! Jewish—we never saw them! Now they are everywhere, at the opera, plays—I suppose the House of Commons will be next!"

"Never!" said a firm masculine voice, from a red-faced beefy-looking gentleman in bottle-green. "That will never happen! They can lend money, but they can't buy us! Jewish money buys almost anything! But not our government, thank God!"

8

Sonia drew a deep breath, and urged her uncle on. At the wide staircase leading to the lower floor and the carriage entrance, she whispered, "Uncle, may we not leave? I have danced, and we could leave now—"

"No, no, my dear," he said absently, patting her hand. "It is much too early. Insulting, you see. Must remain for a time. Ah, there is our host—"

Uncle Meyer led her up to a splendid-looking gentleman with powdered white hair and lean pleasant face. He spoke to them, beamed down at Sonia.

"What a lovely niece you have, Mr. Goldfine," he said. "Where have you been hiding her? And those gems—how did you get your hands on them? Don't let my wife see them!"

Uncle Meyer laughed, well pleased at the jovial tone. "Ah, sir, you tease us. I happen to know your lovely wife has an excellent collection of gems—"

"Never enough, Mr. Goldfine!" And the duke put an elegant finger beside his long nose. "She'll want them, never fear!"

"These belong to my niece, who designed the necklace," said Meyer Goldfine proudly. "She is in jewelry, and does beautifully. Everything she wears, she made herself."

"Well, well, talented as well," said the duke, and gestured to a man standing near them, looking with curiosity at Sonia. "May I introduce you to Sir Jonathan Wiltshire? Sir Jonathan, Mr. Goldfine and his niece, Miss Sonia Goldfine."

They all bowed. The duke and Sir Jonathan strolled with them back toward the huge ballroom. People were staring at them, and whispering again. Sonia kept a smile fixed on her lips. She thought she understood now why her uncle had brought her. He thought she should have more jewelry commissions than she had, and she was advertising her wares! She touched the slender chain briefly, then let her hand drop. Well, she was not ashamed of it.

From very early, she had known she had talent. She always had been drawing and sketching. She had taken her uncle's gems which he usually bought and sold in bulk and formed designs for them. She had learned silversmithing and goldsmithing, and the art of designing beautiful necklaces, rings, tiaras, brooches. Now she had a workroom of her own in his home, and a drawing room where she received ladies and listened to their wishes for jewelry. She could supply any precious gem from the Goldfine stock, plus corals from Italy and India, ivory from Africa and the Far East, pearls from the Orient. Her designs were feminine and gracious—never bulky and heavy, but light and beautiful.

Sir Jonathan, to her surprise, asked her to form a set with him and several other couples. Shyly, she went with him. He was tall, dignified, graying. He spoke little, but kept looking down at her thoughtfully as he led her through the dance. As they met another couple, Sir Jonathan smiled and called the gentleman "Alastair."

Sonia raised her eyes shyly to meet eyes so deeply blue they were like her sapphires, she thought, startled. Alastair! What a beautiful name for him! He was tall, blond-haired, tanned, with a rugged frame.

He walked like a soldier, ramrod-straight and quick. His chin was proud. Sir Jonathan saw her looking after him, and said, "He was colonel of my regiment. He sold out a year ago after his father died and he came into the estates."

"Oh—I see." She watched him later, as he stood with a young man enough like him to be his brother, and two gay young girls, also blonde and blue-eyed. What a handsome family, she thought longingly, as Sir Jonathan whispered they were his sisters. He seemed devoted to them, and watchful, frowning at a young man who staggered tipsily as he tried to invite the younger one to dance, shaking his head at him.

He was protective of them, she thought. How nice it would be to have someone care so much. But she was fortunate also, she added to herself. She had Uncle Meyer, and her two cousins, Jacob and Abner. They were both married, and she loved her sister-in-law Beryl. Bettina was more difficult; she was sickly and fretful after bearing three children. But she was lucky to have relations, devoted and caring for her.

She thought they would leave soon, but Uncle Meyer became engaged in conversation with an elderly gentleman who wanted to talk about the war with Napoleon. She stood patiently, on one foot and then the other, as they argued in low tones about how long the war would last, whether it was possible to defeat the French who had such a splendid record in battle. She smiled when they remembered her, and let her gaze wander about when they forgot.

She kept looking for the handsome blond ex-colonel. How handsome he was, how tall and straight and fine. She saw him dancing with his older sister, laughing down at her, teasing her, for she blushed and shook her fan at him.

She looked about for Sir Frederick and Sir Jonathan, but they had disappeared. She had noticed several card-rooms, with gentlemen bending intently over cards and dice. Gambling—it was the vice and downfall of more than one Regency buck, her uncle had said disapprovingly to Jacob, time and again. They could not resist taking a chance. They bet on horses, on the outcome of a battle, on the turn of a card. On whether a fly would alight on a gentleman's nose, Jacob had said, laughingly. Uncle Meyer had not thought it was funny.

A red-haired young man came up to them, waited until Uncle Meyer noticed him.

"Ah, Sir Philip!" said Meyer, smiling. "Allow me to introduce my lovely niece, Miss Sonia Goldfine."

The dashing youth, bending over in his tight white pantaloons, kissed her hand, beamed at her, and asked her to dance with him. Uncle Meyer nodded. "Yes, yes, run away. Our talk is dull for her, we speak of the war," he explained to Sir Philip Ryan.

On the dance floor, Sir Philip said, "You find the war boring?" and he sounded reproachful.

Sonia gave him a quick shy smile. "Not really. Only it is so exciting here, I wonder that they can even think about wars and battles. Have you ever seen such an assembly?"

He gave her an indulgent smile. "Yes, many times," he said. "But you—are you just presented?"

She bit her lip, turned a little pale. "No—ah, no," she finally let it go at that.

He gave her a quick look as they turned in the dance. "Ah —of course," he muttered, flushing red. "Ah, splendid music tonight," he said, and parted from her in the next move. When they came back together, he had a quick line of patter about the warmth of the September evening, the splendid supper, the fine gathering, how jolly everyone was.

He took her back to her uncle, and he was still talking of

fierce matters to the elderly friend. She stood patiently, waiting for him to be done. Surely they could return home now. But Meyer seemed absorbed, staring out absently at the gathering as they talked.

She opened her fan, moved it slowly to and fro to cool herself. The air had grown stifling hot with the many people in the room. It must be late, past midnight. She shifted to the other foot.

She noted the blond man, Alastair. He was moving across the room toward their end of the hall. How graceful he was, how handsome, how serious, now that he was not laughing at his sister. How blue his eyes were, she thought, as he came closer, and the lights of the candles lit his face.

Sonia wondered wistfully who he would ask for the pleasure of a dance. She cast a quick look near her. Was it the blond lady with the lavender dress, and the brief hem showing her shoes? Or the red-haired lady in green, with the splendid emeralds? They were too heavy on her slim neck, but she seemed very proud of them, arching her head. She would have a headache tonight, thought Sonia. If she had had the designing of them, she would have created something in light gold, a pendant of that one fine emerald, and a slim chain connecting the others. The smaller emeralds should not be clustered like that, they were too heavy.

She started violently when the blond man stopped in front of them. Meyer turned quickly to him with a wide smile. "Ah, sir, there you are," he said, as though he had been waiting for the man. "Lord Fairley, you are fortunate in your beautiful family. Your sisters would grace the finest ballroom in the country."

The man bowed, slightly, as though rather bored with the compliment. "Good evening, Mr. Goldfine," he said, and greeted the other man also, by name. Then he turned to Sonia.

Meyer said, "My dear, may I introduce you to the Marquess of Fairley, Alastair Charlton. Lord Fairley, my niece, Miss Sonia Goldfine."

He had come over to them! She was stunned with the wonder of it. She acknowledged his greeting in a low voice. "How do you do, Lord Fairley."

He did not smile, he seemed rather stern and detached. He said, "Miss Goldfine, may I have the pleasure of a dance with you?"

He made no fine compliments, he did not bother to make conversation with her uncle. She gave him a quick wondering look from beneath her long dark curly lashes, and nodded.

"Yes, sir," she said, and waited.

He held out his arm, and she put her slim hand on the fine blue cloth. He led her out and they formed a set. He did not speak for a time, as he guided her through the movements. He was graceful, moving lightly and quickly, moving her with a gentle ease. When she leaned on his arm briefly, it seemed like iron, it was so hard. He was fit and hardy, she thought, probably from years as a soldier.

"May I say how lovely you look this evening, Miss Goldfine?" he said halfway through the dance.

"Thank you, sir."

Then unexpectedly, he said, "I think I have seen you before, at the opera, and at a concert one evening. Do you enjoy music, Miss Goldfine?"

"Oh—very much, sir. And do you?"

"Yes, I like it immensely. And the plays, do you attend often? I believe I have seen you recently at a Shakespeare play."

A smile trembled on her red mouth, her luminous gray eyes shone up at him. "Oh, yes, I went in the spring. Was it not splendid? The farce that followed quite put me out of sorts, it spoiled it all."

He smiled down at her, and his blue eyes turned warm from frosty cold. "I felt the same way," he said gently. "Shakespeare is without peer, he should not be spoiled so."

The dance ended, and she was sorry. He put her hand on his arm, and they strolled slowly back to her uncle. She noted that her uncle was staring at them keenly, watching them shrewdly. She smiled at him.

"You are most fond of your uncle," said Lord Fairley, as a statement.

"Oh, yes, sir! You see, when my parents died, he took me in and treated me as a daughter. I owe him all," she said simply.

"All?" he repeated.

"Yes, he raised me, taught me languages and mathematics, saw to it that I was trained in jewelry-making when I showed signs of talent. He is—very dear to me."

"I understand," he said.

"You have—recently lost your father, I believe," she dared to say. "May I express my sympathy?"

He bowed, but his eyes turned cold again, and his mouth had a briefly bitter downturn to it. She was curious. "Thank you, Miss Goldfine, you are most kind."

He returned her to her uncle, stayed to talk for a few minutes. She was left out of the conversation, but at least she could gaze at his face, at the handsome profile turned to her, at the bright deep blue of his eyes.

He finally bowed, spoke to her, and departed. She sighed, and turned back to her uncle.

"I believe we can leave now, if you are weary," said her uncle, her arm in his. His dimming eyes gleamed in satisfaction. "Have you enjoyed your first grand ball, my dear?"

"Oh, it was splendid," she said truthfully. They made their way across the floor to the doorway, spoke to their host and hostess. The duchess stared more at Sonia's jewels than at her, as she accepted their gratitude for the evening's pleasure.

"She will be knocking at your door," said Meyer, in the carriage. "She will want some jewels like yours," and he chuckled and rubbed his hands together. "Ah, this was a fine evening, a fine evening."

Sonia smiled at him through the dimness, but her suspicions were confirmed. He had wanted to show off what she could do with jewelry, to help her get more commissions. Dear uncle, how solicitous and thoughtful he was for her! But her thoughts strayed to her last partner, the tall handsome ex-colonel, Lord Fairley.

She leaned back into the corner of the luxurious velvet upholstered carriage, and closed her eyes, as though tired. But with the soft silk cloak wrapped about her, she hugged the memory of the last dance.

How handsome he was, how kind. And he liked music and plays, just as she did. She dreamed, hopelessly, of just such a young man coming to visit her at home, talking with her of the matters they both enjoyed. Courting her, wanting to marry her.

She had never met anyone she wanted to marry. Meyer had not insisted, he knew how grief-stricken she had been at the death of her parents. She had seemed indifferent to everyone but her uncle and her cousins, not wanting to become involved with anyone again. Her emotions were in cold storage, frozen inside herself. The men she met, she had remained aloof from, and from any idea of marriage. She thought they mentally calculated how much she was worth —for her father had left her everything, and she would inherit one third of her uncle's wealth. She was talented, earning money from the jewelry. She did not need to marry, she had thought.

But tonight, for the first time, Sonia thought how it would be, should the strong arm of a fine young man hold her up, and a handsome face smile down into hers, and blue eyes light up at words from her. It was an impossible dream—but she hugged it to her nevertheless.

Chapter
2

〰〰〰〰〰〰〰〰〰〰〰〰

SONIA rose early each morning, eager to get to work on her designs. She had many commissions now, and she enjoyed working on them. Most of the ladies did not seem to mind how long she took, for the designs were so exquisite that they could wear them proudly for years.

Sometimes the highborn ladies brought her family jewels for her to design new settings. That was a challenge, to take out the age-old gems, study them, and set them into new slim delicate designs.

She also had a rich stock of gems from all over the world, some in the rough, some smoothed by jewelers in London for her. When she found a new gem of special beauty, she would study it for weeks, even months, thinking of an appropriate setting for it.

She ate her breakfast, drank some coffee absently. Her uncle had already gone to the City to his banking establishment. He worked long and hard, returning home in the evenings for their early dinner. Sometimes she read to him, from his favorite philosophers and historians, and they usually retired early. That was their routine, and she had settled into it after her cousins had married and left for their own homes.

This large, handsome townhouse actually belonged to Sonia. Her father had bought it, but had not lived long enough to enjoy it. He had brought her from Vienna, with jewels sewn into their clothing, fleeing in the night from the beautiful city which had become hateful to them.

Uncle Meyer had moved his family into this larger house, and after his younger son, Abner, had married, he had given his own house to the boy. And now Bettina complained—that it was not big enough for their growing family! Sonia smiled and sighed. One could give Bettina the moon, and she would complain that someone else had more stars than she.

Sonia went to her workroom after finishing her coffee that morning. She was thinking about the ball, the splendid gems. From looking at the glorious assembly, one would think no one else in London needed another gem. But she was wise enough in the ways of the world to know that the more jewelry one had, the more one wanted.

Flowers soothed the emotions, gentled them. One could walk in a garden without wishing to pluck every glorious bloom. However, jewels excited envy and admiration, and one wanted more and more.

She sat down at her worktable, and drew her latest sketches to her. She unlocked a drawer, and took out the tray of jewels on which she was working. A countess wanted new settings for her emeralds, and it was a difficult task. She was a demanding woman. Sonia had had to stand by while two men had counted solemnly every gem in the set, and written on paper how many gems there were, and of what size and weight. It had been humiliating; usually it was more tactfully handled. The countess had watched every move they made.

Still—the emeralds were lovely, and a pleasure to work with. It was not their fault that their present owner was unpleasant and greedy, with a thin scarlet mouth and plucked eyebrows. Sonia turned over several of the gems gently with her tweezers, and studied the largest ones.

A pendant, with a slim chain of gold, the small emeralds set in the chain. A brooch, with this fine stone in the center, perhaps in a flower design—no, for that woman, something unusual—a fish? Or a snake? She smiled at her fancies. She must look at the family crest again. Perhaps she could simplify that design, and make a charming brooch of the family crest. A dragon, with a slim gold horn, and jeweled eyes.

She drew and sketched for a long time that morning. Tiring of one project, she locked it away, and took out some rough jewels her uncle had purchased for her. She spread those out on velvet, and studied them closely through her jeweler's glass. Some were very splendid—her uncle had good buyers. Sonia must take over that part of the work soon, for her uncle was busy, and growing older and more weary. It was not fair to have him do this, also. She must begin to work more with the merchants.

Sonia had lunch on a tray at her workbench, to her abigail's silent disapproval. Early in the afternoon, Leah returned to her, a triumphant gleam in her dark eyes.

"Now, you must stop working, Miss Sonia! Your cousin has come to call, and his good wife."

"Abner?" sighed Sonia, thinking the worst. Abner used to be so happy and carefree. Now his nagging wife had pulled him down to her level. All was gloom and doom, they had only complaints, and loved to pour out their vials of poison on everyone, making them as miserable as themselves.

"No, no, it is Mr. Jacob," Leah was quick to reassure her. "I have put them in the drawing room, and tea will be served."

"Oh, splendid! I have not seen them for a week." Sonia locked away the gems, and took off her light muslin apron. She tied her thick hair, and without a look into the mirror she hurried to the drawing room.

Jacob stood up to greet her, his grin broad. "Well, Sonia, we must pull you from your work! Father says you work too hard, and Leah is scolding us for not making you go out to dine with us."

"She is always scolding me," said Sonia, with a smile. She kissed his cheek affectionately, then bent to Beryl, seated on a blue velvet chair near the fire. "Dear Beryl, how are you?"

The pair was smiling, exchanging significant glances. It

struck her that Beryl was blooming, her cheeks pink, her eyes sparkling.

But politeness must win out over curiosity. They exchanged greetings, asked about mutual friends, told their news. Beryl asked about the ball.

"We have heard you went to the home of the duke! For dinner and dancing! We were amazed. Father approved?"

"Oh, yes, it was his idea," said Sonia. "I was surprised . . . I think he wished to win more commissions for me."

Jacob's eyebrows raised, but he made no comment. "Well, well, you had a pretty fine time, by the sounds of it, dancing with all the lords."

"How did you hear?" asked Sonia, smiling.

"I have my sources." Jacob's mouth smiled as his finger tapped his ear significantly, like his father's gesture when telling of some bit of important news.

They both laughed at him, and went on talking eagerly. Leah brought in a tea trolley of silver, Sonia's favorite, with the china she had chosen from her uncle's storehouse from a shipment fresh from China. Delicate blue and white porcelain, with a slim elegant dragon curling about the cups and plates, among delicious oriental flowers.

They drank tea, ate spicy cakes, and talked. Finally the talk died down, and Beryl looked at Jacob.

"We have news for you," said Jacob, with an unusual blush behind his black beard. He got up to stand at the fine marble mantel, with the green flowered vase behind him.

"Oh, and what is that?" asked Sonia, already guessing. She held her breath, hoping. They had been married two years, and Beryl had longed and wept for a child.

Beryl blushed, and beamed, and her eyes sparkled. "We are to have a child, dearest Sonia!"

"Oh, how happy I am for you!" Sonia jumped up, went to her cousin's wife, and kissed her warmly. "A child! How happy I am! I thought you were so happy today! Now I know the reason! The best of good wishes for a successful birth!"

"Thank you, my dear!" They accepted her wishes happily, and began to chat of their plans. Beryl hoped it would be a boy, Jacob would be happy for his first child. Already Abner had three sons, and though his wife nagged and complained, he was happy in that. Now the elder brother would have his child, and perhaps more!

Sonia was gently envious of them. To be married and devoted to each other, as they were, made for such a happy state. And now to have a child! She thought of Jacob as a brother. Certainly, he had always treated her as his sister, quietly helpful to her, devoted to her and his father.

"And when do you expect—?"

"In June, next June," sighed Beryl happily. "When the roses bloom. Oh, I pray every night—"

"And so shall I," promised Sonia. Beryl was a dear girl, so gentle and devout. If only all went well. . . !

The talk finally turned to other matters. Jacob worked with his father in the City, at brokerage and other financial matters. The state of the country and of Europe was of deep concern to him, for financial and family reasons.

"Napoleon has romped all over Europe," he said gravely. "We must stop him soon, or he will land in London with his troops! No, no, I jest," he said quickly to his upset wife. "No, no, he will not come here."

But Sonia knew that Napoleon had just such ambitions, and so did Jacob. At one point in 1805 the French had been dangerously close to invasion. Troops had been gathered with landing boats on the coast opposite Dover. Then had come word of movement of enemies, and Napoleon had dashed south to Ulm to defeat the Austrians there, and then on to the battle of Austerlitz.

Napoleon might try again. Just now, he was engaged in battles in the Peninsula against Spain and Portugal. The British had rallied in support of the Portuguese, their allies for centuries. And now in September 1809 they waited word from the armies there, as to the progress. Arthur Wellesley had been sent there, to rally and command the British and Portuguese, and the battle of Oporto and then of Talavera had electrified all England. His successes gave them new hope of drawing Napoleon into a final battle to destroy his hopes of conquering Europe and Britain.

"We have had word of cousins in Vienna," said Jacob to Sonia. "You will tell Father tonight, before I see him tomorrow. They are in some need, and I must arrange to send money to them."

Sonia nodded, her face turning grave. Their cousins had helped her and her father escape. "Is Frederico—"

"He is well," said Jacob. "And his wife, but their baby son has died. And one of his wife's relatives was caught in a pogrom—she is dead. I wonder if we should attempt to get them all out of Vienna." And his bearded face looked older than its years.

"If any money is needed," Sonia said quickly, "you have but to ask. There is plenty."

Jacob smiled and patted her shoulder. "I know, my dear cousin. You are most generous. I will let you know. But Father will probably arrange all."

"Oh, I hate it all," burst out gentle Beryl, with unusual passion. "Why must Jews be so hated that they are herded in ghettos, and not allowed in society? Cousin Dina married a gentleman of noble birth here in England, but she is shunned! She says she does not care, that her children are all. But it is dreadful! And no Jew may sit in the House of Commons, because he cannot take the Christian oath of office! Even if he could be elected!"

"It is something to be endured," said Jacob soothingly. "Do not distress yourself, Beryl," but he looked thoughtful, his hands clasped behind his back.

"How long must we endure?" asked Sonia quietly. "I heard talk at the ball—I hope Uncle did not hear them. But they spoke of us as daring to come to their ball, pushing our way into their society! We were *invited*."

"Of course you were," said Jacob, looking at her thoughtfully. "I am surprised that my father accepted the invitation. Perhaps he had other reasons—"

"Yes, he wishes me to receive more commissions. But I prefer to be treated as a businesswoman," said Sonia, her head haughtily high and her gray eyes unusually angry. The slurs had hurt. "I shall not push myself into their company, believe me!"

"Were they rude to you? Did they treat you hatefully?" asked Beryl, touching Sonia's hand comfortingly. "Do not go again, dear Sonia. We shall have a dinner for you soon, and introduce you to some nice man—"

Sonia burst out laughing, her fury forgotten. "Oh, do not matchmake, dearest Beryl!" she begged. "I do not wish to be introduced to a series of nice young men! I manage quite well by myself."

Beryl teased her, but Jacob looked sober and thoughtful. Uncle Meyer returned home early from his office, and was happy to see his son and daughter-in-law there, especially when he heard their news.

The talk turned to more happy matters. They remained for dinner, and it was a gay, merry family affair. The next morning, Sonia went to her worktable in a happier frame of mind. The ball had made her discontented, she thought. She would not like to go again.

She took out the small leather bag of gems her newest merchant had brought to her. They were splendid indeed, from the Orient, and some very unusual. She had paid a high price for them, yet they were worth it.

She examined them more closely, rolling them out on a white velvet cloth. She picked up one gem, and studied it with her sharpest jeweler's loupe which magnified any flaws readily. There were no flaws in this gem! A stunning star sapphire, it had been cut lovingly into cabochon shape, and the rounded curve showed the beautiful white lines of the star shining on the deep blue. She picked up her cloth and carefully polished it a little more, studying it again and again.

A truly magnificent gem! This was the finest star sapphire she had ever seen, in gem or in rough. It must be more than forty carats, she judged, and weighed it. Yes, just over forty. How could she use it?

She fingered it, thought about it. Finally she set it aside. It was so special, she must keep it for a special cause, for someone she really liked. Not like that countess. Someone special.

For some reason, as she gazed at the sapphire with delight, she thought of the deep vivid-blue eyes of Alastair Charlton. Lord Fairley was quite beyond her reach, as Bettina had said crudely of some beau. However—it was pleasant to think of him. She allowed her thoughts to linger on him for a few minutes.

23

How tall, how handsome, with such a grave smile on his face, and the dark blue eyes lighting as they spoke of music. His manners were as polished as this gem.

She sighed to think how far apart their worlds were. She was a Jewess, from the ghettos of Vienna and Eastern Europe. He was a marquess in the great royal families of England, Protestant, born to great houses and greater positions. England had treated Jews rather well in recent years. Many had fled Europe and come to England because of its tolerance of Jews. Yet—yet how far apart they were. They might walk the same streets, but not together. They might ride down the same highways, but not in the same carriages. They might marry high—but not to each other.

"Oh, I am becoming foolish," she murmured, and took her sketchpad and went out into the garden. The September day was warm, and it was pleasant in that secluded patio, under the trees. She drew in a deep breath of the late roses, and began to sketch a design, incorporating a rose and a butterfly.

Alastair Charlton had dismissed his carriage two blocks away, and walked slowly to the house where Meyer Goldfine lived. He glanced up at the handsome house of stone and marble pillars with grim distaste. He had preferred to go to the countinghouse, but Meyer Goldfine had insisted on seeing him at his home.

Morning. A glorious September morning in London. He should be happy, his cane swinging lightly. Instead, he felt as though heavy weights pressed down each shoulder.

He rang the bell, and a maid answered, smartly dressed in white apron and cap. She curtsied and took his cane and tall hat.

"This way, my lord," she murmured, and led him into a book-lined study.

Meyer Goldfine rose to greet him, with a grave smile, and a bow. "Come in, my lord. You honor my house."

"I would have preferred to come to your place of business," said Alastair curtly, his mouth in a thin line.

"And have the world see you coming to visit a Jew-merchant?" asked Meyer snidely. "No, no, the world speculates too much on what it sees. It is better to meet privately. Pray,

24

sit you down, my lord, and we will go over these papers." He indicated the chair on the other side of his desk.

Alastair looked at the papers on the desk and sank into the chair. He had never felt this fear, even in battle. Those white scrolls and that ledger might hold the fate of himself and his entire family.

For the next two hours, it was worse than a battle. Meyer Goldfine showed him the papers, the ledger, and his own figures. The man had bought up most of Alastair's outstanding debts, and those of his deceased father. The sum was enormous, more than three hundred thousand pounds. Alastair's face grew more white, he felt drained of blood.

"So that is the picture, my lord, I am sorry to say," said Mr. Goldfine, leaning back wearily. "Your father, God rest him, went deeply into debt, and did not pay even the interest. I fear your extravagances since coming into the title have not helped."

Alastair drew his hand over his face. His forehead was damp. "What am I to do?" he muttered, half to himself.

"You might go to a solicitor for advice," said Meyer, watching him with half-closed eyes. "There are items you might sell—your hunting lodge, some of your horses . . . "

"Yes, yes, I might do that." Alastair drew his chair closer, and began to calculate. Meyer told him figures, he wrote them down, looked again. "No, that would not even be a savings of half a hundred thousand pounds," said Alastair, quite unable to believe it. It had been but a year since he had come into the estates and thought all his troubles would be over. His stern father, distant, more absorbed in his gambling and his light women than his family, had receded into the background of his mind. But here it was—the whole sordid picture. Gifts to women, mad bets on horses . . .

He held his head. "I have so many obligations," Alastair said, half to himself. "My younger sister to bring out—the townhouse, and the place at Fairley. My God, I can't give up Fairley! It has been in the family for five hundred years—"

"I can suggest wise investments," said Meyer Goldfine. "If you would entrust your finances to my banking house, I might help the situation."

"I have a solicitor and a broker," said Alastair stiffly.

Mr. Goldfine shrugged his stooped shoulders, and toyed with a pen. "Of course, there is always marriage," he suggested, as though at random.

"Marriage?" Alastair frowned. "I had not thought to marry until my younger brother and two sisters were settled. No, no, there is no one I care to marry."

"I am speaking of a marriage that will improve your financial situation, my lord," said Mr. Goldfine. "It is not unusual, even in British society, for this to happen. Is there some heiress, some wealthy family with a marriageable daughter—" He left the question dangling in the air.

Alastair showed his distaste. "None that I know of," he said curtly. "I do not care for such a marriage. There must be some other way—"

Meyer Goldfine fitted the tips of the fingers of one hand carefully to the fingertips of the other and looked into space. "I am thinking of my niece, Sonia, whom you met at the ball, my lord," he said. "Now, there is a difficult one to marry. A beautiful young lady—and I must thank you for asking her to stand up with you—"

Alastair felt as though bitten by a mosquito's sharp sting. "I promised I would, in exchange for this meeting," he said stiffly, drawing himself up.

"Ah—yes. You were kind to her, however, and I am grateful," said Meyer gracefully. "Her first outing of that sort, you see. The deaths of her parents struck her hard in her young years. She is quiet, reserved, works hard at jewelry designing. She dislikes going out, she suspects me when I introduce her to some young man. I think it will be hard to arrange a marriage for her—in spite of her great wealth, her talents, her skill as a homemaker, her gentleness, and her beauty." He paused, eyed Alastair under his graying heavy brows.

Alastair moved restively. "I am sure she will have no trouble," he said, without interest. "A wealthy woman, of beauty —she should marry well."

"Ah, yes, one would think so. But always she finds some reason to refuse to meet a man a second time; he has no intellect, he has no kindness, he is a snob, and all that—" Meyer laughed gently. "She must be guided into marriage, as a young filly into harness. But—we were speaking of your problems. A marriage to an heiress might solve them all. I have most of your notes, there are some others I can obtain. Marriage might solve all."

Alastair stood up abruptly. "I do not care for the solution, nor is it practical," he said rudely. "I know no woman I care to offer for, none that is wealthy and amiable—"

"Come here." Meyer beckoned to him. Alastair followed him reluctantly to the long window of the room. It overlooked a garden of some size and great beauty. Under a tree was a bench, and upon the bench sat Sonia, sketching, her dark head bent as she worked intently.

"My niece," said Meyer, smiling contentedly. "She works all the day. Presently she will come in to see to my dinner. She keeps me very comfortable, she is a great housekeeper. She never fusses over me. Evenings she reads to me, in several languages; she is skilled in many tongues. Most intelligent woman, and a beauty also, I think you will admit?"

"Yes, yes, but how many girls like that are about?" asked Alastair. In spite of his distaste for the conversation, he remained staring at Sonia, who was unaware of them at the window. Now she raised her head to gaze after a yellow butterfly. He noted the fine round chin, the white skin, the dark curl of her hair, the broad forehead, the graceful hand, the arm where the lace had been shaken back, the slim form in the white muslin gown.

"Few, few indeed," said Meyer. "You could marry her, I think. Yes, yes, she might marry you. She admired you at the ball."

Alastair felt as though he had been struck over the head. He flung around, to gaze down at the slight form of the merchant. He noted the smile on his lips, the fondness of the gaze as he looked at his niece.

"Marriage—to *her*? You must be—mad," he choked out. Marriage to a Jewess, when he was a firm Protestant? Marriage to an heiress for which many would mock him? To sell himself in marriage to a girl he had met once? Never!

"No, not mad. I am concerned for Sonia. She stays more and more to herself. I do not wish her to be a spinster," sighed Meyer. "Much as I love her companionship and her

27

concern for me, I wish her to marry, be happy, have children. She was made for marriage and children."

Alastair put his hand to his throat, pulling at the neat neckcloth in a newly designed Waterfall. He felt as though he would strangle. He must be mad. He could never marry her —he could not. Marriage—selling himself in marriage—and to a Jewess, attractive though she might be . . . He thought of her luminous gray eyes, shining up at him as she spoke of plays and concerts. A pretty girl—but the entire time he was with her he had been aware of who she was and *what* she was. . . .

Chapter
3

•=o=•=o=•=o=•=o=•=o=•=o=•=o=•=o=•=o=•=o=•=o=•=o=•

"WELL? What do you think, Lord Fairley?" persisted Meyer Goldfine, gently.

The title recalled Alastair to himself. He was Lord Fairley, a marquess, with duties and responsibilities to his family name, his estates. He could not marry a Jewess—it was out of the question. For his sons to be half-Jewish! No, it would never do, it was not to be thought of.

He shook his head decidedly, turned from the old merchant, averting his gaze from the eager gentle face. "No, never," he said, horrified. "I could never marry a Jewess. Never."

Meyer nodded, gravely, and turned back to seat himself at his desk. "Well, no doubt there is some other solution," he said, and began to arrange the papers neatly into a high pile, then into folders.

Alastair watched him, biting his lips. He longed to fling the entire lot into the blazing fire near them. His debts, and those of his father—how could they have grown so? And the interest would grow daily. He must do something soon!

"Well, I thank you—for your—concern," he managed to say haltingly. Meyer glanced up, and smiled, and nodded.

"Of course, of course. I will see you to the door," he said, getting up again, holding on to the back of the chair until he had himself steady. Then he hobbled to the door, held it courteously for Alastair. "Do let me hear when you have reached some solution, my lord. I will await your word."

"Yes—thank you."

The maid came, and showed him out. The door clanged shut after him, like a cell door, he thought, and shuddered, remembering prisons he had seen. Some in the Peninsula were of white-washed stone, empty but for a heap of filthy straw. He had seen a prison near the coast of England where men clung to the bars and stared out hungrily from grimy bearded faces at passers-by, begging for bread. The bright sunlight of London seemed a mockery now.

Three hundred thousand pounds. And more interest due within a month. It would pile up and up until he smothered in debt. He came to his carriage and swung himself in.

"Where to, my lord?" asked the coachman, dubiously. He had never seen his lordship so down in the mouth, so hang-dog. He had a shrewd guess what his master had been up to in the neighborhood: it held homes of the Jew-merchants and money lenders. All knew his lordship's father had flung money right and left, and now the new lord was slow in paying wages and food bills.

Alastair gave an address curtly and sat huddled in the carriage until it drew into the quiet mews. He got out, and told the man to go home, he would hire a hack if needed. The coachman obeyed.

Alastair went up to the front door and tapped. It was opened by a maid. Unconsciously, he compared her appearance with that of the white-aproned older woman who had cared for the house he had just left. This girl was slovenly, in a cast-off white muslin dress too tight for her, showing too much of her hanging breasts.

"She'll see you, my lord," muttered the girl, and tramped before him up the stairs heavily, breathing thickly through opened mouth as she went. "He's here, madam," she said, flinging open the door at the top of the stairs.

Alastair heard the door shut after him. As he went into the dimly-lit room, Mrs. Daphne Porter rose from her lounge and held out her hands to him. He took them in his, thankfully, with a feeling of coming to a refuge. He kissed them, smelled the perfume of them, touched the rings he had given her. She had a passion for emeralds and rubies. Today, she was in crimson silk which outlined her full form boldly. And rubies covered her beautiful slim white fingers.

"You are late, darling," she pouted.

He flung himself into a chair, and compressed his lips. They had been intimate for some time now, since his return from the wars and his inheritance of his father's title and fortunes. His sensitive mind winced at thought of that fortune. How had his father managed to fling it away so quickly? When Alastair's grandfather had died but ten years before, the fortune had been one of the more respectable ones on the island that was England. All had seemed sunny and bright, the future radiant. And now . . .

"You look cross, dearest," said Mrs. Porter, touching her lovely waves of blond hair with careful fingers. She lay down again on the chaise longue, languidly arranged the folds of crimson silk. "Did you not find me the rubies I wanted? Just a slim bracelet, love. Aren't there any in London?"

He stared at her, a little dazed. He was faced with disaster, prison, the loss of everything in the world. And she wanted rubies! He could have laughed aloud, bitterly.

"No, I have not found them. I have been occupied with business," he said shortly. She looked at him, and she was wise in the ways of men. She had studied them for years, more devoutly than a priest his prayers. They were her livelihood, ever since her elderly husband had died conveniently, leaving her a small income, just enough for her to gown herself and rent a nice place to receive gentlemen. Other grateful lovers had given her more: jewels, a shooting lodge in Scotland, a small house in the country. Now, she wanted more—marriage with a gentleman, such as Alastair.

Feed the brute, and let him love her—those were her antidotes for any crossness. She rang for the maid, and watched with a slight frown as the girl slopped the tea and set out a plate of mediocre sandwiches and cakes. She would have to speak to her again. Then the girl would threaten to quit unless she was paid more, then she would have to placate her with another cast-off dress.

Problems, problems, always problems, thought Daphne.

Alastair ate some sandwiches, drank some tea, and seemed to cheer up a bit. When the maid had taken away the tray, Alastair came to sit beside Daphne and fondle her hands. Daphne watched him with a slight smile on her crimson lips.

"Business hurt your head, dearie?" she cooed, and stroked his forehead lightly. Her eyes were narrowed, those bright green eyes which had been the subject of several sonnets.

"Yes, quite," said Alastair, thinking of the morning conference. He sighed, impatiently. There had to be a way out, there must be. If only Daphne were wealthy—but she was not. He kept thinking involuntarily of the solution Meyer Goldfine had suggested. No, not that girl, not a Jewess, but someone wealthy. He turned over in his mind the names of several girls.

Even as his arm went about Daphne's slim waist and firm white shoulders, and as he bent to press a kiss on her neck, he was thinking. There was little Betsy Challoner, she was rather sweet. But her father was not so well off, and with his two sons and four daughters to settle—no, that was out.

Lydia Palmerston—older, more sophisticated. No, her brother had gambled much, and their father was troubled about the fortune. Alastair had seen him going into a Jewish broker's not long ago. Meyer Goldfine was right: when one was seen going to them, it was bad news.

Then there was Angela Baddersley. She was sweet, pretty, rather a goose and stupid. But her father was like that also, and still managed to hold on to his fortune. Might not be a bad match, except that Angela bored him immensely. And her father was notorious for hanging on to what was his, disliked paying his debts. He was not apt to pay Alastair's debts eagerly. . . .

"You are upset, darling," said Daphne gently, as he embraced her and laid her back on the longue. "Tell me about it."

"Oh, nothing much," he said evasively. "My brother is acting up, playing the clown. It is the devil to be responsible for him and my sisters."

Daphne smiled, stroked the blond hair back from his forehead, and cleverly pressed her fingers to his temples to soothe his headache. "Poor love," she cooed. "I could help you with your sisters. Are you trying to marry off Edwina?"

He flinched. He hated the talk of "marrying off" his sisters. He was fond of them, and eager to make good matches for them. Edwina was twenty-two, gentle, a sweet loving girl, and beautiful as well. His father had almost married her off to a widower of forty-six, and Alastair had rescued her just in time. Edwina had been so grateful, weeping on Alastair's shoulder, vowing she would have killed herself if she had been forced to marry that horror of a man. And young Henrietta, so spirited and shrewd and gay. He would hate to have her forced into any marriage she did not like. He wanted to present her to Society this winter. She had been forced to wait a year following their father's death.

Now—now he thought of her eager violet eyes, her catchy voice when she was excited. If he defaulted in his debts and had to go to prison, what would happen to the girls? Maurice could probably find some job, or buy a captaincy in some regiment. But the disgrace would tinge him also.

Oh, was there no out for him? No solution at all?

Daphne drew him down into her embrace, and there in the dimly lit parlor, with the fire flickering comfortably, and the scarlet walls seeming to reflect their passion, and the lounge so soft in its crimson velvet . . .

He let himself go with a sigh, and ardently kissed her. He drew aside her skirts, fumbled with his trousers.

"Oh, don't muss me up, darling," murmured Daphne, smoothing his hair. "I do expect guests this afternoon, then I want to go out to Lord Baddersley's ball tonight. It should be amusing."

It was as though she had flung cold water in his face. He had been all prepared for a long session, ending in her bed, in comfort. He got up slowly, his face flushed, adjusted his clothes. "I beg your pardon," he said icily. "I thought you were as ardent as I felt myself to be."

"Oh, when you pout, you seem so very young," sighed

Daphne, a glint in her narrowed green eyes. She swung her feet to the floor, and settled her dress gracefully about herself. A slim hand smoothed the lace of her bertha. Another gesture smoothed her blond hair. "Don't be cross with me. I just don't want to be interrupted when we—are involved," and she glanced upstairs.

Sure enough, guests did drop in shortly thereafter. They remained for luncheon, and others came later in the afternoon. Alastair, fuming, remained for tea, and then went home to change for the evening.

He returned in time to escort Daphne Porter to the Baddersleys' for the evening. She was now wearing her favorite striking black, with silver trim, the rubies on her hands and in her small beautiful ears. Glances of admiration and some bold looks followed her, as Alastair escorted her on his arm into the hallway.

Lord Baddersley bent over her hand, kissed it as his wife stared coldly at the woman. Alastair caught the look, understood. The woman was becoming notorious. She was not the sort one invited to balls. In fact, he began to realize, no matter how one felt she was not the sort one married. No matter how exciting she was, how thrilling, how intriguing, she was not the sort one married.

He fixed a smile on his face and asked one of the younger girls to stand up with him. Over her shoulder, he saw Daphne giving one of his rivals a dazzling smile. He held her wrist in his hand and was pointing to it. She nodded. And Alastair felt a deep pang of jealousy. Was the cad preparing to buy a bracelet for her, one of rubies?

Alastair managed to ask his host's daughter to dance, but Angela was more insipid than ever, and more stupid. She could not manage more than a sentence of conversation at a time. He wondered if her children would be just as idiotic. How horrible, to have an idiot as a son and heir!

He stood up with several other young beauties, and was a little horrified at himself for studying them critically with a view to matrimony. Most of them had small fortunes. He knew to a thousand pounds the dowries of each of them, for the talk over cards and at horse races was frequently of marriage and the heiresses currently in favor in London. He flinched for himself and for all the other men of his acquaintance. And also the women. The season was frankly a marriage mart, and the highest prizes were much sought after.

"You're sober tonight," smiled one of his friends, Sir Frederick Toland. "Worrying about Maurice? He's all right, he'll settle down."

"I expect so," said Alastair, who had been worrying about himself. "Seen him today?"

"At the races," laughed Sir Frederick. "He cannot resist a bet, but really, he hadn't a chance today. His nag was a sleepy-eyed dunce if ever I saw one. And to bet such a sum on that! He wouldn't, if he hadn't been in his cups. I expect you gave him a piece of your mind."

"Not yet, but I shall tomorrow," said Alastair grimly, for this was all news to him. Maurice gambling heavily—how much had he lost? Another problem, to add to the ones that weighed all too heavily on him.

He was coaxed to come along to the gaming room, but refused firmly. He knew his own weaknesses along that line. Some sharp-eyed fellows were there; and they would fleece him, and no gentleman could accuse another of cheating at cards, not at the ball of a friend.

He remained in the dancing room, though his legs grew tired. He had not slept much the night before, and he kept looking at the ladies there as though he had never seen them before. Betsy had such a sharp long nose—was that inheritable? And Angela—how had he endured her before? He watched Daphne more jealously, for she was so stunningly beautiful. He could find no flaw in her, except that she had no fortune of her own, and he needed one. How he needed one. . . .

Alastair went up to the lovely Mrs. Porter and took her arm. She turned from the bevy of men surrounding her, to gaze up at him. She laughed her high charming laugh.

She tapped his arm with her silver fan. "La, you are so sober tonight, Alastair!" she rebuked softly, so none else could hear. "What is wrong with you? Laugh! The world has not come to an end."

His mouth stretched in a false laugh, and she giggled. "Does that please you?" he asked, half-savagely.

She half-closed her eyes, and tapped his arm again. "Come again tomorrow," she whispered in his ear. "And bring me a darling bracelet of rubies, and all will be forgiven! I promise to make you very happy, love!"

Someone claimed her attention imperiously. "This is my dance, Mrs. Porter. You promised me—faithfully—"

She laughed, and glided away with him, her face charming as she glanced back over her shoulder at Alastair, standing numbly where she had left him.

A bracelet of rubies! And he could not now afford a single unset little gem! A bracelet of rubies! He wanted to laugh, but thought he would sound hysterical.

He turned and walked out of the large ballroom, into the hall. He felt stifled, choked. He took a deep breath of air, found it powdered and hot. He must have air—he must have air—

He found himself walking stiffly down the stairs, like a man in a nightmare, into the lower hall, where a butler and footmen waited, faces impassive, hands in white gloves, ready to help the ladies and gentlemen into their cloaks.

Alastair accepted his black velvet cloak, and swung it around his shoulders. He had not meant to leave, he had not said farewell to his host. And he had walked out, walked away from Daphne! It did not seem to matter.

He had dismissed his carriage. He would hire a hack—no, he would walk. It was about two miles, the walk would do him good. His brain seemed fogged and dazed.

He strode along, in his black cloak over his blue silk suit, the silver trim shining in the street lights. A beggar crouched in the shadows, crept forward. "Sir, oh, sir, I begs you," he whined. "I's hungry tonight—"

Alastair tossed him a silver coin and strode on, scarcely remembering later what he had done. The blessings of the beggar followed him, he did not hear the words.

"What can I do?" he muttered to himself, swinging his cane savagely before him. "What the devil can I do? What answer? I found myself looking over the marriage mart tonight. Oh, God, am I sunk so low? Yet what other answer—what can I do?"

He was responsible for so many. His brother, his two sisters, aged aunts and uncles and cousins, the many retainers, there must be more than a hundred at the townhouse and in the country. The footmen, maids, cooks, grooms. . . .

"Good evening, my lord!" The deferential words brought him up short. Why, he was before his own door, and had no recollection of having walked there! Had he gone mad?

He muttered some response, walked in, gave the butler his cloak and cane, and went up to his rooms. The beautiful apartment in his favorite blue and silver gave him little pleasure tonight. He strode unseeing across the Persian carpets, to the long windows, stared out at the deepening purple sky, to the stars, the slim sickle of new moon, and did not see them.

He went to bed, to lie awake, and think, and think. His brain seemed to go round and round and round, like some desperate animal in a trap.

"What can I do? What can I do? With so many dependent on me? What right have I to marry for happiness and love and joy? I must marry for heirs—"

Fairley needed an heir—he needed money. He was responsible for so many—yet whom to marry? Could he marry for money? How would he ever have respect for himself again?—Pride, he thought, devilish pride. He should go to some marriage broker and ask her to find him a bride, fair if possible, but full of money! Maurice could marry and have sons, and Fairley would go to them. Yet—yet, he wanted children, he wanted children of his own, he had always thought that one day he would find the perfect woman and marry her, and they would have a happy home—such as he had never known with his stern father and frail mother. To lose everything, he thought, tossing restlessly on the wide bed. To lose —everything. . . .

He slept late, woke with a headache, and went down to luncheon, having missed breakfast, with a fiendish temper. When Maurice told his sisters about his bet and how much he had lost, Alastair lost his temper.

"How dare you be so stupid?" he cried, as his sisters stared at him and Maurice flushed with temper. "How can you? Do you think we are made of money? To make such a crazy wager, and lose thousands of pounds—"

"My God, Alastair, you talk as though we were for the poorhouse," said Maurice sullenly.

"Speaking of money," said Edwina, hopefully changing the subject from wagers. "Henrietta and I wish to shop for dresses today, dear Alastair. You said we might buy something really grand for Henrietta's presentation this winter. And we need other dresses, day gowns, tea gowns, ball gowns. I thought the new lady from France might be a splendid dressmaker. I can see Henrietta in white with silver trim, and me in cloth of silver—"

Alastair held his head. "Do you not any of you understand me?" he shouted, then saw the footmen staring at him. "Come to my study," he said, curtly, flung down his napkin and left the table. As they followed him, he shut the door with a bang.

He surveyed them, his lovely sisters, his handsome brother, and set his mouth grimly.

"Now, I see I must explain it all again. We are in debt. Do you understand me? We are—deeply—in debt! We cannot afford to throw away money—"

"But dash it all, Alastair, you have tossed away twice this amount and laughed about it!" protested Maurice sulkily, throwing himself into a deep crimson chair near the desk.

"Do you mean we cannot have any new dresses? But mine are so shabby—and all last winter's are black!" wailed Edwina.

"Am I not to be presented?" protested Henrietta, her full pink lips quivering uncontrollably. She stared at him reproachfully, her violet eyes swimming with tears.

He passed his hand over his damp forehead. "We are—very low in funds," he said, more calmly, deeper in despair than they could realize. "You must be patient, you must not toss money about. Of course, you will go ahead and purchase some dresses, Edwina, but be careful! Father—Father was deep in debt—"

"Oh, you do sound like Father now," said Maurice, discontentedly. "It was all right for him to throw money about on horses and females. But when we have a little fun, it's all wrong for us! You spent plenty last month on the beauteous Mrs. Porter—all those rubies, you know you did! But when I go out and bet a little on the nags, you cry poverty! You've lost your sense of humor, old boy, that's it!"

"I've lost more than that," said Alastair, sitting down heavily at the desk. "I have been to the money-lenders, and they won't advance any more. The size of the debts—" He paused and bit his lips. He could not tell them, it might slip out and be all over London. He sighed heavily. "It is enormous, and we must pay the interest this month. I tell you, I am not joking. We must cut back on expenses, and—well, cut back."

"Now you are being a wet squab," said Maurice, standing to stride about excitedly. "I don't believe it is so bad. Father was always moaning about money, but he managed to have himself a good time, even when—" He stopped abruptly, his mouth set.

They all knew what he meant—even when their mother was dying. Their father had been notorious for his affairs, and he was not one to sit and hold his wife's hand at her sick-bed. The night she had died, he had been with one of his mistresses.

He had continued in his profligate ways, and had died in a drunken rage at a gambling party. Alastair had been called home from the wars, to sell out from his regiment and take over the title and the many duties of his new position. He had found out only gradually the extent of his father's debts. Today—and yesterday—now that he knew, he felt the full burden of the responsibility on his shoulders. He looked at his brother hopelessly. His sisters were quietly weeping.

"Well, well," he said heavily. "We will manage somehow. We must manage somehow."

Chapter
4

—•—•—•—•—•—•—•—•—•—•—•—•—•—•—•—•—•—

SONIA went down reluctantly to the drawing room where she received clients. She had sketches in hand, her pencils, and blank paper.

"Think of it as a business. Uncle manages to do so, and not think of them as guests," she told herself firmly. She stood at the closed door for a moment, drew a deep breath, then went in, smiling.

The several women stared at her curiously. They sat on the deep couches, or in comfortable plush chairs, waiting for her.

"Good morning," she greeted each one of them by name and title. "Lady Morrison, you are most welcome, I have not seen you for a time. Mrs. Hendrick, how do you do?" She went down the line, speaking, bowing her head slightly, then went to her small desk at the end of the room. It made her feel more comfortable, and she had space for her drawings. She laid them down before her, and folded her hands.

Lady Morrison was first. "My dear Miss Goldfine, you did such splendid work for me," she gushed graciously. "Everyone remarks about the jets you did so swiftly, and the pearls are beautifully restrung. And with the pendant—beautiful!'

"Thank you. I am so glad you were pleased with them.'

She waited for them to get to the point, managing to smile at their praise and remarks. She was always keenly aware that they looked down on her as a businesswoman and a Jewess. Their remarks were full of patronage and sneers.

"At the opera the other evening—oh, we went to the opera, Miss Goldfine, and our box was across from that of Lord—"

She managed to keep a smile fixed on her face. She had been there also, she had seen them, though they had cut her. She always remained quietly in her box, and stared right at the stage. But Leah would whisper to her, pointing out the women who were her clients and the jewels of her own design that they wore.

Finally one came to the point. "I have received some fine sapphires, Miss Goldfine. I would like you to look at them and tell me what might be done with them." Mrs. Hendrick stood and came over to her with the jewel box. She opened it on the desk. "They are already counted and weighed," she added, and put the list beside the box.

Sonia picked up the list, scanned it, then gazed at the jewels. Even without her jeweler's loupe, she knew they were not first quality. The colors were dull, there were obvious flaws. She touched them lightly with her tweezers, turned them over on the jeweler's cloth before her. "Um, yes," she said absently. Several large ones were irregular in shape, they might make pleasing designs: ladies always liked flowers or snails, or dragonflies.

"They are beautiful, aren't they?" beamed the woman.

One of the women said in a low voice, but audible to them both, "Her lover has good taste!"

The other women laughed, Mrs. Hendrick flushed, her eyes sparkled angrily, then she shrugged. Sonia compressed her mouth.

"You will note, Mrs. Hendrick, that the shapes are irregular. That lowers their value in the market," she said firmly. "And these are flawed, note the scratches and the faults. Those should be noted on the list."

42

One of the women laughed nastily. "Maybe he doesn't have such good taste after all! Cheap stuff!"

Mrs. Hendrick bent over the gems, peered at them near-sightedly. "Why, I thought they were perfect!" She sounded distressed.

Sonia hardened her heart. If she set the gems, and then later a jeweler told Mrs. Hendrick the true value, they might accuse her of having substituted poor gems for good. "I'll write down the size and weight of the larger ones, and the flaws," she said firmly. "Also the combined weight of the small ones. Then you will sign this list, please."

Mrs. Hendrick clucked over this, but had to obey. Lady Morrison came over to witness for them, peering at the gems. "Well, she is right," she said reluctantly. "Not without flaws. Yes, yes, I can see that."

The matter was taken care of, then Sonia began to speak of designs. "Should you like a slim necklace of silver, with the best sapphires in a pendant design? I might suggest a rose, or a lily—"

"No, no flowers! Everyone has flowers! They said you could do something different, something that will have folks talking about my jewelry!" Mrs. Hendrick was flushed and eager, after the first disappointment.

Sonia glanced through her sketches, musing. This was the part she liked best, doing something different and creative with the gems. As she thought, she caught snatches of the conversation.

" . . . saw Lord T. with Mrs. P. the other night, now there's a pair for you! What he sees in her is beyond me— coarse and over-blown! But she's willing, and he has a wife who is always expecting, with nine children, what can you— well, I know my husband, and if I can't accommodate him at times, off he'll go to the whores—"

Sonia flinched at the conversation. She tried to block it out of her mind. The doings of Society did not intrigue her, and who went with whom, and who was unfaithful to whomever. Their language was filthy, their chuckling coarse as any fish-wife's.

"You're not married, are you?" asked Lady Morrison, picking up one of the sketches to glance over it.

Sonia started, realized the woman was addressing her. "No, my lady. Now, Mrs. Hendrick, may I suggest that I study the gems for a time, and come up with some unusual—"

"I would have thought you would be. You have money and presence, and I thought Jews always married early," said Lady Morrison, tossing down the sketch and picking up another. "Something about having many children and marrying well, isn't it?"

The other women turned from their gossip to stare at Sonia. Their eyes were bold, curious, as though she were some dog or horse they were evaluating. Not another woman, more sensitive and gentle than themselves.

Sonia ignored the question, and studied the gems through her jeweler's loupe. "This might make a brooch," she said, moving one large gem and three smaller ones into a design. "They are similar in color."

"Well, do make up some sketches for me, and I'll come back and decide," said Mrs. Hendrick self-importantly.

"I would think you would have beaus hanging on your skirts," persisted Lady Morrison, staring down at Sonia at the desk. "You're quite pretty, for a Jew. Your nose isn't long at all, is it?"

One of the women caught her breath. Sonia stood up, smiled faintly with an effort. "If that is all, I have much work to do. Mrs. Hendrick, please believe I shall exert every effort to create a splendid series of designs for you. Shall I send you a note when I have completed something for you to look at?"

She moved them to the door, by moving there herself. Reluctantly, they left their gossiping, and picked up their reticules and gloves to depart.

In the hallway, the neat maid approached. "Pray, ask Simeon to see the ladies into their carriages," Sonia managed to say.

The ladies half-bowed haughtily to her and departed, muttering. Sonia caught the clear high voice of Lady Morrison. "You notice she answered none of my questions? Snobbish, they are, all these Jews, for all they are here on sufferance! Lord Morrison says we should never let anymore into the country—"

The maid closed the door after them and gave Sonia a keen look, shaking her head.

"I will be in my workroom," said Sonia, and escaped, with the jewel box and her sketches. She felt a little sick, and sat at her table for a time, staring unseeingly at the sketches. How nasty women could be! It had been deliberate. She wondered if, because Lord Morrison owed her uncle money, Lady Morrison was so snappish. It often happened that way.

As she had grown older, her shyness had increased. She had been sheltered and protected by her uncle and two cousins. Still she had heard the talk. In England it was not as blatant as the vicious words she had heard on the streets outside the Jewish ghetto in Vienna. Here, there were no open threats, no blows, no gangs of ruffians attacking in the night. But the words—yes, there were still the words.

England had welcomed the Jews who had fled persecution in Spain and Portugal. Later, it took in Jews from the Netherlands, France, Austria, the German states, and Russia—as well as poor Polish Jews who had not even had a homeland after other countries callously carved up Poland to suit themselves. England, in her spirit of freedom and individual liberty, had welcomed even those of other religious faiths, allowing them to worship as they chose, to live and work and pray. Jews could not vote here, and some found it difficult to purchase land and houses. None could be called to the Bar or matriculate in the ancient honorable universities. The few professions open to them were money-lending and brokerage, the making of jewelry, the peddling of goods from town to town.

Yet, they were free here in England, free of special harsh taxes such as the other states of Europe imposed on them. They could go from town to town, live where they chose, or could rent. They could send for relatives and friends, help them come to England. It was better than waking in the night, fearful of hearing the sounds of the roughs coming to beat on the doors, "Come out, Jews!" And the cries of the beaten and murdered. . . .

Her own mother had died—she had been too late coming home from her sewing. They had caught up with her outside the ghetto—beaten her to death. The gentle woman, the sweet and smiling wife and mother, now only a picture in a frame—a bloody mass on the ground, defiled and violated and killed. Sonia pressed her hand to her mouth, feeling sick again, as she had as a child.

Nightmares had pursued her for years. Her father had lost all will to live once his beloved wife was dead. He had gotten Sonia to England, bought the house for them, and not lived to enjoy it, nor gain his sense of composure and serenity ever again. He had caught a fever and died. From then on, Meyer Goldfine had taken care of Sonia—lovingly, compassionately.

Leah Stein, her abigail, came to her with a luncheon tray about one o'clock. "Your uncle is delayed at his office. He will come home about four," she murmured, studying the girl's pale face with gentle worry. "Something troubles you? Those gentiles?"

She could make the sound of the word like a spitting curse. Sonia smiled faintly. "They are coarse and unlady-like," she said, making a face. "I don't know why I let their stupid words bother me. And they are ladies—*ladies!*"

"Pooh! A lady is a lady inside herself, not from a title someone hands to her on marriage or birth," said Leah sagely. "Those ones, they are little smelly dogs. Forget them."

She stood over Sonia until the girl had eaten some luncheon and had her coffee. Sonia felt better and worked on the designs with a more cheerful heart. What would she do without work? It was not a curse but a salvation. She mused on the words of the Torah as she worked. The first five books of the Bible told the story of her ancient peoples, and she thought about them often. What wisdom was there, what wordly knowledge as well as faith!

At four o'clock, Leah came to her again. "Your uncle wishes you to come to his study. He has a guest."

Sonia made a face. "Of what faith and nature?" she laughed.

"You will see," said Leah, unexpectedly mysterious. She looked over Sonia, brushed her hair again, urged her to change from the mussed white muslin to a demure pale blue with azure ribbons at her throat and waist. "There, now, you look lovely."

"He is not matchmaking again, is he, Leah?" asked Sonia, suspiciously, hesitating while putting a diamond ring on her finger and diamond studs in her ears. "Not again?"

"Stop fretting yourself. You uncle is a wise man," said Leah. "Relax and have a good time. Do not be all tight inside with your stomach in knots."

Sonia vaguely suspected that her dear Uncle Meyer was going to present her to yet another in his long list of bachelor acquaintances, all of them (according to him) charming, intelligent, eligible, handsome, and admirers of her beauty and mind. Well, she must just brace herself to be cool and aloof once more, and put the suitor off. She would not be married off to any man, nor endure what her mother had gone through. How desolate her father had been because of her! If love did that to one, it was something to be avoided, not met eagerly. One should be friendly but distant, holding slightly back. She loved Uncle Meyer and her cousins, she was close to Leah. They were enough in her world. Others could hurt. . . .

Downstairs, she tapped at her uncle's study door. "Come in, come in, my pretty!" called her uncle.

Sonia grimaced, then carefully smoothed out her face before entering. Her uncle must have some man in there—she must be careful. . . .

She entered, shut the door after her. The dimness of the room caused her to hesitate. Then, she saw the men rising at her entrance. Her uncle had been in his favorite wing chair near the fire. And the other man. . . .

She stared, her gray eyes wide and luminous, startled. It was a moment before she could move forward. Alastair Charlton was in pale blue and silver as usual today—handsome, blond, tall, cool. His white ruffled shirt was immaculate. The white neckcloth was tied high at his bronzed throat, in a beautiful fall of lace. At his wrists were small studs of sapphires. What a prince of a man he looked! Like one in a fairy tale, so handsome, grave, and beautiful. Yes, *beautiful.* She could look at him forever.

He bowed, she bent her head slightly, meeting his look, then glancing away again. How bright blue his eyes were, so shining a blue, like her star sapphire, with lights in them.

47

He held a chair for her, a small embroidered chair, just her size, and she sank into it. She looked at her uncle helplessly.

Uncle Meyer was smiling benignly, his fingertips together, as he sat in his big chair, feet propped up on a stool. He looked very satisfied and happy.

"You know Lord Fairley," said Meyer Goldfine, beaming at her. "He stopped in to talk some business. You have been busy today, my dear, so Leah tells me."

"Yes, another commission," she said, then felt choked and put her hand to her throat.

"Good, good, she is so popular, she is sought out by all the ladies, and by gentlemen also," said Meyer to his guest.

Alastair bent his head in acknowledgement. "She does beautiful work," he said gravely. Sonia was conscious that his gaze kept shifting from her uncle to her, then back again.

She wondered if he had come to ask for some work for his sisters—or his mistress. She pressed her handkerchief between her fingers. How hateful—to do something for a mistress of his! She would feel so—so angry, so full of jealousy. . . . What was she thinking about? A mistress of his, how fortunate a woman! To receive the caresses of his curved sensuous mouth, the touch of his big bronzed hands. . . . She looked away, into the fire. She suddenly felt burning hot.

They did not speak further of commissions. They talked of music, of an art exhibition which had recently opened. Alastair spoke well, he had ideas. Sonia listened intently, forgetting her lack of ease and embarrassment. Meyer encouraged him. He spoke of books they had both read. Even Alastair looked at him with respect when he began to explain some philosophy.

They had talked for most of an hour before Lord Fairley turned to Sonia, with his request. "Miss Goldfine, I have asked your uncle's permission to have the pleasure of your company at the opera Friday next. I have bespoken a box. Will you come?"

She gazed at him, her gray eyes wide and startled. He was asking her to the opera? *Her?* He seemed serious.

When she did not answer, he went on, "I understand there

is a new soprano from Italy, supposed to be exceptional. When I heard she was singing, I thought of you at once. I know you care as little for the farces as I do. However, the rest of the evening may be very worthwhile."

Sonia managed to look to her uncle. He was nodding. "You may go, Sonia, and take Leah with you. She will be your chaperon. Splendid woman," he added to Alastair.

"Well—I—don't know—I don't— Uncle—what do you think?" she managed to say faintly.

"Of course, you would like it, my dear. You get out seldom enough, " said her uncle benignly.

He meant for her to go. She wished she understood his motives. Did he seek even more commissions for her?

"If—Uncle wishes, I will go," said Sonia, at last.

Alastair spoke up quickly. "I should rather, Miss Goldfine, that *you* would consent because *you* wish it." He looked at her, as though expecting some definite answer.

She was all the more bewildered. Excitement began to build in her, causing a flutter in her throat.

Her manners had been well-drilled into her. "I should be most happy, my lord, to accompany you."

He smiled for the first time that day. "Thank you, Miss Goldfine. I shall look forward to the occasion. May I come for you about eight o'clock?"

She agreed. With a few more pleasant words, he took his departure. She did not understand at all. How could he wish her company? How was her uncle involved? Could Lord Fairley be interested in her—that way? As a suitor? How was that possible? No, no, she must be mistaken. There must be some other motive. He wished to commission some jewelry, or he had some business with her uncle—that must be it.

Her uncle took an unusual interest in how she would dress for the opera. Sonia finally settled on a splendid white satin gown, slim-fitted to her waist, then in a discreet wide skirt to her silver slippers. The bodice was low, showing her white shoulders and fine white neck, the satin crumpled into folds to form white sleeves above her elbows. She wore white gloves, and her diamonds, a fortune in diamonds. She would

49

have settled for modest diamond studs in her ears, and perhaps a ring, but her uncle insisted.

"No, no, my dear, the diamond necklace you created, and the two bracelets—your arms set them off. All the women will be crazy with jealousy," and he chuckled. "I wish I could be there to see them all turn green!"

"Uncle, you are being wicked," she scolded him gently. But he only chuckled, seeming quite happy.

Leah accompanied her, discreet in black silk and a modest jet necklace of her mistress's creating. The carriage drew up promptly at five minutes until eight o'clock, and the footman accompanied them downstairs.

Lord Fairley was as splendid as herself, in his blue satin suit, diamond stud at his beautiful neck-cloth, white linens shining. He placed her white ermine cloak about her shoulders, took her on his arm out to the carriage, settling her inside as carefully as though she were something precious.

At the opera, they were stared at until she was embarrassed. She was glad to slip into the box near the railing, settling herself on the velvet chair with relief. Lord Fairley took her ermine cloak, put it with his on the hooks, then handed her the program. He sat down beside her, with Leah behind them.

He began to speak about the soprano, where she had come from, her experience. Sonia lost some of her shyness, asked him questions eagerly. They chatted until the music began, then sat in rapt silence.

"Ah, that was quite fine, was it not?" was his comment at the end, smiling down at her.

She nodded, entranced, reluctant to return to the world of reality. "Quite, quite beautiful," and drew a finger under her eyes. She had wept a little during the sad final scene.

"Would you care to stroll during the intermission?" He was standing, holding out his hand to her.

She was startled once again. She never went out at intermission, preferring to remain aloof from the crowd, lost in her own dreams. However, he seemed to expect it. Leah remained in the back of the box, frankly studying the audience below her.

They went out, she on his arm. "Quite a crush," he said,

shaking his head. "Here, now, hold to my arm, or I shall lose you." He sounded as though that was important to him. How courteous and gallant he was, as to some lady of his close friendship.

She clung to his arm, and they strolled up and down the elegant lobby. She caught curious looks in their direction, saw Lady Morrison. But the woman cut her, turning a shoulder on her. She would not wish to speak to Sonia Goldfine, the jeweler.

"There you are, Alastair! I say, Miss Goldfine, how radiant you look tonight!" It was Sir Philip Ryan, whom she had met at the ball, the dashing red-haired fellow who had been so kind. She smiled and curtsied to him, and to Sir Jonathan Wiltshire behind him. They bowed deeply, then began to chaff Alastair Charlton.

"No wonder you didn't want to come with us! You had snared the elusive Miss Goldfine," said Sir Philip, wagging his finger. "Are you coming to supper later?"

"Not at the same place as you," said Alastair, in his own teasing tone. "We shall choose some quieter place, where the chaps aren't so rowdy."

Sir Jonathan spoke of the music. Sonia felt able to reply in her quiet low tones. Behind them, a German in uniform came up to clap Sir Jonathan on the shoulder and speak in a heavy accent.

He was introduced to them all. He beamed and spoke in English. Sonia answered him in German.

"You are enjoying your stay in London, sir? It is a beautiful city, is it not? What do you think of the opera?"

He stared incredulously at her, commented in German. "But you speak my language! You are German?"

"No, I came from Vienna, many years ago."

"Ah, Vienna—that most splendid city—"

Alastair broke in. "I beg your pardon, but we are not all so well-versed in languages. May we speak English?" He was smiling, but Sonia felt a tension in him.

"Of course, of course," said the German princeling. "I was so surprised, so happy, to hear my own language spoken, and with such a fine accent—"

Alastair got her away from them with difficulty, as the signal sounded for them to return to their seats. In the box, he helped her settle in her chair, then asked, "Do you speak many languages, Miss Goldfine?"

"About eight or nine, my lord," she said.

He looked surprised. "Eight—or nine . . . ?"

"Yes. After the first two or three, the rest are not difficult."

He kept staring down at her, even as the house darkened. They listened to the farce, laughed a little, but she winced at some coarsely frank lines. Alastair leaning to her, whispered in her ear, "Not to our taste, eh?"

She smiled, shook her head, and was glad when the lights came on. Alastair sent for refreshments, some orange squash and biscuits, and they nibbled during the intermission. Several gentlemen came to their box, to laugh and talk, but they themselves did not go out again.

Another section of opera followed, which they enjoyed more, then a light melodrama concluding the program. It was late as they got up to leave.

Lord Fairley asked, "And now you will go on to supper with me, Miss Goldfine?"

She stiffened, glanced at Leah. She did not keep strict dietary laws, it would be all right. Yet—it was after midnight—

"I believe it is too late for me, sir, I am sorry."

"Not even for some champagne? A light supper, in a quiet place?" He did seem disappointed, and that feverish, excited feeling came to her again. He had asked her because he wanted her company! How could that be?

"Thank you, no, sir."

"Very well." He put her cloak about her shoulders, and led the way out. There was a crush waiting outside for carriages, and Alastair frowned as people thronged about them. He put his arm lightly behind Sonia's shoulders, to protect her.

"I say there, don't push us into the street," he said sharply, to some men behind them.

They mumbled an apology, glancing at his stern face. Sonia felt sheltered behind his iron-hard arm. The carriage soon drew up, his coachman on the box. Alastair helped her in, then Leah. He sat opposite them as they were driven off.

All too soon, they were at her home again. He showed her

52

to the door, waited until the sleepy-eyed footman opened to them. Then he bent and took her hand, and kissed the glove lightly.

"I have enjoyed tonight. I hope you will consent to another such evening, Miss Goldfine?"

"I should—like that," she managed to say, and then she was in the hallway and he was gone, the carriage rumbling away over the cobblestones.

She went up to bed in a daze, feeling close to tears. He wanted to go out with her again! He had enjoyed the evening! He *liked* her! She had heard whispers as they strolled, even as they talked to his friends. She had heard the words, "Jewess! In trade!" several times, but Alastair had not seemed to hear.

Leah helped her undress, then left her. Sonia slowly put away the diamonds, then sat in the window seat for a while, watching the waning moon.

How could it be? She felt nervous, apprehensive. He could not be serious about her, not about her as a woman. He must want something from her uncle—yet—yet. . . . What if he was serious about Sonia? What if he was? She wiped the tears from under her eyelids. Her nerves were on edge, she was excited about the opera and the beautiful, melancholy singing of the final songs. That was it. She was wrought up.

She closed her eyes, thought of the handsome, serious face of Alastair as he listened. He had smiled, at the farces, frowned, was as rapt by the beautiful singing as she was. They had felt in tune, somehow. Yet—yet. . . .

They were of different religions. He was a marquess, of one of the great houses of England. She was the product of a ghetto, a trading house. How could he be serious? It must not be true—she must not dream—she must not dream. . . .

Yet when she fell asleep, she did dream—that a handsome prince in blue and silver came to her, took her hand, and said, "I love you," in a deep, exciting voice. She hated to wake up and realize it had been only a dream. She must, she really must, settle down again and be sensible. Dreams like that did not come true. She would only be hurt, if she went on like this.

Chapter
5

THE next morning, Leah brought to Sonia in her study a huge box of flowers. Sonia opened it, took out the card.

> With gratitude for a lovely evening.
> —Alastair Charlton

The flowers were masses of white roses and lovely starry white jasmine. She bent over them, tears springing again to her eyes. It was a conventional gesture, but how she loved it! Delicate long stemmed white roses, and the fragrant delicate jasmine. . . .

Leah looked satisfied and yet troubled all at once, as she brought two vases of blue porcelain to hold the flowers. Sonia arranged them, managed to say brightly, "How kind of the marquess! It was most thoughtful."

Leah gave her a keen look. She knew Sonia better than anyone else did in the world. "Yes, most kind," said Leah in a bland voice that meant she was thinking deeply.

Sonia did her sketching that morning, but her gaze kept drifting to the glorious blooms on her table. The scents were pervasive, like a memory of something beautiful. Her mind kept going back to the evening, his gentleness and protective manner, the joy of sharing the emotions of the singing. They were alike in their tastes. How strange it was.

Jacob and Beryl, Abner and Bettina invited her out with them several evenings later. They were to attend a serious drama, and she looked forward to it eagerly. Bettina could whine, but she was a good judge of theater and an intelligent critic. It could be a delightful evening.

The four of them came for her promptly, Jacob was always on time, or ahead of time. He was teased for it, but all respected him. He was much like his father. Beryl praised Sonia's gown, rapturously.

"How beautiful you look, dear Sonia! The blue satin, the swansdown trim, your diamonds! They set you off, like one of your jewelry designs!"

Sonia smiled, but was pleased by the compliment. The men said little, but stared at their "little sister" complacently. Bettina began to say that she, too, could look splendid had she but the money to spend on dresses and jewels. Beryl said sweetly, "But you have as much as Sonia, I know, because Papa said so."

Sonia changed the subject hastily. She did not want to start the evening with a quarrel. They hurried out to the carriages, set out early for the theater. Jacob had obtained a fine box near the stage, so they had little need of their exquisite opera glasses. They were so close they could see the faces clearly, and, more important, hear the lines distinctly.

They were early enough to be able to settle in their box seats, watch the audience coming in, and comment on the gowns, who was with whom—all the latest gossip. Bettina followed the tattling in the gazettes quite avidly, and would expound on it if encouraged.

"Oh, there is Mrs. Porter," she exclaimed under her breath, leaning past Sonia to point with her opera glasses. "You have heard of her? A recent widow, the woman in the green satin and emeralds. There, with the blond hair."

Sonia glanced at the woman, away again, then at her

again. She stood regally in the box across from them, smiling at some remark made to her by one of three gentlemen with her. A rather dowdy woman stood behind the group.

"So that is Mrs. Porter," breathed Jacob, unusually curious. "One wonders what Lord Fairley sees in her. They say he escorts her everywhere."

Blood rushed to Sonia's head, there was a queer ringing in her ears. Mrs. Daphne Porter—she knew enough of Society to have heard of her. And that was the—mistress—of Lord Fairley! She stared at her until the woman's image was imprinted on her mind: queenly, sensuously beautiful, full-blown and of seductive quality. Was that what Alastair Charlton liked in a woman? It was a wonder he had bothered to invite Sonia anywhere! They could not have been more unlike!

She heard Bettina's whispers as in a daze. "Escorts her all about—gifts her with rubies and emeralds—often at her soirees, they say he pays the rent on her flat—devoted to her—"

Sonia was biting her lips. She wanted to weep. So much for dreams! He could not have been serious about her. He probably wanted some commission from her, or something from her uncle.

"Ah, there he is, Lord Fairley!" Bettina's whisper was so shrill, Sonia was sure she could be heard three boxes away. Sonia glanced unwillingly toward Mrs. Porter's loge, but saw no striking tall figure of a gentleman. "No, no, behind us, in the center!"

"Don't point, for my sake," groaned her husband, Abner, crossly. He half-hid mockingly behind the curtains. "You will have the audience watching *us* tonight, rather than the play!"

Bettina scowled at him, and made some sharp reply. Sonia did not hear her. She had glanced backwards obediently, to see two tall blond-haired gentlemen enter the box toward the center of the ring. The young man with him looked enough like Alastair to be his brother—perhaps it was his brother. She wished she dared raise her opera glasses, as Bettina did, and frankly survey the loges. It was enough for the moment that he had not gone to the box of Mrs. Porter. He stood to permit two young girls to come in.

"His sisters, I do believe," said Bettina.

Sonia drew a deep breath, and turned her attention deliberately to the stage, as the house lights were dimmed and the orchestra began an interval of light music preceding the play.

Deliberately, also, she made herself listen to the dialogue, watch the acting, become absorbed in the story. Her nerves still quivered. She must be on edge, but would not show it. Alastair Charlton was beyond her reach, she reminded herself, quite beyond her.

The first act ended with restrained applause. Much of the London crowd went to be seen, rather than to see, and the drama was beyond them. They stirred, yawned, stood up to join the promenade.

Jacob asked if the ladies cared for refreshments, then went to order for them. Abner remained to keep them company, chatting with more animation than usual. Bettina was discussing the play with sharp wit when a knock came at the door of their box.

Sonia half-turned, expecting to see a waiter with their tray. Her eyes widened and widened as a gentleman stepped in— Lord Fairley, in a striking white satin suit, with diamond and sapphire studs at his neck-cloth and wrists. With a look in his blue eyes, and a smile for her.

He bowed to her. "Good evening, Miss Goldfine. I expected to see you here, I knew you could not resist such fine drama."

Abner was staring, Bettina had her mouth half-open. Sonia rose to greet the nobleman, moving past her cousins.

"Good evening, Lord Fairley. How pleasant to meet you again. May I make known to you my cousins—" And she managed the introductions, though she felt rather faint with excitement. Jacob returned with the waiter as they were being completed.

She thought Lord Fairley would exchange a few remarks and depart. Instead, he accepted a chair in their alcove, a cup from Jacob, and seemed prepared to remain for the lengthy intermission.

Bettina soon recovered her poise and began to comment on the play, all the time gazing at him with her sharp eyes, storing up his appearance for later gossip. "I thought the hero was rather too full of tensions for the first act," she said. "He must save himself, or he will have nothing to build up. Do you not think so, Lord Fairley?"

"The poor fellow has a great many problems. One must allow him his emotional display," said Lord Fairley mildly, glancing at Sonia. Was there a twinkle in the deep blue eyes? She half-smiled in a vague conspiracy with him, then glanced down at her cup again.

"I should like to read the play at leisure," said Beryl. She set down her cup with a shake of her head at her husband. Jacob had been unusually quiet for him, content to listen and to see to their comfort. "Yes, I should like to read and study it. The lines have much more meaning than one can catch in a moment."

Lord Fairley agreed with this. They all talked with some ease, and Sonia was able to make a few comments on the actors. When the lights dimmed for the second act, it came as a surprise. Lord Fairley moved with ease to the door, saying, "I must return to my family. Thank you for allowing me to share the intermission with you. Miss Goldfine, my best regards," and the final bow seemed to be directed to her alone, before the door closed after him.

The second act began. Sonia sat with her hands clasped, her eyes on the stage, but the fine acting was somewhat lost on her for a while until she was caught up in the drama again. To have paid a call on them! How the audience must have stared!

Bettina commented on just that at the second intermission. The lights had no sooner gone up when she leaned forward to whisper sharply to Sonia, "Did you see how we are stared at? Lord Fairley drew all eyes to us! There are surely holes in my back from all those opera glasses on me!"

Beryl laughed at her kindly. "Everyone stares during the plays, Bettina. Lord Fairley was only paying us a kindness. But I did not know he had met Sonia," and her eyes went to Sonia, with a question in them.

"He had called to see Uncle," said Sonia, with some composure. "Uncle insisted I should accept his invitation to the opera last week. Lord Fairley enjoys music."

They all stared at her, thoughtfully. "Father insisted?" asked Jacob. "He wished you to go, with a gentile?"

"He said so," said Sonia quietly. She was thinking of the comments about Mrs. Daphne Porter. That was the woman who had Lord Fairley's real attentions, and a pain in her heart warned her. She was close to being hurt by this. She smiled brightly. "Is he not grand? A marquess, no less, and with such elegant manners."

"A marquess? He seemed very easy, polished, yet not haughty," said Beryl, and Sonia could have hugged her.

"I wonder—" murmured Jacob, but did not tell them what he wondered.

In early November of 1809, Alastair had made up his mind. His other creditors were dunning him, he had found no other way out. And Miss Goldfine was a credit to her sex, a lady in every way, low-voiced, modest, inoffensive. He liked her fine mind, and enjoyed the sharing of music with her. They had tastes in common, he thought her above the low farces, and equal to the high drama he himself enjoyed.

It had to work out—and it was the only solution. So one fine morning, he dressed carefully in navy blue wool, his silk shirt, a white lace stock, and sapphires. He would not go poor-appearing to his fate. His mouth twisted slightly as he surveyed himself critically in the mirror. Rather pale, not so tanned, his eyes a bit sunken, and his cheeks hollow. He had not eaten well lately, and too many nights he had lain awake, to toss from one side of the bed to the other.

Now the die was cast, he must go through with it. Well, he would go gallantly, with head high. His brother and two sisters, and all dependent on him, must not be disappointed. His own happiness was of little account, he had no right to any happiness. As for heirs—if they were a disappointment, then the estates must go to Maurice. He would see to that. Maurice must marry well and high. He would see to that, also.

He had sent a note to Meyer Goldfine, asking when he might see him. Meyer had said he would be at home this morning to him. So Alastair had his coachman drive right up to the door, and stepped out into the walk.

He looked more critically at the house, and found no fault

with it. Modestly large, gray stone, with narrow pillars, it was grand without ostentation, handsome without gaudiness. Inside, it was well-kept, with beautiful appointments, furniture, Persian carpets, and paintings. It showed good taste. It augured well. He found himself counting desperately through all these points. This would be good, this looked well, this turn of the card might work. A gambler, he thought, restraining his bitterness.

He was shown into Meyer Goldfine's study. The elderly gentleman rose to meet him, the dimming eyes smiled. He held out his hand. Alastair took it, shook it gently, with appreciation for the fragile quality of the aging bones.

"Ah, sit down, sit down. You have found some solution, your letter said?" Meyer Goldfine sat down carefully in his favorite chair, his feet went to the hassock. Alastair waited to see him seated, then sat down in the overstuffed chair opposite. He found it comfortable.

"Thank you, yes, sir. Your wisdom is greater than mine," he said steadily, managing to smile.

The keen eyes studied him, the graying head nodded. "Thank you. Which portion of my many attempts at wisdom do you find palatable?"

Alastair smiled more naturally. He had a fine dry wit, this old man. "I cannot pull out of my own accord and will. I must find a partner to help me," he said steadily. "At the moment, I believe the only solution I have is to marry well and —pay off my debts, that I might begin again."

"Ummm, ummm," Meyer murmured, nodding. "And you have found such a young lady, ummm?"

Alastair drew a deep breath. "I find your niece, Miss Sonia Goldfine, both attractive in mind and spirit, sir," he said, and found the words not too difficult to say. "Do you think she would be willing to marry me?"

The old head was bent, he could not see the eyes, hidden behind the dark lashes. "Ummm," said Meyer Goldfine thoughtfully. "You enjoyed her company, eh?"

"Very much so. We have many tastes in common. She is a lady, modestly and sweetly attractive. She would—make a fine marchioness, I believe, if she is willing to—take this step."

Meyer Goldfine kept his head bent. "We must discuss some matters first, before we ask her—opinion on the matter, my lord," he said gently. "Firstly, in the matter of your debts. I have taken the liberty of repaying some of them quickly, so the interest will not mount up higher. Certain men would not deal with me; you must repay them yourself. Let us go over all the financial matters." Pulling himself up with a little difficulty, he hobbled over to the desk and sat down there. Alastair followed him, to sit across from him, heart thumping unpleasantly fast. This was the crucial moment. After the settlement, there must be no drawing back. He was a gentleman, his word was his bond.

They went over the figures for more than an hour. Then Meyer Goldfine said, "As settlement on your marriage to my beloved niece, Sonia Goldfine, I am prepared to pay all your debts for you, amounting to over three hundred thousand pounds. In addition to that, I will settle on you, free and clear, another two hundred thousand pounds. You may do as you wish with it, use it to settle your brother, or present your sisters and dower them."

"You are—most generous," said Alastair. It was more than he had dared to hope.

"In regard to my niece—she is wealthy in her own right. My banking house handles her investments, which are extensive. In the marriage settlement, it shall be written that these are hers, to do with as she chooses. If the marriage fails, none of the money will go to you or yours. I regret my bluntness, it is necessary, my lord," said Meyer Goldfine, moving a paper carefully on the desk. "None of her funds shall be touched. I know your propensity—er—to gamble. I want the fortune she has to remain intact, to go to her children, and yours, God willing."

Alastair folded his hands over the knob of his cane, clenched his fists to control himself. Finally he managed to say in an even tone, "That is your right, and hers. I shall not touch the money belonging to her."

Fury had raged in him. He had wanted to storm away, telling the little old man to go to hell. But pride restrained him. And he had said to himself that he would go through with it, no matter what. His family must be made secure against the future, whatever he had to sacrifice.

"Do not be angry," said Meyer gently. "My dear Sonia is very precious to me. She has suffered much in her life. I want her to be happy in her marriage, and not suffer more. There is much love and womanliness in her. She will make you very happy, should you allow her to do so. I will pray daily for your joy in the marriage."

Alastair swallowed. "I thank you, sir," he said stiffly.

"However," continued Meyer. "I am a practical man as well as an uncle. The marriage could fail. If it does, you will still have the two hundred thousand pounds, and your debts will be paid. I do not wish the settlement to bind you for life. If the price is too high for both of you, it is better to dissolve the marriage, rather than to make both of you chafe against the bonds." He smiled slightly at Alastair's surprise. "You thought I would not say such a thing? We Jews believe in the sanctity of the marriage bond. Yet we are too practical to insist that every marriage should be kept whether it is perfect or not. Marriage is not to be entered into lightly, but if a mistake is made—" He shrugged. "There are remedies."

He spoke then of a written marriage settlement, in which all would be spelled out. He would have attorneys draw up papers, which he and Alastair would sign. It would be an agreement between them and would be binding on them both. Alastair's debts would be all settled on his wedding day.

Goldfine wrote out a rough draft of the settlement, showed it to Alastair. They discussed it. Alastair said, "You are being most gracious and generous. I thank you for it. This will mean I can begin again, to manage the estates and households as I would wish, without fear of having all taken from me."

"I ask only that you make my dear Sonia as happy as possible, should she accept you," said Meyer.

Alastair started. He had forgotten the girl! He had not even proposed to her! He stared in alarm at Meyer Goldfine.

"Enough of business. You will speak to Sonia today?" asked Meyer.

"Yes, yes, I should like to."

Now that the settlement was being put within his reach, he was anxious to get it all over and done with.

"I will ask that Sonia come to the drawing room. You may be private there with her." Meyer rang the long cord for a maid.

Sonia was working in her rooms when the maid came to her. Her uncle wished her to come to the drawing room. She sighed, a little impatiently. Her work was going poorly, she kept thinking. Her mind wandered to the fine young marquess who had showed her attentions. She understood he was just being kind—yet—what if . . . But no, he was attentive to Mrs. Daphne Porter, he could not have anything much to do with a young girl like Sonia, inexperienced and naive. She knew nothing of the ways of men and the heart.

If her uncle was going to present her to yet another of his "fine young men with prospects," she would retire to the country! She shoved back her curls from her broad white forehead, smoothed down the hair in back, gave an impatient look to her white muslin gown with the simple blue ribbons, and descended the stairs to the first floor.

The footman, face impassive, showed her into the drawing room and shut the door after him. Sonia stared at the tall figure near the windows. Her heart seemed to stop still, then began again with a frightening leap.

"Oh—*you*—" she breathed. Her manners came to the fore. "Lord Fairley! Forgive me, I was—startled—"

He came forward, took her hand in his, raised it to his lips. She wore no gloves, she felt the warm lips on her fingers and a thrill shot through her. She sank into a chair near the fire, for the early November day was damp and chilly. Lord Fairley took a seat next to hers.

"Forgive me for calling unannounced," he said gravely. He was looking at her anxiously.

She contrived a smile. "You are always welcome. Have you been discussing business with my uncle?"

He gave a start. "Yes, well—we have. Your uncle gave me permission to speak to you."

Misunderstanding, she gave him a shy smile. "But of course you may speak to me. Did you enjoy the remainder of the play the other evening?"

"Yes, yes, it was splendid. However, it was on another matter—"

She waited, her heart thumping. Would he ask her out again? And what would the world of London say, if Lord Fairley appeared once again in the company of the Jewish designer of jewelry? How the tongues would wag! She was not sure she should go. She wanted to go—yet . . .

He cleared his throat. "I have requested permission of your uncle—to pay my addresses to you," he said solemnly.

She stared at him, her gray eyes wide, her hand to her heart. "You—wish—*what?*" she managed to whisper in a choked tone.

He stirred in the chair. Color came to his tanned face. "I am sorry to—shock you, Miss Goldfine. I have long admired you, despite—the differences in our stations. It seemed to me that it did not matter—our differences of faith, our positions —the fact that we are of different upbringing. We have much in common—do we not?" he asked desperately.

"Oh—sir—I cannot think what to say," she murmured. She was sure she had fallen asleep at her desk and was dreaming. This prince in a story, this grave charming man, with his deep blue eyes, his handsome face solemn—he could not be asking for her hand in marriage!

He sighed, and passed his lean tanned hand over his forehead. She was surprised to see his face was damp, as though in some deep emotional stress.

"If you say no, there is no more to be said," he said, lowering his head. "However, if you wish to think it over . . . Believe me, Miss Goldfine, I deeply admire your nature and your mind. You are a very intelligent and fine woman. Your uncle is immensely fond of you, and speaks highly of you. Your reputation in the city is a credit to him and to you. If you wish to hear more of me, I can recommend several friends, my record in the war—"

"My goodness," she said faintly. "I would not dream of asking—I mean, everyone thinks highly of you—and—and you have been extremely kind—and Uncle speaks so of you—"

"You will consider my offer, then?" he asked anxiously. "I will promise to take every care of you, to consider your wishes in every way an honorable man can. You may know— I have one brother and two sisters to settle in the world. Per-

haps—" he smiled slightly, "that very consideration might
cause you to draw back. One sister is in particular quite a
handful!"

"Oh, sir, I am sure they are charming," she blurted out,
drawn out of her shyness and amazement by his humorous
speech. "I should be happy to assist you in their care. I know
you are devoted to them—"

"Very devoted. I am responsible for them," he said. "After
thinking of nothing much but battles and estates for some
years, the care of three young persons is much on my mind. I
shall be glad of your advice and assistance."

Now that they had spoken more at ease, she was able to
think again. He must be serious! He spoke of marriage, and
her helping him with his family. He was looking at her with
respect and anxiety about her answer. Could he possibly be
attracted to her, could he love her?

"You will think seriously about my offer?" he asked.

"Oh—yes—"

"And—there is no other man in the offing?" he blurted out,
blushing like a schoolboy. That endeared him to her. "I do
not mean to cut out some chap, but I am sure if you would
allow me to escort you about and we could converse more—"

He did mean it! He was serious! He reached out his hand
for hers. Timidly, she put her slim long fingers into his. "I—
should like—like that," she said.

"And you will consider my offer of marriage?" he asked
solemnly.

Something made her say it: the squeezing of his fingers on
hers, the tone of his voice, or the melancholy blue of his
eyes. . . .

She said, "I should like—to marry you, Lord Fairley."

He stared down at her. "You—would? You would?"

She swallowed, and glanced to the fire shyly. "I think so. My
Uncle approves."

"Oh, he has approved, he told me, or I should not have
approached you, Miss—may I call you Sonia?" he said, more
naturally. "It is a splendid name, and suits you so well!"

His spontaneous outburst calmed her. She managed to say,
"Please do, and thank you. I—I feel rather—overwhelmed. I
did not know that you—you liked me well enough—I mean

did not think—" She longed to ask him about Mrs. Porter, but that would not do!

"I think we shall get along very well together," said Alasair Charlton thoughtfully. He was still holding her hand and they were talking in low tones when her uncle tapped lightly on the door and entered.

Sonia sprang up, blushing. "Oh, Uncle—Lord Fairley has said—asked—I mean—"

"I have been honored by her acceptance of my offer," said Lord Fairley, standing beside her and taking her arm in his hand naturally. He looked across at her uncle. Sonia felt rather than saw a slight tension between them.

Her uncle smiled. "Well, well, if that is what you both wish," he said, benignly. "You must stay for a little luncheon, Lord Fairley, and we will discuss the happy event. My dearest Sonia, to have you married happily and settled at last! I shall be so very pleased!"

Her uncle kissed her cheek. Lord Fairley watched them, then bent and kissed Sonia's cheek also. It was a solemn moment. She wanted to laugh and cry. His lips on her cheek! How sweet that was, that gentle touch. And she would marry him, and live with him, and he would kiss her often, and love her and cherish her. . . .

It was a dream. Her handsome prince, coming to wake her with a kiss. How beautiful he was, this prince of hers, this marquess who was so courtly and thoughtful. And to belong to her! She would belong to him and they would live together forever and ever in great happiness!

They had the same tastes and interests, he would escort her to operas and plays and concerts. They would chat with their friends and family and each other.

Her gray eyes shone like stars that afternoon, as she listened to the conversation of her uncle and her fiance. She was engaged to be married! It was a wonder, and she could not believe it entirely.

Chapter
6

◦●◦●◦●◦●◦●◦●◦●◦●◦●◦●◦●◦●◦

THE plans seemed to move forward with stunning quickness. Sonia had thought they would be engaged through the winter and perhaps be married in the spring or summer.

Instead her uncle said, "I see no need to wait. Lord Fairley needs you in his household. It is sadly in need of a firm hand, I believe. And why wait? You are both of age and know your own minds."

Jacob came, to be closeted in the study with his father for two hours. He came out, flushed behind his beard, his eyes angry. He sought out Sonia.

"I cannot believe you have agreed to a marriage such as this," he burst out. "What pressure has Father brought on you? To marry a gentile!"

"Oh, Jacob," and her tears came. "What a thing to say! Lord Fairley has been most courteous and kind. He asked me so gently and courteously and—"

"That is not the point," said Jacob brusquely. "You know he has need of money and you are wealthy—"

She drew herself up, dried her eyes. "That is unworthy of you, Cousin!" she blazed, anger seizing her. "Not a word has been said of money! Uncle has told me that my fortune is my own, no matter what happens. It will go to my—my children. Lord Fairley wants no part of it!"

"Indeed?" Jacob looked puzzled and disturbed. "Gossip says that he is short of money and in debt. He has been seen at the money lenders, though not recently, I believe—"

"Jacob, you will not insult him in my hearing!"

Jacob sighed, patted her shoulder. "You know I love you as my own sister," he said quietly. "This marriage troubles me. It is not like Father to agree to your marriage with a gentile. You realize you must be married in *his* rites. Only Father and I may attend, with the rabbi's permission. There will be no *chupah* under which you two will stand, there will be no bridal party of your relatives and friends—"

Sonia stared at him, her face paling. Nothing had been said about this to her. "No—of course not," she said slowly. "How could there? I—I must be married in—in his church, I suppose—"

She put her hands to her face. No, she had not thought of this. Now she began to consider it seriously. No bridal canopy covered with flowers, no rites such as Jacob had enjoyed when he married Beryl, none of the joyous ceremonies she had witnessed since childhood when other relatives married. No singing of the songs she knew, no processions, no feasts. She would be among strangers, marrying a stranger, in strange rites.

"I must speak to Uncle," she said, and Jacob was satisfied.

She went to her uncle, who frowned when she spoke of the matter. He studied her face with his keen eyes.

"But Sonia, my beloved daughter," he said very gently, "You are a girl like the daughter whom the Lord never gave to me. He brought you to me and you are like my own. Would I consent if I thought you would be unhappy? I thought you liked and respected this young man, or I should never have given my consent."

"I do—like him." She thought, she *loved* him. She gazed at Alastair with all her heart in her eyes until she felt embarrassed for herself. He was so serious, so handsome, so

70

princely. Yet—he was not a Jew. "I just—never thought—Uncle, we cannot be married in the synagogue, can we?"

He shook his head sadly. "No, he would never agree. Sonia, you may keep your religion, and go alone to the synagogue with Leah. But your children must take his faith, and be brought up in it. Do you understand that?"

No, she had not looked that far ahead. The mists of her dreams fell away from her. She rose unsteadily to go to the window and stare out into the garden. "How much—must I give up—uncle?" And her voice quivered.

"Some of the rites," he said steadily. "You will give him a ring, as you wish. But your ring must be on your left hand, as the Christian custom is. Not the right hand. You will not observe the dietary laws in his household, you will give up your customs for his. His relatives will be yours. His habits yours. His friends yours. In your own sitting room, you might have a corner of your own in which to worship. But if he wishes, you must attend his church with him."

She felt coldness gather about her heart. "Uncle, you would never have agreed to this kind of marriage—for Jacob or Abner, would you?" She did not turn to look into his kindly worried face. Still she stared unseeingly at the bright flowers in the autumn garden, the asters and late roses that drooped their heads.

"No, that would be different. A Jewish man must marry one of his own kind," said Meyer Goldfine decidedly. "A woman is different. She can give up to the man. A man cannot give up to a woman."

She bent her head, leaned against the cool glass. He came to her, putting his arm about her waist.

"It will not be so hard, Sonia," he said quietly. "You have never participated deeply in the faith. It scarred your youth. You can begin again in your marriage, have love and trust and confidence with this man you respect, eh? He will take care of you, he will guard you, he will respect you. You will forget the troubled past, live for him and for the future and your children."

She could not speak, her voice choked. He squeezed her gently. "My dearest Sonia, I hope much for this marriage. You have always refused the other young men I brought to you, the Jewish men. I think, underneath, you wished some-one different, someone to help you forget the past. Eh? With Lord Fairley, you can have a new life."

"You believe this, dear Uncle" she whispered. Perhaps he knew her better than she did herself.

He nodded. "You need someone different, someone intelli-gent and honorable, someone with a mind to match yours. I think in Lord Fairley you have met your match. I will pray daily that this is true."

Comforted, she was able to go ahead with the wedding plans. She kept her set smile when the Christian ceremonies were explained to her by a minister, a man who was cold and formal and obviously thought little of this marriage of Lord Fairley's. Nevertheless, he was proper, careful to explain ev-erything several times, going over the wedding ceremony with her and making sure she knew her part in it.

For some reason, both her uncle and Lord Fairley were anxious to have the wedding take place at once. She would wish for more time to think, she felt rushed and confused. Whenever she mentioned this, her uncle would gently tease her.

"Ah, my dear, I do not want you to think, maybe change your mind. You have depended too much on your intellect! I wish you to feel emotions instead, and to be eager to be with your fiance and husband."

She blushed deeply, agreed to a change of subject. To be with *him*—alone—she scarcely dared think of it.

Leah prepared her for the physical side of her marriage, as she had no mother to do so and no aunt. Beryl came one day, speaking gently, precisely, ignoring Sonia's embarrass-ment, to teach her lovingly what her marital duties would be.

The dressmakers came almost every day, hurrying to pre-pare an exquisite wedding dress of white silk and lace, with chiffon draped over all. The wedding veil was of Brussels lace, fine as a spider's web.

There was one engagement party, in Lord Fairley's home. It was the first time she had been in his townhouse. She felt timid and anxious as she stepped out of the carriage. Only Leah came with her. Jacob, for some reason, was angry about the marriage. Beryl would not go without her husband. Meyer was not well, was keeping his strength for the wedding ceremonies themselves.

Lord Fairley met her at the door, and smiled to see her pale anxious face. "My dear, how lovely you look," he said, taking her arm. The butler removed her cloak carefully, with awe at the splendid white ermine. Sonia stood revealed in a beautiful gown of pale blue satin, with sapphires and diamonds at her throat and wrist. Lord Fairley took her aside into a little room. He seemed rather pale and serious himself, she thought, though splendid in his blue satin and sapphires.

"I wished to give you your engagement ring, Sonia," he said, taking out a small velvet box. She held out her right hand automatically, and he smiled, and took her left. "No, the left hand, my dear! You are indeed confused tonight."

She said nothing. Jewish brides wore their rings on their right hands. She would feel odd with the rings on her left—but she must accept his customs, her uncle had said so. She made no protest as he put the fine diamond on her finger and raised her hand to his lips.

They returned at once to the hallway. His sisters were coming down the stairs. Sonia looked up shyly at them, she had not even met them!

Lord Fairley presented them formally. "Sonia, my dear, may I present my sister, Lady Edwina. And this is Lady Henrietta. My dear sisters, this is my bride, Miss Sonia Goldfine."

Sonia held out her hand. She did not mistake it; there was hesitation before Lady Edwina, grand in blue velvet, took her hand and murmured something. Lady Henrietta hesitated even more, and her violet eyes looked as though she had been crying.

"How do you do?" murmured Sonia, as Lady Henrietta dropped her slim hand hastily. No, she had not imagined it. They looked coldly, proudly, disdainfully at her.

They proceeded to the drawing room full of guests. A blond young man came up, looking much like Alastair, only more immature and amiable, unformed.

"Maurice Charlton," said Alastair. Someone else called him "Lord Maurice," and Sonia wondered if she should address him like that. To be safe, she did.

He wore flashing blue satin, trimmed with gold rather gaudily, but it suited his dashing good looks.

The brother and two sisters stood with them in a receiving line. Edwina murmured names to her sister-in-law-to-be, in a cool polite social tone which spoke well for her training. Everyone was staring openly at Sonia. She kept her head up, her smile pinned on, longing for a reassuring touch of Alastair's hand.

When the guests had drunk their health and eaten of the cakes and pastries, they departed. An uneasy silence came over the remaining few. Leah had remained in the background, an alert abigail, watching everything with her curious eyes.

Edwina turned to her brother. "Did all suit you?" she asked, in what seemed a mocking tone.

He frowned at her. "It went well," he said curtly.

"I cannot believe it is true!" blurted out Lady Henrietta, and put her handkerchief to her eyes. "It is such a shock, you cannot mean it! It is all some terrible nightmare!"

"Henrietta!" he thundered, striding toward her, while Sonia stood still, paralyzed with shock. "You will say no more!"

"I don't care, she isn't one of us! How could you, how could you do such a thing?" And Henrietta began to weep frantically.

Maurice took her arm. "Say now, you better be quiet. Our stern brother is scowling at you," he said, with a grin. He had been drinking rather heavily and his voice was slurred.

"She feels deeply," said Edwina, giving Sonia a look of scorn and dislike. "I must say, it was a great shock to all of us. What is the haste in all this? Why should you marry so soon? Think it over, Alastair, it will be evident that this is not the right solution!"

"You will all be silent," said Alastair, in a clipped deadly tone. He had turned pale beneath the bronze of his face. "Sonia, I beg your pardon. They are overwrought, and perhaps have had too much to drink. Allow me to call your carriage for you. May I escort you home?"

She was so shaken by the unconcealed dislike of his sisters that she could scarcely speak. "No—my lord—it is—not necessary—"

Leah came forward, Sonia's cloak over her arm. "Our carriage is outside, Miss Sonia," she said protectively, shooting a look of dislike and disdain toward the others. "We'll be on our way."

Alastair had a white line about his proud mouth. "May I call upon you tomorrow afternoon, Sonia? I will wish to apologize for the crass behavior of my sisters and brother!"

She did not want to cause trouble between him and his family. She summoned a pallid smile. "It is not necessary. I understand," she said gravely. "Goodnight, my lord."

"Alastair," he insisted.

"Goodnight, Alastair," she said. He handed her down the steps and into her carriage, and waited until she had driven off, then returned to the lighted house.

He must have said some stern things to them, for the next time Sonia met them all were excessively polite. She could not help feeling they liked her no better, but would obey their brother's dictates. She lay awake nights before her wedding day came, tossing and turning. Was she doing the right thing? If her uncle had not daily reassured her, she would have broken the engagement. There was too much against them; it might never work out.

Alastair sent flowers to her, notes, and came often to see her and speak of future arrangements. He confided his troubles about his sisters. Edwina was too shy, for all her proud manner. Henrietta was inclined to frivolity, inclined also to young men who were not at all suitable. Sonia listened, hoped she might one day be wise enough to give good advice about them. It did comfort her that he confided in her.

The wedding day came, and she dressed for her marriage, with both fear and hope winging in her heart. She could scarcely speak for terror as they approached the church. There seemed to be a crowd about.

"Oh, I thought we had not invited many," she murmured fearfully to her uncle. He patted her hand.

"Your future husband has many friends and relatives," he told her. She turned her face from him, though it was already hidden behind the cobwebby veil.

Her friends had not come; they were holding aloof. Only Jacob and Uncle Meyer would be there. Her heart was down to her white satin shoes. Alone, friendless—how could she go through with this? Yet, when they entered the church and she saw Alastair standing tall and proud and handsome at the altar—waiting for *her*—she forgot all else.

She made the strange responses in a steady tone, tried to ignore the buzz of whispers behind them. She missed the bridal canopy of flowers, but flowers were set in vases all about the altar. Surely, surely, it would all work out. They were of like minds, after all, and he was kind. . . .

The reception was more difficult, for she did not have her back to people there in Alastair's home. No, she must face them across the room, and later in the huge dining room, with the mammoth white cake to cut. . . . All went in a daze, of white and silver, and talking and laughing, and the buzz of gossips in which she caught words.

"Yes, yes, Jewish, isn't it amazing! And he is a marquess! Where will they enter next? Pushing their way in—pushing —much money, I hear—money, that's it— Wealthy family— from Vienna, speaks all kinds of foreign languages! English? Of course not, not with those looks! Dark and heathen she looks—Pretty? Well, if you like the type—"

Alastair did not show by one muscle of his face that he heard anything. Yet, his hand over hers was firm and hard, unnecessarily gripping hers as she tentatively cut the cake with his dress sword. She caught the stares, the mockery in some looks. Several of the men looked her up and down in the shimmery white dress. Their eyes were not easy to meet.

She was glad, fervently glad, when it was all over, and Alastair showed her up to their apartment. He had commanded an entire suite of rooms in one wing of the house, and had had her chambers redecorated for her. All silvery blue and white, with touches of gold on the draperies and furniture, gold vases on the mantels of the fireplaces. He looked about anxiously as they entered.

"How charming," she said spontaneously as they entered, and his anxiety eased. The rooms looked like a refuge to her. "I could not have chosen better, I will enjoy the colors here."

He smiled down gently at her. He put his hand on her hair, and in the first intimate gesture he had made, he stroked his hand over her head to her neck, and held her closer to him. "I want you to be happy with me, Sonia. If there is aught you wish, you have but to say it."

She wanted to say, "Love me, oh, but love me—" But she could not say it. She turned shyly from him, to examine the lovely rosewood table near the window. He followed her.

"I thought you could draw and sketch here," he said. "I know you will wish one room to be your workroom for the jewelry you make. Shall you wish to bring the tools and equipment from your other house?"

She hesitated. "Oh—not just now," she said cautiously. In the back of her mind, she was thinking of what Jacob had whispered to her this morning. "If it doesn't work out," he had muttered in her ear, "you can get a divorce. Father will arrange it, I know, Sonia. Don't feel tied!"

He had been angry and resentful about her, he had argued with his father, to no avail. And he had come to her wedding in his somber Jewish dress, with his prayer shawl, no matter how people stared and snickered at him. Dear Jacob! Kinder than any brother could have been.

"I thought we might dine upstairs tonight," said Alastair, quietly, to her back. "It might be more comfortable for us. I am weary with all the chatter, are you not?"

She turned around, pink flushing her cheeks. "Yes, yes, I am a bit weary. But won't—they—mind—"

He looked a bit grim. "No, they won't. Besides, we shall please ourselves. It is our home, Sonia. I had thought in a few weeks we might retire to my country home, just the two of us. A godmother of Edwina has offered to chaperon the girls for some weeks while we get away. Shall you like that?"

"Oh—so much," she said impulsively, her gray eyes shining.

"Good. I hoped you would like that. I must see to the estates and, besides, I think we should be alone for a time to get acquainted with each other," he said, simply and naturally. He touched her cheek with his long fingers. "I shall change to my robe and be comfortable. I think your abigail is coming up."

He disappeared into his rooms, and she went to hers. Leah came up soon, and helped her change from the fragile wedding gown and veil into a slim robe of white satin, with long lace sleeves to her fingertips. Leah was unusually silent that night, her face sober. Sonia scarcely noticed. She felt trembly and excited inside. This was her wedding night!

They dined together, quietly, and Alastair kept the conversation going in an easy and calm way. She was grateful to him. Her hands shook when she held a cup, and the wine was cool in her throat.

Later, Leah helped her undress, and put on the white silk nightdress. In the wide bed, Sonia felt lost. She had always had comfortable beds, but this was such a very large one. . . .

Leah left her, and only a candle burned beside the bed. Sonia lay with her hands behind her head, contemplating little gilded cupids on the ceiling, and the pale blue of the sky beyond them. It was a charming scene, with garlands of rose and silver. If one might only escape to such a pretty paradise—alone. . . .

The door opened, and Alastair came in. He wore a robe of deep blue, and his hair was wet from washing. He brushed it back with his hand. Her heart began to thump. She gazed up at him with wide luminous gray eyes, rather frightened.

He took off the robe and, in just his nightshirt, lay down beside her. He turned over easily, blew out the candle, then put his arm about her.

"It went off well, don't you think?" he said, in such a natural tone that she wanted to giggle hysterically. She was not a giggly woman, never had been. Perhaps it was the wine. She never drank much wine, but so much had been poured today and so many toasts drunk.

"Yes, very well," she said, in a sort of squeak.

"Sonia, you have no mother to guide you. Did some woman talk to you—about tonight?" he asked quietly, his hand smoothing gently over her body under the sheet.

She felt strangely hot and tremulous. "Yes—Leah—and Beryl did—" she whispered.

"Good. I shall be gentle, and you must be willing to tell me if I hurt you. We have our lives before us; we need not be hasty about this," he said, and she thought he was smiling in the dimness. "You are very lovely, have I told you so?"

There was a deeper note in his voice, a caressing tone she

had not heard before. It gave her some confidence. At his urging, she turned and lay against him, and felt the hard muscles of his thighs against the softness of hers. His hand moved over her back, down to her hips, and drew her closer yet.

He moved his lips against her cheek, then to her mouth, held it in a long kiss. She felt she melted against him, and when he indicated how her arms should entwine around him, she complied. One did obey one's husband, she thought, in a daze. And she wanted to—she felt excited, curious, wondering. He kissed her again, her lips moved in response.

"How sweet you are! Your perfume is so light, yet so pretty. Is it lilac?" he murmured against her neck.

"Ummm," she said, unable to think. He chuckled softly and the sound rippled through her body.

He murmured to her, his hands stroked over her body, his lips kept on finding warm places to caress. He opened her nightdress and kissed down to her breasts. She caught her breath sharply as he took a nipple in his lips and pulled gently at it. Her hands went to his head, and she dared to move her fingers through the thick blond curly hair. How silky it was, slightly damp, curling to his strong neck.

She would have been content to remain like this. However, he seemed to have other ideas. His kisses grew more urgent, he turned her on her back, and lay over her, drawing back the silk of the nightdress, until she was bare beneath him. His hand moved more intimately over her. She gasped again and again. His fingers—how they thrilled her! Leah had told her what would happen, and so had Beryl, but somehow she had not thought her heart would pound so, and her thighs burn, and the whole of her melt against him.

When he brought the two of them together slowly, carefully—she felt some pain. But she would not have stopped him for the world. For long moments, she felt part of him, a vital part of his body. It was dangerously exciting. When he drew back cautiously, she could have wept. She clung to his hard shoulders.

"Far enough for tonight," he whispered. "Have I hurt you, my darling?" He sounded anxious.

"It hurt a little—I don't mind—" she said honestly.

79

He got up, brought a towel wrung out in cool water, and washed her carefully. If there had been a light, she would have blushed and resented it, but in the darkness—his hands felt gentle and tender and she did not mind. She adored him for his care.

"There, now you will sleep," he said. He put the towel in the bathroom. She thought he would go to his own room, and felt disappointment.

Instead, he returned to her bed and lay there, holding her in his arms against his hard body. He did not sleep for a time, seeming restless, moving in the bed.

But Sonia was happy, her head was on his shoulder, and his hand was on her back. She went to sleep in his arms. He was there when she wakened once in the night. He slept deeply, his arm still about her. In the morning, he was still there.

She opened her eyes, saw his face beside hers on the pillow. They gazed gravely into each other's eyes. Then he began to smile. "Good morning, my wife," he saluted her.

She flushed, and put her hand to brush back her hair, loosened in the night. He stopped her.

"Let me play with your hair. I love it all down like that," he said, and his hand moved in the long curly dark strands. "It is almost to your waist," he marveled.

He moved over her to kiss her again, and his caresses became more passionate. The wind blew in, flowing curtains drifted from the windows. They seemed alone in a world of silence.

Her arms went about him. He pressed his face to her breasts, murmured, "Sonia, I want you badly. Will you mind—"

"Please—do what you wish," she whispered lovingly. His kisses grew more ardent, burning against her, and his body moved urgently against hers.

He was more direct this morning. Her body felt warm and yielding. She did not mind it when he entered her. He thrust again, again, then his whole physical being shuddered in hers, and she felt the sweet release of his passion.

"Have I hurt you?" was his first question, as he regained his breath.

"No, no, you did not hurt me," she reassured him. Her hand moved slowly, exploring, along his hard back, to the muscles there and the lean spine.

"Oh, you are a darling, you are so sweet," he whispered. He lay back, holding her to him, and she felt the final shudder sweep through him. He seemed relaxed and happy. She smiled against his chest. She had made him happy! Somehow she knew it, and it made her feel bold and confident. His hand was moving through her hair, stroking over her bare shoulder. They lay in lazy contentment.

After that first night, Alastair came to her room every night. Sometimes he kissed her and made love fiercely, sometimes he held her gently and caressed her for a time before they slept. But she made him happy, she felt sure of it, and the knowledge kept her going through the difficult days. At least, nights he belonged to her!

The housekeeper resented her, and kept going to Edwina for orders. The girls were proud and aloof, watching with reproachful eyes as she tried tactfully to take over. Alastair wished it—he had said so—but sometimes she could have cried as she tried to draw up the meals, direct the servants, plan for a dinner.

They gave their first party as man and wife. Sonia was anxious for it to go very well. In her pride, she may have overdone it, she thought later. But she wanted him to be proud of her!

She chose a cloth-of-gold dress, trimmed in mink, with topaz jewels at her throat and wrist and in her small ears. As she descended the stairs that night, with Alastair following her down in his blue satin and silver trim, she felt proud, confident, her head erect. She was his wife, and she belonged to him. He had chosen her.

Edwina and Henrietta came down soon after. Gasping, they stared at their new sister-in-law. "Sonia, you look— stunning!" whispered Henrietta, her violet eyes wide. "I never saw—such a glorious gown, and your jewels—"

"Thank you, Lady Henrietta," said Sonia, with composure.

Edwina was more moderate, but her blue eyes gleamed at the sight of the jewels and the mink. She was beautifully gowned in blue silk, with a modest silver chain and pearl pendant. "You do look fine, Sonia," she said.

Alastair interrupted their talk. "You must begin to call my sisters by their first names, without the lady before it," he said to Sonia. "We shall have no more formality within the family. Eh? That is only right. They are your sisters now."

Sonia glanced hopefully at the two girls, only to be chilled by their cold looks. Maurice soon came down, clattering down the stairs, dashing in his pale blue and gold. His mouth dropped open as he saw Sonia.

"I say—you look like a queen," he said frankly. Alastair smiled proudly at Sonia.

"You do me proud," he said simply, and she was satisfied with that. No matter what else everyone thought and said, if Alastair was satisfied with her, she must be happy. She turned to greet their first guests, her hand on Alastair's arm.

Chapter
7

DECEMBER had scarcely begun when Alastair removed to the country. Sonia was glad to go with him. His sisters remained cold and aloof, carefully polite, but no more. She was happy to get away, to be alone with Alastair.

Their carriages rattled cheerfully along the country roads, some white-glazed with ice. The leaves had fallen from the trees; only the evergreens stood tall and stately with dark green limbs erect. An ice storm had swept through the Cornwall area, leaving some devastation.

Alastair watched the country with absorbed interest as they rode, growing more cheerful as they approached his estates. He pointed out places to her on the last day of their journey.

"There—there is the farm where I first helped with the haying. There is the school my father had built for the children of our estate workers. There—now you can see the spire of the church in our village. Oh, look, you can see the manor house on the hill. See it there, against the blue?"

She looked with even more eagerness than he, delighted

that he was sharing his childhood, his life story with her. They rolled up the winding hill, the horses straining, and entered the smooth area before the manor house. She caught her breath at the sight of it.

At a distance, it had not looked so huge. Close-up, it seemed mammoth. Two wide wings spread out from the large central section. Built of Cotswold stone transported many miles, it glowed in the late afternoon sunshine of the wintry day. In the bleak countryside, it seemed like a topaz gem in a silvery dark setting.

Trees were set about it, with flower beds in formal pattern. "It seems a bit grim now," said Alastair, leaning forward eagerly to look out the window past her. "But in the spring and in the autumn, by Jove, it is beautiful! Spring brings the apple and apricot and plum trees, and the hills are full of drifting blossoms. And in the autumn, you shall see the maples turn to red and gold, and the beech to pure gold. The hills are alive with flame then."

The countryside seemed to bring out the poet in him. She looked at his deep blue eyes, his shining face, and knew that he loved this place, his estates, Fairley.

He jumped down before the carriage had stopped rolling, opening the door with a jerk. The servants were waiting for them, a butler in formal dress, and others lined up behind him.

"Welcome to Fairley, Sonia," said Alastair, turning to give her a hand down. Seeing her awkward after the long ride, he reached into the coach, boyishly caught her by the waist, and lifted her out with a grin.

She felt a warmth here she had not felt at the townhouse. She smiled at the servants lined up to greet her. She went down the line slowly, looked in each face, shook each hand, and murmured the names after Alastair. They bobbed curtsies, or bowed low, gazed at her curiously, but with some friendliness, she thought. They went into the wide halls, to be met by the house servants, and the ceremonies were repeated there.

The housekeeper was a broad-faced woman of buxom appearance, clad in rustling black, with keys at her waist. She bowed, then introduced Sonia—"Lady Fairley," as she kept saying every few words—to the footmen and the maids. Leah followed them silently, her cloak about her, watching alertly to see how her mistress was greeted.

The rooms were old-fashioned in appearance, there had been no repainting and remodeling for many years, yet she liked them the more for that. In the vast drawing room stood heavy furniture of mahogany which seemed to be rooted in place as though there hundreds of years. A log fire burned in the huge fireplace. The mantel was of dark wood, highly polished, topped by flowered Chinese vases in the famille rose pattern. Someone had found some late asters to set in them, with dark green ferns. The gesture touched her.

The winter drapes had been set up. They were dark crimson, showing off the crimson of the Persian rugs on the floor, the shining hardwood of the window frames and door frames. The furniture—sofas and chairs—had been tapestried in lighter crimson silk, with touches of pale gold. It was a cheerful room, welcoming her after the long cold ride.

Upstairs, their rooms were equally welcoming. Hers were in blue and gold, with a blue canopy over the large fourposter bed. The simple lines of the carving told her it had been made about one hundred years before. The matching chairs and small dressing table were in the same style.

"This was my grandmother's room, and her mother's before her," said Alastair, showing her in. He cast a worried look about. "I had not realized how old-fashioned it looked. If you wish changes—"

"Oh, no, oh, no, it is perfect as it is. It is so—warm and welcoming, like a nest against the cold," she said spontaneously. His face relaxing, he smiled down at her.

"You must tell me if you wish aught changed," he said gently. "These are my rooms—" He flung open the door in the side wall. She peeped in timidly, to see handsome crimson silk hangings, an equally immense old-fashioned bed with simple carvings, oil lamps, a few candlesticks of silver on the tallboy. The bathroom was very simple. The tub would have to be filled with kettles of hot water. There were wash basins of porcelain on a blue-painted wooden stand.

She slept well that night, though she missed Alastair. He was weary also, and had gone to bed in his own bedroom.

Yet she felt his presence close to her, as the rooms were not so huge and only a door was between them, not several formal rooms.

She wakened, to a thick dark day with rain sweeping down across the hills and valley. She felt amazingly happy for all the gloom of the day. They were alone in the country, with none of his relatives about to spoil her pleasure, and she hummed as she dressed.

She heard Alastair humming in the bathroom, and smiled. When he was happy, he sang or hummed in an off key that was curiously endearing. He could not carry a tune, but grumbled away at the melody in a sort of husky baritone. When he was unhappy or troubled, he was silent. She knew already some of his moods, and to hear him humming was reassuring.

Mrs. Pendennis, the housekeeper, was a typical Cornish wife, cheerful, bustling, always busy about her tasks. She beamed at Sonia happily, and wanted to show her everything the first day. She was as different from the stiff starchy housekeeper at the London townhouse as night from day, thought Sonia.

"There, now, himself is back home," said Mrs. Pendennis. "And how much troubles for him to settle! Sure, they'll all be after him to settle matters for weeks. You'll be wise to make things smooth for him at home, you will," and she nodded her graying head, beaming from her flushed rosy-cheeked face.

She had the cook make typical fare for them, as Alastair wanted it. They had thick Cornish pastries, meat pies, fish dishes as strange to Sonia as could be. And for desserts, there were bottled fruits which had been gathered in summer and preserved, blackberries, currants, plums, cherries, besides fresh apples from their own trees, stored in the cool cellar. Whenever the occasion warranted, there were buttery cakes, covered with whipped cream so thick that Sonia thought she would surely gain weight. How delicious they all were, eaten in the fresh cold air of the manor house, with the smell of the logs in the fireplace, and the laughter of the maids in the kitchen. This was a happy place.

Alastair was busy about the estates. He discovered that

Sonia could not ride, and promptly proceeded to teach her. She had a very gentle elderly mare, who could not be coaxed beyond a sedate walk, and she bounced up and down happily beside Alastair as he rode his stallion. The riding habit she wore had been his mother's—it fit her quite well. She adored the high black hat with the plume.

On rainy days, which came often, she remained indoors, learning the complicated ways of the household. It was such a huge estate, with a huge household to match. The maids were hired from the village. They had to be trained in sewing, cooking, waiting table, cleaning, making beds, and whatever else Mrs. Pendennis deemed proper.

"Sure, we lose them as fast as we train them," she said sorrowfully. "Either a young man has his eye on the girl, or she goes off to the big city to get a job where she'll meet more men. Pity!"

Christmas was coming. Sonia felt disturbed about celebrating this holiday, then told herself that she must be sensible. It was a time of rejoicing, of gift-giving, of being thankful. It was like her own Festival of Lights, and she would quietly think of it to herself like that.

She had a gift of her own making for Alastair. She looked about for other gifts for him. That kept her occupied during the December days. She embroidered and hemmed some fine linen for stocks, set his initial lovingly into them. She made him some silk shirts. Leah helped her ruffle the fronts and wrists.

Sometimes she even had time, on an especially bad stormy day, to work on jewelry designs. Alastair seemed anxious that she should not give up her work, asking her several times if she would like to send for her equipment.

"No, no, no commission is urgent," she told him. "I completed all I had and refused several. When we return to London, I might take it up again."

"I want you to be happy, and the jewelry-making seems to do this," he said, gently. "Your uncle told me how much it meant to you."

She thought this was very sweet and thoughtful of him. Yet, for all their pleasure together, a barrier was creeping up between them. He was away all the day, coming home soaked and tired, often later sleeping alone in his bedroom. She knew the work was difficult, and there was much to straighten out from years of neglect. Yet—yet why was he not so close to her as before? Or were they just becoming settled married people?

Alastair had been brooding deeply about two incidents which had occurred before they departed from London. Unable to keep away from Mrs. Daphne Porter, he had gone to see her.

She had been cold and cruel, accusing him of marrying for money. "You care nothing for me," she had said, her green eyes flashing. "All your compliments, all your assurances—and you married that—that Jewish woman within a month! No, I shall never believe in a man again!"

She had sounded over-wrought, dramatic, almost hysterical. He had been quite unable to calm her. She had sent him away, declaring she would never receive him again. And that stung. They had been intimate for a year. Even now, he had hoped somehow she would continue to see him secretly. He was paying her rent, he had bought clothes for her, and jewels. Somehow, he could not stop doing that. He continued to pay into her bank account, though he knew he was being a fool. This was not his money, he thought bitterly. It was the price of marrying Sonia!

When he returned to London, her anger would have cooled, he thought. He wanted to take up the relationship again. In her best moments, she soothed him, excited him, made him feel more alive and masculine—he wanted her. He wanted her blond beauty in his arms, her red mouth opening under his, his hands on her full breasts, to see her green eyes slumbrous when he took her.

At times like that, he could not go to his wife. He would lie awake, and listen to the rain beating against the windows, and long wildly for the woman he had left in London. She was difficult, exciting, unpredictable. He wanted her!

The other incident had stung deeply, in another manner. He had been doing errands in town before departing. He had run into Sir Jonathan Wiltshire and the man had walked right past him. Alastair, laughing, had gone after him and grasped his arm.

"I say, Jonathan, you are in a daze! Didn't you see me?"

The older man, tall, dignified, his hair graying, had turned and deliberately removed Alastair's hand from his arm. "I wonder you can ask that," he had said, his tone both sad and rebuking. "What have you done, my old, old friend? What have you done?"

Alastair had stared at him blankly. "Done? What do you mean?"

"Marrying a Jewess!"

Alastair had felt the blood draining from his head, he had felt quite dizzy. Jonathan, softening a little, had drawn him into a coffeehouse nearby, and they sat down over cups.

"How could you do such a terrible thing?" Jonathan had asked him. "To marry outside your class! You of all men! I could not believe the report!"

"I—it was necessary," had said Alastair, holding tight to his dignity. "I hope you will come round when we return to London. I shall need my own friends about me."

Slowly Jonathan had shaken his head. "I cannot come. I cannot. To see a woman like that, in the place where your mother ruled! Intimately associated with your sisters! Have you forgotten all honor? Have you forgotten what is due to your family name? Are you no longer a gentleman? I cannot but believe that the Jews dunned you for money, forced this on you—"

The words had echoed unpleasantly in Alastair's ears night after night. He worked from dawn to dusk, worked himself so hard that he was exhausted. Still he lay awake, hearing those reproaches. *Have you forgotten what it is to be a gentleman? Have you forgotten your family name? Have you forgotten what is due your heritage? How could you? You have forgotten all nobility, all honor. . . .*

He writhed, flung his arm over his eyes. Had he? Had he not just done what he had to do? Should he have gone bankrupt, and let his sisters take posts as governesses as other poverty-stricken former gentlemen had done? His brother—to go down in debt to the gamesters?

This must be what all London whispered about him. No wonder men had cut him, and women tittered behind his back. How could he think he could have done such a thing to

89

the strictly regimented society of England and not have them stab him? He had betrayed all their values—he had married outside his class—and for money!

She was a Jewess and in trade. Her uncle was a broker, and a shrewd one. So were her cousins. All his former friends must know of her fortune. Many must have guessed that lack of money had driven him. God, how far could a man fall! If only he had died in battle! At least then, his name might have kept some honor.

Such thoughts tormented him night and day. He rode like a demon across the chilly wind-swept countryside, and drove his men as hard as himself.

Christmas was coming. What a hollow mockery! He had left gifts for his brother and sisters at the townhouse, to be produced by the housekeeper at the proper time. He had not spoken of the occasion to his wife. After all, she did not keep Christmas!

Yet—as the holidays approached, he noted a keen sense of excitement in the air. The cook was baking huge cakes for the holidays, rich fruit cakes that scented the air of the manor house. The housekeeper came to him, asking about the gifts of money for the servants. And Sonia was sewing things, and hiding them from him with an enchanting giggle and a blush, when he happened early into her sitting room.

Wearily, he resigned himself. He must spend Christmas as usual, watch the holly and mistletoe hung about, plan a Yule log, and think what to get for his wife—his wealthy wife, who could buy and sell him!

He went into the nearest town, searching. He had to have some appropriate gifts for her. In a dress shop, hopelessly looking once more, he found the proprietress taking pity on him.

"My Lord Fairley, there is a new shipment of warm woolens in from Scotland. Might your lady like one of them cloaks, maybe of blue and green plaid? Mighty handsome they be," and she spread out one after another.

He fingered the fabric. Yes, it was warm and beautiful. She had no such thing, she wore velvet and ermine! he thought bitterly. But these were handsome, and would keep out the chill rain. He purchased one of them, in what he hoped would be her size.

Christmas came. The gifts appeared suddenly in the drawing room, along with a handsome tree which Sonia and the housekeeper had helped the maids to trim. Excitement bloomed in Sonia's cheeks, as he came in from work, early.

"Do you like it?" she asked anxiously, her slim hands clasped before her in a pleading gesture.

"I say—it is stunning," he said, eyeing the tree. It was tall, fragrant, looked much as his mother had decorated trees years before. He recognized the ornaments, the silver bells, the fragile angels, little golden horns, a tiny wooden sleigh which had been his favorite. "You must have worked hours," he said, more warmly. "However did you find all these?"

"Mrs. Pendennis ordered them brought from the attics," she said happily. "I have never decorated a tree before—she showed me how. It was such fun!"

Then he remembered— No, she would not have had a tree before. He bit his lips, and thanked her even more warmly. How many customs must she be forcing herself to observe for his sake? He wondered if the wedding had been strange to her. The pastor had told him that she seemed an intelligent woman, but he had had to go over and over the service with her before she understood it. Of course, it must all have been very exotic to her.

He got the housekeeper to help him wrap the presents he had bought for Sonia. "There now, how pretty," said Mrs. Pendennis, with satisfaction and hidden relief. "She'll like this cloak, just right for her, it is. And such pretty handkerchiefs, all lace! You know what a lady likes, to be sure, my lord!"

Know what a lady likes, he thought gloomily. Daphne liked rubies of the first water, sapphires and diamonds. All gems, the finest gowns, the best furs. A flat in a fashionable neighborhood, servants.

He tried to suppress thoughts of Daphne. He could not see her for at least another month. There was so much to do here and he must return again in the summer, to make sure all was going well. But soon, soon, he could return to London, and to Daphne. Such a fascinating, entrancing, unpredictable woman! He could scarcely wait to go back to her. . . .

He must be very careful in his movements. Now he was a married man. His new relatives were shrewd. They would not like any insult to Sonia so soon in his marriage. And if she did not produce a child soon, he would be in trouble. Meyer wanted a child of the marriage to prove it was going well. He felt a very cad. He liked Sonia, he enjoyed making love to her, for she was amazingly responsive. And her mind was quick and agile, delighting him. But he did not love her, of course he did not love her. How could he?

On Christmas morning, he rose early, feeling very restless. He strode back and forth, before taking his bath and dressing. His valet found him most particular about his shave, his neckcloth, the set of his blue velvet coat.

He went down early, to find Sonia there before him, having breakfast in the dining room. He was surprised, he had not heard her movements. Were there shadows under her gray eyes, or was it the lighting?

"Good morning, my dear," he said, feeling horribly guilty. "A Happy Christmas to you." Then he remembered, and looked worriedly at her.

She smiled over her coffee cup. Her lips were steady. "A Happy Christmas to you, Alastair," she said in her low musical voice. "May this New Year bring you much joy and happiness."

"And you also," he said, sitting down at his place. The footman brought him his usual plate of eggs and ham, poured his coffee, and he settled to his meal.

After breakfast, they retired to the large drawing room, to admire the tree. "Is it—I mean—may I give you my gifts now?" asked Sonia, after a little time. Her cheeks were pink, her gray eyes eager.

He smiled at her, relieved. "I have a few things for you also, my little wife," he managed to say, teasingly. He went to the tree, picked up the large box with the cloak and brought it to her. He had the pleasure of hearing her exclaim with delight as her hand smoothed lovingly over the fabric.

"It is perfectly beautiful," she said, and stood to place it about her shoulders. The colors suited her admirably, and he said so.

He opened his box of shirts, exclaiming suitably over them, admiring the neat stitches. He found also the neckcloths with his initials on them. Then he discovered the small velvet box wrapped in silver paper.

With a feeling akin to dismay, he slowly opened it. When he saw the ring inside, he stared at it almost with revulsion. She had given him so much, he was out of debt with money in plenty because of her. He had been feeling guilty about that—planning on returning to Daphne, to give gifts to that woman he could not forget. . . .

And now in his hand was a delicately wrought ring of silver with an immense star sapphire set in it. A fortune in itself, he thought, turning cold. She was watching him eagerly, her hands clasped together.

"Your design? he said, turning it over. "How—very charming—" The sapphire was perfect, a huge misty blue, with a stunning crisscross of white lines in it. "It is—it looks a very—expensive jewel."

A shadow crossed her face. "It is a fine gem," she admitted, in a low tone. "When I saw it—I wanted it for you."

He replaced it in the box. "I cannot accept it," he said. He got up abruptly from his seat beside her. "It is too much. You should set it for yourself—it would look good on your hand," he added.

She was looking stunned, her red mouth trembling before she compressed it firmly. "Do you—not like it—my lord?" she murmured.

He moved restlessly to pick up some silver wrap and fold it in his hands. "It is too fine for me," he said.

Her head bent. He had hurt her deeply, he realized. "There is something wrong—perhaps you do not care for star sapphires. Is there some custom, or superstition—"

"No, no, absolutely not," he said hastily. He bit his lips. He was rejecting not only the ring but her artistry, for she had made the ring setting, he felt sure. He picked it up again, examined it carefully. "You have given me so much—I am overwhelmed, that is all," he said, reluctantly.

"You do not like it," she said flatly. The blush was gone, she seemed white and tired.

"I do. I have never seen such a splendid gem. But I cannot accept it, Sonia," he added more quietly. He looked at her bent head. Damn it. Every gift was a fresh blow. She had carefully stitched his shirts and neckcloth, and now this. . . . He felt such a cad, such a low worm.

"Is there—some other design—perhaps in gold?" she whispered.

"No. It is perfect." He slipped it on his finger. He must give in, but it was difficult for him. His pride was taking a beating. "Look, Sonia, a perfect fit. How stunning it is. Are you sure you want me to have it?" he said more lightly, with an effort.

Tears trembled on her dark lashes. She blinked them back with an intense effort. "Oh, Alastair, I wished to give it to you. When I first saw it, I knew it was—like your eyes," she said very shyly. Her slim talented fingers twisted in her linen handkerchief with the lace borders, almost tearing the lace.

He was deeply touched. "Well, then, I must wear it, always, in memory of your kindness to me. It shall be a bond between us, eh?" He forced himself to say it, then bent, took her chin in his hand and raised her head.

He saw the tears that threatened in her gray eyes. Very carefully, he kissed each eyelid, then her red mouth.

"Sonia, you have a generous heart—it will get you into trouble," he said with a sigh. "This is too good for me, yet I shall cherish and love it always. Now, smile for me, or I shall be very cross with myself for making you weep on Christmas!"

She managed a smile. He kissed her again and held her close to his heart. She was very vulnerable, he thought. He had not realized how much, for under her cloak of sophistication, he had not seen the shy heart concealed. She had given it to him, this beautiful gem, because it looked like his eyes! He could not refuse it . . . he must wear it for her.

The rest of the month, and into January, they were much together. Alastair made a determined effort to forget London, and to get the Cornwall estate into as good repair as possible.

Sonia helped him eagerly, and he found himself turning over some of his arduous duties to her.

She not only managed the household and directed the housekeeper. She helped with the estate books, for she had a good practical knowledge of bookkeeping. She suggested economies, and how to make the best use of the laborers, who would rather work summers and not in the cold winters. She suggested he hire more seasonal workers, and let the men off to go fishing when they chose, rather than remain close to the estate, whiling away idle hours.

They went for long walks when the January days turned cold but clear, enjoying the brisk winds against their faces. She wore her warm Scottish cloak of blue and green with a scarf over her head, while he put on his warmest wool suit and high boots. They could stroll along the country lanes, talk about the fruit trees, plan the year's work. And he told her more of his worries about settling his sisters and his brother. They weighed much on his mind.

Sonia had brisk commonsense, and he enjoyed talking to her. Some cold evenings, he would fill his pipe, and smoke contentedly beside the fire, while she read to him in her low clear voice from books of philosophy or poetry or drama. He felt unusually contented. It must pass, for he was not one to remain forever in the country; but for now, it was good.

Chapter
8

●➤●••●••●••●••●••●••●••●••●••●••●••●••●••●••●••●

FEBRUARY came, and Alastair decided they could return to London. He was eager to go, so eager he ordered his valet to pack a week before their departure. Sonia was more reluctant, taking long walks of farewell among the stark apple trees, the flower gardens.

Tears filled her eyes at thought of leaving this place where she had been so happy. Alastair was so anxious to return to London, to see all his family and friends. Would he forget about her? Would she be expected to be stiff and formal again? Would the housekeeper and maids still resent her?

She repressed a deep sigh. This had been two months of heaven, and perhaps it would be all she would ever have. She would have the memory of the sweet days and nights alone with Alastair to comfort her in the hectic days of London. The memories of reading to him, stretching out her slim feet to the crackling fire, the smell of fresh apples in their bowl. A glass of wine on a cold night—and Alastair laughing at some tale he had told her, his blue eyes sparkling with delight. The friendliness of the country folk. The nights when he did come to her—holding her, making love with passion.

Mrs. Pendennis wept when they left, her apron frankly to her eyes. Several small boys ran down the path alongside them, waving and waving until the horses picked up pace and the carriage outstripped them. Sonia leaned from the window, still waving back, until a turn in the road hid their cheerful grinning faces from sight.

She sank back into her place against the squabs, drew the Scottish cloak more closely about her. Alastair was smiling indulgently.

"I am glad the manor house pleased you," he said. "We may return for a couple of months in the summer."

"That will be pleasant," she said eagerly. She was wishing they could remain for the year, to watch the apple trees bud and flower, and fruit come red and ripe. To see the garden blooms, of roses and daffodils and crocus, and the lilac bushes burst into fragrance in the corners of her favorite garden plot. However, Alastair longed for London, and the smart season was approaching. They must entertain and attend other parties, and be seen. It was what he longed to do. She must stifle her sighs so he never heard them.

She was silent on the first day of their return trip. She was gazing with farewell looks at the knife-edged mountains, the snug cottages wreathed in vines, the rustic roads and evergreens, the golden Cotswold stone of a Gothic church glinting in the wintry sunlight. The sadness struck deep into her. Yet surely they would return again. Somehow she felt filled with apprehension about this return journey, as though she were going full-tilt toward trouble.

They stopped at a comfortable inn for the night, and the innkeeper ran about making everyone bustle for them. They ate hugely and hungrily of the platters of roast beef, hot vegetables, cold sliced lamb. For dessert there was rich apple trifle, smothered with thick clotted cream.

"Eat your fill of it, Sonia," said Alastair happily. "We won't have such in London! London—ah, we will be there in two days!" His cheeks were tanned from hours in the sun, he looked happier and healthier than when they had left London.

They arrived in London as dusk fell. The street lights were being lit by the lamplighters from the ends of long poles. The musical cries of sellers of lavender and fish and oranges filled the air. The horses slowed as they approched the sheltered secluded street of Alastair's townhouse. They felt as reluctant as Sonia herself, she thought.

At the sound of the carriage, the great doors were flung open. The housekeeper and the butler stood there, waiting to receive them. They went in, and found a silent house. The young ladies and their brother were out at a soiree, said the butler gloomily. Alastair frowned, but said nothing at this slight.

Sonia was relieved. It would be tomorrow before she faced their cold looks again. She went right up to her room, with Leah supporting her. "There, it was a long nasty cold ride," said her abigail, tenderly helping her remove cloak and bonnet.

"But we are home again," said Sonia pointedly, sitting down to remove her lined boots. It felt good to slip into her soft sandals, to shake out her heavy length of hair. Leah went below stairs to fetch a tray of hot tea and a light supper for her charge.

It developed that my lord had changed and gone out at once. Leah's mouth compressed in anger, but she said nothing to Sonia about it. If Sonia thought her husband had gone straight to bed, it would be just as well.

Sonia knew he had not. She had heard the sounds next door, and had felt wounded. She knew why he was eager to go out. She ate a little, and retired early, to lie awake, bone-weary from the jolting of the coach.

He must have been very eager to see his friends again! Was it some particular friend, some woman, that he went to? She pressed her fist to her mouth, and shut her eyes. She must not think about it, she must not. Women did not protest, they endured.

She finally slept, uneasily, to waken when he returned rather drunkenly to his room. She heard a chair knocked over, and wakened to listen to the sounds. A clock chimed the hour—four o'clock. She turned over to sleep again.

Morning came, and she dressed and went downstairs. She

was no coward, but it took courage in full store to face the housekeeper and maids and wait for the others to come down. After the friendly cheerfulness of Mrs. Pendennis, it was doubly hard.

Nevertheless, she had always done her duty. She took over the reins of the household again, inquired into the accounts, spent hours at her desk in the room behind Alastair's study to get all into order once more.

A great deal seemed to have been spent on exotic foods and more wines than could possibly be consumed in a year, even with the aid of dozens of guests. She questioned the bills, almost went to Alastair about them, then decided not to do so. He might say something contemptuous about her quiet life before her marriage, that she did not understand London Society, or some such rebuke. She could not face that.

She quietly transferred some funds of her own to the household accounts, and paid the enormous tradesmen's bills without a word.

Alastair came into her office later in the week. "There are some bills here. Would you take care of sending drafts on my bank?" he asked. "My secretary has taken off to visit his sick mother, and I haven't a clue about the bank books and all that," he added rather impatiently.

She smiled. He was like a small boy at times, when faced with unpleasant, detailed tasks he did not enjoy. Outdoors, he was in his element. In his study, he paced like a frantic lithe panther in a cage.

"Of course, Alastair, if you wish," she said gently, pleased she could help him. "Do you have account books there? Shall I work in your study, and replace the books when I have done?"

"If you would be so kind," he said. Taking her to his study, he showed her the neat files of his secretary. A number of ledgers were carefully arranged, but others and some bank books had been tossed into boxes and drawers.

She began to take them out and study them, a little bewildered. Alastair must have gone poking about, trying to find what he wanted. She felt sure his precise secretary never would have left them in such disarray.

Alastair went out to see to a horse he might purchase. She

was there in his study all the afternoon, trying to make order of the bills and check books.

As she worked, she began to feel rather ill. More and more ill as the afternoon hours wore on. For she found such huge sums in the account books, some marked PAID in great bold letters, others "Account taken care of by Meyer Goldfine," under the date of November, 1809.

Sonia pressed her hand to her forehead. Hundreds of pounds, thousands, even hundreds of thousands, according to a quick calculation. Hundreds of thousands of pounds! Some had been the debts of his father, some of Alastair—gambling debts, mortgages on Fairley, the cost of horses and stables, jewels sent to Mrs. Daphne Porter, the rent of an apartment for Mrs. Porter. . . .

She felt dazed, bewildered. How could they have gotten into such debt? Still, he was a nobleman, he did have a town-house, a country home, horses and stables. . . .

And as for her—had he really married her for her money? None had been taken from her accounts, she checked them over herself every month, in Uncle Meyer's counting house. No large sums had been deducted from her balance.

It was a terrible puzzle. Perhaps Uncle Meyer had paid a dowry to Alastair for her. Yet, this one was too great, he could never have paid such a dowry—not over three hundred thousand pounds. And for what? To pay such bills, such gaming debts, and for his mistress . . . ?

She fumbled over the books, put them away with her mouth set. As she pushed them into one opening, she found they would not fit in. She pulled out the two books, found a document crushed in the space where they should have gone. She drew it out, opened it innocently—and found her name on it.

She swallowed. She took in the words in one burning look. Then she began again at the beginning and read the several pages, sitting like a child in Alastair's huge chair.

A marriage settlement, such as the Jewish people used, only it had not been read aloud at her ceremony, nor given to her for safekeeping, as was customary with Jewish brides. She read the terms and could not believe them.

A sound at the door interrupted her. Her eyes were great

and somber as she turned to the doorway. Alastair had come in and was striding toward her, his tanned face dark with anger.

"What are you doing? What have you found there?" Blood had rushed into his face, his blue eyes glinted with passion and fury.

"The marriage settlement," she whispered. "I found—the marriage settlement. Oh—Alastair—"

He snatched the document from her trembling hands, glanced down at it. "You didn't know about it?" He seemed to be sneering at her. She shook her head, closing her eyes. She felt faint. "Well, this was between your uncle and me. It is not your concern," he said brutally, shoving the document back where it had been. "If you hadn't gone poking about—"

"I found—papers," she managed to say, opening her eyes and holding up her head with dignity. "I was trying to find the right books—to pay the accounts—"

"I'll warrant!" he snapped and sent the papers on the desk flying with his arm and fist. "Go away! I'll take care of these! I should have known better than to trust you with the contents of my desk!"

She took a deep furious breath. "You asked me to pay your bills for you. I did not think to find such great debts. And the rent for Mrs. Porter's flat is two months behind!" she flared, flouncing up from the chair to glare at him, her fists clenched.

Blood came up higher into his cheeks, he lifted one hand, and she thought he would strike her. She stared at him, unflinching. She would rather have been struck, she thought, than to find what she had found.

"Damn my secretary! He should not have left in such a hurry," said Alastair, but he could not meet her eyes. He looked down at the desk top, and his shoulders, sagging, seemed to lose their proud carriage. "I didn't mean for you to see these, Sonia, really—"

It was a kind of apology, but she was too hurt to accept it. "No? It was a secret between you and my uncle, then? The fact that you were so deeply in debt that you had to marry a Jewess for her money?" she flashed.

The words were out between them, the hateful words that could not be recalled.

He bit his full sensuous lips, and she could not keep from remembering how tender and passionate they had been on her lips, on her breasts. . . .

"That is true," he said flatly. His head came up, he still could not look at her. He stared at the crimson drapes at the windows. Outside the winter darkness had gathered in, and the wind gusted against the panes of glass. "My father—and I—there were such debts—there was no other way out. Now you know. I had to forget everything but my family, my responsibilities. I had to marry, to get out of debt and start again. I have my sisters to launch, my brother to settle. I cannot blame you if you hate me for it."

Hate him? Tears blurred her eyes, and she turned away sharply. That was the trouble, she could not hate him. She loved him. She adored him. And he—he had married her, for the money alone. . . .

He was putting the papers away, crushing them in any way into the drawers, locking them, slamming shut the doors of the cabinet behind the desk where the incriminating ledgers lay. The sounds were like so many blows at her heart. If she had only known—if she had only known. . . .

Surely Uncle Meyer could not have done this to her! She clutched at that thought. Her uncle loved her, he would not have sold her thoughtlessly to any gentile. . . .

"I'll take care of this from now on," said Alastair curtly. "I might have known you would go prying, get into everything. A woman cannot resist looking into secret papers—"

She lifted her head proudly. "Forgive me," she said sarcastically. "I shall not disturb your papers again!" She turned to sweep from the room, the train of her silken gown trailing the carpet grandly. She gathered up her blue skirts in one hand, she reached for the door handle, finding it by instinct rather than sight.

"Oh—Sonia! You will not speak of this to my brother and sisters!" he said sharply. "I have no wish for this to be bandied about in the streets!"

She bowed her head, left him. She could not speak again.

She went up the stairs to her apartment, and stood in the center of a lovely room, fists clenched, taking deep breaths to regain command of herself. Leah came in, found her like this, and swept to her in concern.

"My baby, my pet, my dove, what is it?" crooned Leah, taking her shoulders and turning her face to the light.

"I must see Uncle," muttered Sonia.

She heard Alastair in the adjacent rooms, cursing his valet. Doors banged, drawers were slammed. He was dressing—to go out again? To Mrs. Porter, whose rent he paid? She thought of that arrogant letter, reminding him to pay the overdue rent.

Leah silently helped Sonia to change to an outdoor gown of dark blue velvet. As she left the room, she heard the roaring in the hallway below. Alastair glanced up in the midst of shouting at his brother, glared at her, then slammed out the front door.

Lady Edwina was standing aghast at the entrance to the drawing room. She looked at Sonia descending the stairs, at the dark velvet cloak covering her gown.

"But Sonia!" she cried. "What is it? Alastair has gone out for the evening—and now you! But we have guests—a dozen guests to dinner—"

Sonia had forgotten. She found she did not care.

"You will entertain them admirably, Lady Edwina," she said coldly, and went out to the carriage she had ordered.

Lady Henrietta had come to join her sister. "They have quarreled, I'll be bound," she whispered, so loudly that Sonia heard her before the door closed after her and Leah. Sonia smiled, a wry twist of her mouth. Quarreled? What a meek mild word! She felt she hated them all, the source of her present terrible unhappiness and shame. To be sold—for that sum of money—and no one caring. . . . She could not endure it. She must know the truth.

She had never thought to feel such shame, such horror at her condition. She was a proud woman; she had earned her own living at jewelry-making; she had her intelligence. She haed hoped one day to marry for love, or never to marry at all. But a marriage such as had been foisted on her by a man

104

she had loved all her days—her uncle—it could not be. There was some terrible mistake. . . .

Meyer Goldfine had eaten his frugal supper, and the remains were on the tray at his side as he sat with his narrow feet propped up near the fire. He set aside the book he was reading, to look at Sonia with a smile of pleasure as she came in.

"My dearest Sonia, an unexpected visit—my dear—" He struggled to get up. She shook her head, and sank down into the chair next to his, forgetful of cloak, bonnet, and her distraught countenance.

"Uncle Meyer, did you give Alastair three hundred thousand pounds—to marry me?"

Leah gasped behind her, and shut the door sharply to keep out the curious maid. Meyer turned pale in the face of his niece's fury.

"My child, what is this? Of what do you accuse me? Of course there was a dowry," he said cautiously, eying her warily.

"Uncle, the truth, if you will," she said, drawing a deep painful breath. Her chest hurt her in a curious way, like a pain deep inside that would never go away. "I found some papers, as I worked in—his study. He wanted some bills paid, his secretary had been called away. I found a marriage settlement. Uncle, the truth!"

"Truth? What is truth? How can we discover truth?" he mused, his head on one side as he glanced away uneasily from her pale face, her shaking hands.

"Uncle!"

She was blazingly furious, more angry than he had ever seen. Her fists clenched.

"Now, now, my dear, caution and patience. All shall be revealed and understood," he said finally. He sighed deeply. He hated scenes. He liked everything to move sweetly and serenely, especially now that he had grown old and tired. Scenes were distressing and caused him to lose sleep.

"Tell me, then, from the beginning."

Her voice was taut and commanding. She would not endure less than the whole story. So he told her.

"Very well, my dear. You shall know." He told her what

he had discovered about the debts of Alastair's father, how he had bought the mortages and all other papers he could discover until he had Alastair firmly in his hold. Then he had sent for him, made his ultimatum. And Alastair had given in, courted Sonia, won her, and married her.

"But—why, Uncle?" she whispered, her gray eyes distended wide in disbelief. "I thought—I thought you—you loved me and wished me well? But you have tied me in bondage for life to a man who—who despises me and what I am!"

He flinched. "Come now, you exaggerate," he said sharply. "You have been happy, you have had the look of a bride at times. You have been with him, he has dealt gently with you? Of course. He is a man of the world."

She waved that aside, shivering a little. "Why, Uncle? You must know he despises all Jews," she told him bluntly.

Uncle Meyer nodded, but said hopefully, "As he comes to know you better, he will admire you, and his sons will be his pride and joy."

"His sons!" She choked over the words. "Uncle, why? Why have you caused this to happen to me? Why did you not give me a choice? You know I must have refused his offer, thinking he—"

"He did not love you? But he will," said Meyer calmly. "You are attractive, you are wealthy, you run a fine household, you are peaceful and gentle—most of the time. . . . He will love you, especially when you give him sons!" And he nodded his gray head in the little skullcap.

She persisted. "Why, Uncle?" And Leah's gaze was equally demanding and accusing as she listened to her darling girl.

Meyer sighed, and gave in again. "I have this plan, my dear. And you must be part of it. You see, my sons must marry Jewish girls and continue their line. But you—you could marry anywhere, you might marry into royalty. I planned it long ago. No Jews may be received at Court. Well, you shall be the first! No Jews may serve in the House of Commons and the House of Lords! Well, they dare not refuse your son, for he will one day be a marquess!"

Sonia stared at him, so did Leah, wide-eyed and unbelieving. His words had rung in the quiet book-lined room.

"I—don't—understand—" whispered Sonia, pitifully, her hand on her heart. "You loved me, you raised me—"

He turned his head from her, to gaze into the heart of the fire and into the depths of his dreams. "I love you, my chicken, yes. But you know how Jews are treated in all societies. In England, it is better than the pogroms of Europe, the cruelties, the taxation, the murders—such as befell your beloved mother, my dearest Sonia. But even in England there is such prejudice, such scorn of us. Well, one day, there will be those Jews who will break through the barriers of prejudice and take their rightful places in society. Yes, and at the Bar, and in the courts, and in Parliament, and in the great houses of the land. A Jew may not own land, but your son will inherit land. A Jew may not be called to the Bar, but one of your sons or grandsons may. It is necessary. There must be a start somewhere—and you, Sonia, will be the vessel for the future changes for Jews in England."

"Oh, Uncle, you are mad—you must be mad—" she murmured. Her face went down into her gloved hands.

His eyes glowed with the fervor of his plans, he shook his gray head proudly. "No, we have discussed it carefully, some of us. It must work, others will do this, also. We are not received—but the next generation will be! We are not accepted—the next generation will be accepted and honored. Your son will be a marquess!"

Seeing her silent distress, the overwhelmed slump of her figure, he grew more kindly. "Sit up, my dear, sit up and raise your chin and think of the future! We do not matter! It is the future of our people that is at stake! You have courage and intelligence, in addition to your wealth and beauty. You will win out. I promise you!"

He had used her, as she had never dreamed anyone would do. She felt crushed at his ambitious employment of her, and all without confiding in her. She was a woman, he was a great man, and he had his plans. A woman was a vessel, he said—her uncle had said it!

Yet—yet she felt a deep responsibility to her people. She remembered so vividly the nightmarish scenes in Vienna, the bloody body of her own mother. The shouts, the screams, the nightly terrors. The little petty annoyances and the big problems of the heavy taxations, the little slights and scorns and the big horrors of the persecutions.

If she could do something to help—if by her own sacrifice her people could be brought more pride and place in England—if crushing herself would bring to fruition the wine of their hopes. . . . She must do it, she thought, with the taste of sourness and despair on her lips.

They talked for some time. Meyer told his niece glowingly of his hopes for the Jews of England. What they could accomplish, once at the Bar! What they could achieve, once in the Houses of Parliament! Society would receive them. There would be ways of earning the right to have their own homes, their own plots of land. They would be honored for their achievements, they would not be spat upon and dealt with contemptuously. Was it not worth all the trouble and sacrifice they could make?

He had talked long with Nathan Rothschild about this. The great son of the Rothschilds of the bank in Europe had not approved of marrying into the gentiles. But he wished great things for his brethren in England. He had met with scorn and contempt himself in his efforts to set up his banking house.

"Together, we can do much, my dearest Sonia," said Meyer, his face flaming with eagerness. "Much, much, much! You shall never regret your part in this, I promise you!"

She could not think of it now. She finally rose, kissed him and left his house to make her way back to Alastair's. Bitterness filled her, though she tried to choke it down. To be so used, without her knowledge and consent! Leah sat silently beside her, sympathy welling from her in waves without a single word being spoken.

The townhouse candles were ablaze, torches flared before the house as carriages were being driven up and horses walked.

"Drive about to the back, to the stables," Sonia ordered curtly and her coachman obeyed. She got out, and went in wearily by the back way, past the waiters, maids and cooks. She went up to her rooms.

Leah undressed her, and she sat down at the writing desk in her pretty bedroom. When Leah had left, Sonia went over and over the conversation with her uncle. Music and laughter drifted up from the floor below them as the party went on lightheartedly.

It emphasized her loneliness, it made her feel frightened at the heartsick despair she felt. Meyer had sold her to Alastair, for three hundred thousand pounds. He had his reasons. Perhaps, in the cold light of day and reason, she could understand and forgive him. Tonight, such grace was beyond her. Her head sank into her arms, and she sat there for a long time while the candles guttered and finally went out.

Chapter
9

━●━●━●━●━●━●━●━●━●━●━●━●━●━●━●━●━●━

THE cold formality between Alastair and Sonia did not go unremarked in the household. The housekeeper raised her eyebrows, the maids whispered and tittered, Alastair's valet went about with tight lips and outraged look. He adored his master, whatever the marquess might do, and he would have no scorn spoken in his presence about him. Yet he was fully aware that the door between the two bedrooms remained closed day and night.

It was Alastair's brother and two sisters who were uneasy about the situation. It was beginning to be understood by them that only Sonia's money had kept them going, that the marriage settlement had kept them from poverty, disgrace and hard work far beneath their station. Maurice talked to Edwina, Edwina talked to Henrietta, and finally they held whispered conferences. They must be nicer to Sonia. After all, she was a sweet, gentle, polite woman. Perhaps she would not get so furious that she would leave them.

"After all," declared Edwina, "he married her, and we

don't approve of divorce. It would cause such a terrible scandal—"

"And she can be so sweet," sighed Maurice. "I wish I could find a girl so gentle and amiable! It quite makes one despair of marriage. Only the other day, Peter told me that his wife—"

Edwina gave him a warning frown. "Not in front of Henrietta," she said coldly. Henrietta tossed her head, resolving to hear the gossip from Maurice as soon as she could get him alone.

"I am sure there are many amiable ladies about, Maurice," said Edwina.

"Yes, they may seem amiable when one is courting! But when one marries, one finds a termagant! I tell you, it is enough to put one off—that a girl should turn one face to Society and another to her own family and husband! What a shrew a girl can be!" And he shuddered in his handsome flashing blue coat.

"Do let us keep to the subject," said Edwina. "What can we do to reconcile them, and make Sonia feel more welcome? Daily she goes off to her own townhouse. She says she is working on jewelry. But not to be here for teas . . . People are beginning to talk—"

"Yes, and we do want to be presented this year," muttered Henrietta. "I don't know if Sonia can be, but I want my presentation!"

"We shall be fortunate if either of you are presented," said Edwina, putting her hand to her cheek with a sigh. She felt as though she were growing up too quickly these days, watching the taut control of Sonia, the sullen anger of Alastair. The girl who was her sister-in-law was suffering inside, and it was probably Alastair's fault, much as Edwina hated to admit it. Was he still going to that disagreeable coarse woman, Mrs. Porter? Certainly he was out many evenings when he might be with his own family.

Alastair had been worrying about the same thing. He had quietly discussed the matter with some of his feminine friends, older women accepted without reserve at Almack's. Any one of them would have sponsored Henrietta, but, to a lady, they had refused even to try to sponsor Sonia. One had told him bluntly why; the others had hinted. A Jewess would be trying to push her way into Society, and it would not be allowed.

One kind lady finally explained to him how it might be arranged. "Henrietta will be presented by someone, but your wife at that event may only sit in the background. Then on other occasions, she may come to balls and accept invitations to dances. That way, propriety will be satisfied. She will not be presented to the Queen, nor will any ceremonies be outwardly performed. She may go on as though she had been received. But, of course, she cannot be received."

Alastair had raged inside, though he had bowed and smiled, and kissed the lady's hand on parting. He felt angry and protective toward his wife. She was a sweet girl; she had been quite lovable and amiable during their stay at Fairley. Back in London, she seemed a different person, cold and distant, ever since the unfortunate discovery of the marriage settlement and his account books. He flushed angrily whenever he thought of it. How careless he had been! He had stuffed books and bills away awaiting the return of his secretary. The young man could take care of it all later; the tradesmen must wait.

Edwina looked quite relieved when Alastair came home in time to dress for dinner that evening. He patted her cheek.

"Worrying again?" he asked her dryly.

She nodded, her blue eyes lighting at sight of him. "Oh, Alastair, I did want this evening to go well! Sir Philip Ryan is coming tonight, and he is so—so amiable!"

"Amiable? I would not have described him so, but I am not a young and beautiful girl," he teased her.

She blushed furiously, but gazed fondly after him as he ran lightly up the stairs to change.

He finally decided on his blue and silver. He heard no sounds from the next apartment; all seemed quiet. He frowned, and asked his valet abruptly, "Has—Lady Fairley returned home?"

"I believe not, my lord," said the valet, brushing Alastair's coat with infinite care and studying the set of the linen stock with absorbed interest.

"Where is she?" he asked, discarding his air of unconcern.

"I believe she goes daily to her townhouse, my lord, to attend to her business of making jewelry." The tone was level, impassive.

"I see."

He waited for a time. Sonia had not returned by the time it was the hour for the guests to arrive. He went down alone to receive them with Lady Edwina at his side. He noted the looks; he heard the whispers, and they disturbed him again.

The evening seemed unendurably long. He had much time to think at the dinner table, with Edwina presiding at the low end. By one in the morning, when the last of the guests had departed, he had resolved he must speak to Sonia. They had to present a united front to Society, or gossip would overwhelm them all.

He told his valet to call him at eight o'clock, making sure he got up. The valet hid his surprise magnificently and bowed as he left the room.

Alastair was up before eight, though. He had been unable to sleep much, for worrying about what he would say. His valet came, Alastair dressed and drank a cup of tea in his rooms. He heard low voices in the next apartment. Sonia was up, too.

He sent his valet to ask if he might come in. The valet returned and said formally, "My lady will see you at your convenience, my lord."

Alastair pushed back his shoulders, lifted his chin, and felt as though he were going into battle—one more difficult than any he had ever fought.

He opened the door to her living room and went in. Sonia was seated near the windows, attired in a morning gown of pale lilac muslin, with deeper purple ribbons at her waist and throat. The silver tray before her contained the remains of her breakfast.

"Good morning, my lord," she said formally. "May I serve you coffee?"

Leah brought a second cup and saucer at his nod, and stood stiffly nearby. Alastair gave her a look. Sonia finally said, "Is there something you wish to discuss, my lord?"

"Yes, and alone," he said bluntly.

Leah looked outraged, but gave him a frosty nod and left,

every line of her plump back ramrod-straight. She shut the door after her, retiring into the bedroom.

Sonia waited, poured his coffee, set it before him. He drank it slowly, looking from the window to the wintry garden scene before them. The March wind had begun to tear to pieces what was left of the dry leaves of the autumn before.

Alastair had carefully composed several fine speeches, but they went the way of the dried leaves. He said finally, "We cannot continue this way, Sonia. It is damaging the family . . . it brings to naught all I have worked to achieve. Is there no forgiving me for what I have done to you by marrying you?"

The dark gray eyes were lowered; she seemed to study the design on the plate before her. Her shoulders raised in a shrug, she finally said, "What do you wish me to do, Alastair? Leave you?"

"My God, no!" he said, horrified. He looked directly at her, noted the gray hollows below her eyes, the tired lines of her face. She looked older than when they had married, her fine color from their stay at Fairley had disappeared. "No," he said, more quietly. "We must reach some accommodation. I have been trying to arrange some way to present you and Henrietta. It has been—difficult. Rumors of our—estrangement are about. And other matters are in the way."

"My religious beliefs," she said in a low tone. She raised the coffee cup to her lips. Her slim hand did not shake. She did not seem upset, only resigned. He nodded.

"I have talked to many ladies; they refuse to sponsor you. Any one of them would gladly sponsor Henrietta. So—what shall we do?"

"Ask the most powerful of them to sponsor Henrietta, of course, and forget about my presentation," she said dryly. "I did not think it would be possible. We must think of her future."

He was relieved, and hated himself for it. She took it well, as though she had not expected otherwise.

"I will do that," he said. "I think Lady Jersey herself would sponsor Henrietta—she has her good moments. In the meantime, we shall not keep you in the background," he added with determination. "I know your work keeps you very busy. Have you many commitments at present?"

She hesitated, gave him a puzzled look. "The usual," she said.

"Well, if you will but return home in time to change for dinner and join us as hostess, I think it would be well," he said firmly. "We must appear a family. We shall drop the plan of presenting you. However, you must attend dinners in the homes of others, you must be the hostess in our home. It is not fair to Edwina to ask her to do all this." He appealed to her silently, his dark blue eyes asking for him.

She thought about it, gazing from the window as he had done. A cheeky bird perched on the windowsill near them. She appeared to be studying him closely. He fluttered his wings, gave them a bright beady stare, then darted away in search of a tasty morsel in the wintry garden.

"I will do whatever you wish," she said, in a level tone. "What are the engagements this week?"

Relieved, he told her. She noted them mentally. "I thought we might plan a more formal dinner and entertainment next week, leading up to Henrietta's presentation. About fifty guests of the *ton*, carefully selected, with jugglers and Spanish dancers—there is a troupe at the Gardens, and I will hire them for the evening. What do you think?"

A sparkle came into the gray eyes that had been so lackluster. "Oh, that would be splendid, I should enjoy it," she said, in a livelier manner. "Do let me arrange it, Alastair. I will discuss it with Edwina. We shall arrange such an evening that the guests will not be able to refuse the invitations."

It was an odd way to put it. He had never had guests refuse to come. But he let that pass, and they went on to speak of other means of planning the winter and early spring festivities. With Henrietta safely launched, they could then concentrate on arranging Edwina's betrothal.

"Is she interested in any one man, or is it to be an arranged marriage?" asked Sonia carefully.

Alastair saw the dangers in that subject. He managed to say, "I think she is as yet uncertain of her feelings. Perhaps this winter she may become interested in some man or other.

I shall want to investigate anyone thoroughly. She is a dear girl," and his voice warmed.

"As for clothes, perhaps they will wish to choose more expensive gowns, especially for the presentation," said Sonia. "I know merchants who have silk and satin fabrics which are not shown to many dressmakers. I could have them come and present them for a private showing. As for jewels—"

He bit his lips. "I believe they have sufficient number," he said stiffly.

She turned her head restlessly. "They would be charming to design for," she managed to say, and he saw the movement in her throat. "I should like—like to make some suggestions, and perhaps design something special for them all, including your brother. If you would not object—"

"It is very kind of you to offer," he said, remembering the star sapphire and how he had hurt her by trying to refuse it. This was her gift, the gift of beautiful designs, and he would not turn her down again. "Something delicate and youthful-looking, befitting their age and rank. I know you can do it charmingly."

She seemed to relax, her tense arms curled on the table. She said, "I shall be glad to try. Perhaps an ivory satin brocade for Henrietta, with pearls, small gems suited to her years. For Edwina, she looks stunning in delphinium blue, and her gems could be some aquamarines. I have an unusual number of them of fine quality I obtained recently."

"Whatever you say." He stood up with relief. The gap between them had been closed, at least he hoped so. "We shall go into more detail, my dear, as the weeks go on. I believe there is a dinner tonight. Would you wear your gold dress? I admire that on you."

Her eyelashes fluttered, hid her gray eyes. "Yes, of course, as you wish."

He left her room, and went back to his own, humming. It was done. Sonia was generous; she never did things halfway. She had forgiven him, she would work with him. He felt greatly relieved.

They did work together; she flung herself with enthusiasm into the plans. They had dinners, teas, one grand ball, with entertainment which was the talk of London for three days.

He finally got time to get away one morning. He had not seen Daphne Porter alone since his return to London. Always she had a crowd about her, laughing and talking, drinking and playing cards. He felt she was deliberately keeping him at a distance to punish him for marrying. But he must have it out with her. He wanted her badly, he wanted to be in her arms and forget all his problems.

He took the stairs to her flat two at a time. In his hands were presents—an ivory fan with an unusual peacock design, a length of red silk, two gold bracelets. Nothing terribly expensive, but he felt he could not take Sonia's money to buy something like rubies, such as Daphne had been hinting for.

The slatternly maid would not let him in at first. "She's asleep," said the girl sullenly, turning him from the door.

"Get her up, then. I have something of importance to say to her," he said impatiently, and pushed past her into the drawing room. A negligee lay over one end of the lounge, cards were scattered on the floor and some dice. She had been gaming last night, he thought, sniffing the stale air with disgust. Sonia kept everything immaculate and sweet-smelling; he didn't know how she did it, after the throngs they had in.

He sat down, pushing aside a gauzy scarf to do so. He set the gifts on the small table beside him. He had to wait over half an hour, but when she came out, it was worth it. She wore a crimson velvet gown, bordered in swansdown. It was gaudy, but it suited her blond beauty.

"What is of such importance, Alastair?" She yawned behind her hand. She accepted his kiss on her hand and cheek, then lounged into a chair, crossing her legs, so the gown swung open, showing her lovely long legs. He looked at her hungrily. Forgetfulness—that was important.

"I brought you a few things, Daphne. You always have such a crowd about—I thought I would come in the morning for a change," he smiled.

She tore open the papers, cooed over the length of silk, slid the bracelets on her arms, then opened the fan and looked at him over the brim. "Is this all, my darling?" she smiled.

Her eyes were naughty, vividly green in the darkened room. He came over to sit on the arm of her chair. "No, there is *me*. Look—let's go to your room," he said rapidly, urgently.

He had not had her since his marriage, and he wanted her badly. She shrugged her rounded plump shoulders.

"Darling, so hasty. And you didn't bring me rubies. Bad boy," she scolded. "You didn't forget again, did you? You have some in your pockets," and she began to put her hands in his coat and trouser pockets.

He flushed, and sat up straight, finally sliding from the arm of the chair to stand erect. "No, I didn't bring gems, Daphne," he said quietly. He strode away, to gaze unseeingly from the window out into the mews. A carriage was waiting there—he had not seen it before. Didn't he recognize the coat of arms on the panels? He frowned down at it. He turned about, to catch sight of a jacket of a distinctive shade of green lying on the floor near the window.

That green jacket, with the gold braid elaborately on the shoulders . . . he had seen it before . . . he had teased the owner as he was being fitted at the tailor's, calling him a peacock. Something went cold and hard in Alastair.

"Darling." Daphne stood up and came to him, leaning against his arm. She lifted his bronzed hand. "Your ring, that's it! That is my present! You silly boy, to keep me waiting!" Eagerly she tugged at the star sapphire on his finger. "It's beautiful . . . let me see it!"

The star sapphire Sonia had presented to him, of her own exquisite design and making. . . ! His fingers closed into a fist, Daphne could not remove the ring, and she pouted at him.

"No," he said harshly.

"But I want this ring, love! Let me try it on . . . come on, darling," she coaxed and pouted in a way that had driven him wild with desire a few short months before. Her red mouth was so full and luscious. . . .

"No. I cannot. It is—a gift." He kept his fist clenched and she could not open his fingers.

"Oh, let it go, then." Angrily she flung his hand from her. "But don't think you can come up here and dictate to me! You'll pay for me, and don't forget it! I wanted marriage, and you married that woman, that—"

"Don't say that, or her name," he warned, in deadly cold tones that once would have quelled any trooper in his regiment. "Forgive me for intruding. I will leave now." He picked up his morning top hat and went to the door.

"Alastair! Come back!" she cried mockingly. "When you have enough gems for me! Come on back!" And she laughed.

He turned, surveyed her, in that crimson robe with her blond hair down her back. In a few years, she would not even be pretty. Lines already marred her face, her overindulgence in liquor had made her chin plump and sagging.

"I will not be back, Daphne," he said evenly. "Oh, you might inform Sir Philip Ryan—in the bedroom—that your rent is three months overdue. I will instruct that the bills be sent to him directly from now on!"

He opened the door and went out, with her screaming after him. "Alastair—come back! You cannot refuse to pay the rent! You hired the flat. You have to pay!"

He smiled grimly as he went out to the street. A petty revenge, but it suited him.

His coachman was waiting. "I'll walk for a while, then get a hack. Go on home," he said, brusquely. He walked on, toward the river.

London was having one of its foggy days, when everything was blotted out as though gray wool shrouded its buildings and lampposts. He strode on, his cane swinging in warning to any would-be footpad, staring into the mist. In spite of the fog, he seemed never to have seen so clearly.

He walked for a time along the riverbank, his heels ringing on the cobbles. When the fury had cleared, his mind was clean, drained of all desire for Daphne. He had seen her clearly, and the picture was not at all pretty. That he had—had wanted that slut—dreamed of her while he was at Fairley, longed for her, desired her, rushed back to see her! And all she wanted was her rent paid, and gems for her plump neck and thick fingers. Love? She did not know what it was.

The gray mist clung to his top hat and fine wool suit; it settled in raindrops on his boots. Still he strode on, thinking, remembering, cringing as he thought of how he had fallen for that vapid face, that ringing laugh, the amusements she offered, the forgetfulness in her arms.

How he had brought about his own downfall! Lavishing gifts on *her*. . . . His foolish desire for that greedy wench had taken him deeper and deeper into debt. Not only gaming, but that woman also had brought him to this state. He was like his father—he was following in his footsteps . . . neglecting a fine wife at home while he chased after a hank of blond hair.

Had he been possessed of a fortune, he might even have married Daphne Porter! He felt sick at the thought. To have her the mistress of his home, the mother of his children— that bitch! To ask Edwina and Henrietta to receive her and be guided by her!

He sighed, and ran his hand over his dampened face. It was cold; he had best find a hack and get home. He was tired, hungry, lost. He turned about, and began to retrace his steps.

The fog closed about him, yet he had never felt so free, so sure of where he was going. He was going home, to the woman he had married. Sonia! She was all gentleness and ladylike poise, her gray eyes cool and confident and intelligent. His wife! How had he been drawn to her? How had it happened that fate had allowed him to marry her? She was infinitely above him—a gentlewoman, a wife of whom one could be proud. Already Edwina and Henrietta were turning to her, confiding in her.

He came into a better district, of business houses and flats, and was able to find a hack. He got in and directed the jarvey to his home.

He took off his hat, and ran his hand through his damp hair. Sonia. How could he remake his life with her? She had been hurt, finding out about that marriage settlement. And he had insulted her. Could she ever forgive him, and be his wife again?

He had married a Jewess for her money. Now he admired her for her intelligence and goodness. His life was all afoul, for he had done such foolish things in the past. Would she understand this? He honored her. Did she know that? The past months had been so difficult for her. He smiled a little, tenderly, as he thought of her happiness at Fairley, her shyness in the townhouse. She tried to appear so confident, but she was like a sparrow, quick to take alarm and fly off, her gray/eyes flickering with fear.

He must go slowly, and woo her all over again. He had started off right, for she had been loving and sweet in his arms—until that horrible incident in his study.

From now on, he thought, he must devote himself to Sonia, and to his brother and sisters. He must think only of them all, and settle down. He had had a lucky escape, and he was thankful for it with all his heart. He grimaced at the thought of Philip Ryan. He would not do for Edwina, if he was frequenting Daphne Porter! No, he would not do for dear Edwina, so gentle and trusting and good. Sonia must help him find the right man for Edwina, someone who deserved her.

He was late for luncheon. They were sitting down at table when he came in, wet and weary, from his long walk. "I'll only be ten minutes—wait for me," he said, putting his head in the door of the dining room.

Sonia nodded. "Of course. We have only just sat down to soup," she said, her gaze averted from him.

He hummed as he dried himself, changed to another suit, and dashed down the stairs again. He came in as they were at fish, and said, "I'll have a double plate of that—it looks delicious!" His voice was so gay and happy that Edwina exchanged a look with Henrietta, while Sonia looked up to his end of the table in surprise.

The conversation was amiable, of clothes, and the next dinner, and who had talked of what at tea yesterday. He had never felt so contented and happy. He teased Henrietta about a beau, told Edwina she must look smart or her sister would beat her to the altar, and informed Maurice that he definitely would escort his sisters to the plays this coming week, no matter what else he had planned. He caught Sonia's sober gray gaze on him in wonderment, and grinned down the long table at her.

No problems were so bad that they could not be worked out, he thought.

Chapter
10

━◦━◦━◦━◦━◦━◦━◦━◦━◦━◦━◦━◦━◦━◦━

SONIA was almost frantically busy, but it kept her from brooding. She could even sleep at night, so tired that after a glass of warm milk she dropped right off.

Alastair did not come to her, but he did stay home more often, and that was something. He had persuaded Henrietta's godmother, the formidable Lady Barnstable, fairly recently widowed, to present her to Society. They were all busy from morning to night.

Lady Barnstable—Sonia's mouth curled into a smile at thought of her. She had feared to meet her, and when she did she found her sharp-tongued, speaking her mind freely. Yet this small, dynamic person in her purples was a dashing figure. A widow at fifty, she was now fifty-two and coming out of her mourning gray.

She had agreed to bring out Henrietta. It had been a fortunate choice. No one snubbed Lady Barnstable—she had too many friends in high places. So long as Sonia kept in the background, all had to go well.

Sonia went daily to her townhouse, where she worked all morning and afternoon on her jewelry designs. She had completed sets of gems for Edwina and Henrietta, made smart unusual cuff studs for Maurice and Alastair, and finally composed a drawing room piece for Lady Barnstable. The lady was exceedingly wealthy and possessed boxes of jewelry. Sonia had thought long about what to give her.

She had seen the lady's gardens, with beautiful trees, shrubs, and plots of exquisite flowers, and had heard her speak lovingly of her blooms.

"I hate the winter," had said Lady Barnstable. "Only then do I lack fresh flowers from my gardens here. In my country home, I have a greenhouse, and have flowers sent up to London daily. But the poor things often freeze on the coach."

So Sonia had captured her idea. Now she had completed the gift. It was about eight inches tall, with a rock crystal base like a flower pot. From it grew a jade stem. The lilies of the valley were formed of pearls, drooping on more jade stems. Tucked in the base were flowers of carnelian, jasper, amber, and tourmaline.

It needed only a little more work and it would be complete. She turned it about on her work table, her gray eyes shining. She did hope the lady would be pleased. Once enlisted in Henrietta's cause, Lady Barnstable had worked ferociously hard to present her and find young men to introduce to her. Because of her, Edwina and Henrietta were now enjoying their happiest time in London.

Someone tapped at the door. Leah went to open it. It was one of the refugee women whom Sonia had taken in. There were so many Jews escaping from the Continent, now that the pogroms were increasing in ferocity in Austria and the German states. French troops were on the march everywhere. Any Jew with money tried to escape lest everything be taken from him.

The slim woman bobbed a curtsey, and said in German, "Mr. Goldfine presents his compliments, and would you join him in the drawing room, my lady?"

All the refugees were very impressed that their hostess was a British lady with a real title, as well as one of themselves. Sonia gave Leah a quick glance—they were both surprised.

Uncle Meyer rarely came home in the early afternoon, once started on his work at the office.

"Please inform Mr. Goldfine I shall be there within five minutes," she said.

Another curtsey, and the woman went out.

Sonia put her jewelry away reluctantly, took off her working apron, revealing her muslin gown of lilac with the blue ribbons. "Do I look all right, Leah?" she asked anxiously, for she was without a mirror.

Leah brushed with her hand at the soft curls on her charge's forehead. She straightened the skirt of the gown, gave her a long critical look from head to toe. "You look splendid, my dove," she said.

Sonia went with her to the drawing room. She heard the deep tones of two men. She hesitated. Who could be with Uncle?

She tapped lightly on the door. Her Uncle Meyer called out, "Pray to come in!"

She went in to find him standing with another man. She knew the other by sight, and gave him a deep curtsey.

Her uncle made the introductions with an unusual degree of formality. "My niece, Lady Sonia Charlton, Marchioness of Fairley. May I introduce to you Mr. Nathan Rothschild? Mr. Rothschild, the Marchioness of Fairley."

They both bowed again. Sonia had seen the astute face with the sagging lower lip, the sharp blue eyes, the curled reddish hair of this man in his mid-thirties. She had heard much of him since she had come to London. He had set up his own banking house. When he bought, he was imitated and followed. When he sold, all London sold, or so they said. He stood by a pillar at the Exchange and everybody watched him. He was stout, ungainly, yet somehow commanding in air and manner.

They all sat down, Uncle Meyer in his usual chair, the others on either side of him. Leah stood in the corner of the room, a watchful presence never far from her charge.

"I have heard of your exceeding generosity to our unfortunate brethren," murmured Nathan Rothschild to Sonia.

She bent her head. "I was also once a refugee," she said simply. "I know how they feel."

"I understand you have hired a tutor to teach them English, besides giving them food and lodging."

"It is necessary in England," she said, with humor in her luminous gray eyes. "The British think all other languages barbarous! They must learn English in order to live and work in England."

He nodded. "I am glad you understand that. Others do not. Well, well, we are grateful to you. You are as good as you are beautiful. Your uncle constantly sings your praises to me and to the members of the Congregation."

"I am shocked by my uncle," said Sonia demurely, somehow feeling free to speak to Rothschild in spite of his formidable reputation. "I had not thought he would put himself out to bore his friends."

The bankers laughed, and Sonia smiled. She understood that this was all preliminary to whatever he had come to say.

She sat back, then, let the two men talk. Since obviously she had been invited to listen, she likely would have some part in a decision or later event. She was content to listen and watch their faces.

They spoke of the efforts of Viscount Wellington on the Peninsula, leading the British and Portuguese troops against Napoleon's French invaders. Rothschild was doing his utmost to get gold bullion and specie to the British general to pay his soldiers. Rothschild turned to Sonia.

"You see, one of Napoleon's great policies, which have worked for him so far, is to have his troops live off the land. His Frenchmen go foraging around the villages and countryside, stealing chickens, pigs, grain—all they can get—and live on it. In the German states, in Austria, this worked, because the farmers were prosperous. The land and its fruits fed them well. In Spain, it is a different matter."

She had read of Spain, and wished she could see the beautiful buildings, the rare gardens and fountains, part of the Moorish legacy. "How is it different, sir?"

"In Spain, the people are very poor; the farmers are hard put to feed their own families. They have little to send to the towns. When the French ravaged the land, the farmers had little left. They complained bitterly, but Napoleon turned a deaf ear. Now some of the Spanish have turned guerilla—

that is, they hide in the mountains, and pounce on the French invaders. Spain is bitterly divided, especially since its own king no longer rules."

They went on to speak of other matters there, and Sonia found it fascinating to hear two men speak knowledgeably of the far-off war as though they had been there. She had heard that Rothschild had his own couriers, and received information of battles even before the Prince of Wales or the King and his council. She could well believe it—he spoke softly but so definitely about what he knew. His eyes flashed with intelligence.

"Is more money needed to send to the Peninsula?" asked Meyer Goldfine. "We will be glad to give a loan on generous terms."

"I thank you. It is not necessary. The British government will furnish the money, and gladly. The problem is getting the money to the port of Lisbon. We send it on ships, and the ships are sunk or captured. The French are keen to intercept. They know by instinct—or by paid informants!—which ships have gold on them."

"But you have other means of getting the gold to them?" asked Sonia, before she knew she was going to speak. Her eyes flashed with interest and enthusiasm.

Rothschild turned to her. He studied her intently before he nodded. "We have our ways, yes. You will speak of this to no one but your uncle, my lady," he added firmly.

"But of course! I will not speak of it to anyone."

He studied her more thoroughly. "You speak several languages, I believe?" And he then addressed her in German. She answered fluently. He tried her in French, in which she was proficient. He nodded in pleasure.

"She also speaks Spanish, Italian, Portuguese, any language you can name," said her uncle proudly.

Rothschild did not smile, nor seem to notice the interruption. He spoke to her in each language, finally in Hebrew, and was pleased by her answers.

She was more and more puzzled. Why had she been called in to listen to them, and to speak with them? She had been about to offer money to him, but he did not seem to require that. What could she give him for the cause of the English troops? She was not answered.

He rose at the end of two hours, thanked them for their company, and bowed over Sonia's hand. After he had departed, Sonia returned to her room, for her uncle had sunk into meditation, his head on his hands.

She went home early that day, for tonight was a ball at the very home of the Prince of Wales, whom people thought would be named Prince Regent at any moment. The King of England was mad, so they said, and a ruler was needed while he remained ill. But no one could agree on what should be done, so matters lagged. Yet Prince George might one day be King George IV, and it was important to be in his favor.

Alastair was on the outer fringes of the society that clustered about the Prince. He had been most pleased when he had received invitations for them all to attend the ball. And Sonia's name had been on the invitations! She had scarcely believed it.

Surely the Prince and his social secretaries would be aware of the fact that she was Jewish. She knew some of the lords were more tolerant of the Jews than their ladies. Was the Prince one of them? Tonight she would find out.

She was anxious to appear well. She had hesitated over half a dozen of her finest dresses, only finally to discard them. At Alastair's suggestion, she had selected a topaz silk taffeta with an overdress of sheer gold gauze. With it she wore topaz earrings, a delicate tiara of topaz and diamonds, and rings of topaz. When Leah had dressed her, the abigail turned her gently to look at herself in the full-length mirror.

"You look like a queen," said Leah, proudly, her eyes flashing.

Like a Jewish bride, thought Sonia. Her dark curly hair was fastened high in the current style, with a coronet about her head and soft curls falling to her throat. The delicate jewelry set off her sensitive oval face, her red mouth, and her luminous gray eyes. She was taller than the average, and she carried herself beautifully.

Alastair's valet tapped at the door, and then Alastair came in. He too looked splendid. He was grave and anxious at first, but then smiled at the sight of her.

"My dear, your appearance is perfection!" he said, taking her hand to kiss. He was magnificent himself in midnight blue velvet, with the star sapphire on his hand. He seemed to wear it all the time now, she noted. She was shyly pleased.

He never came to her bedroom except formally, in the daytime. He did not come to her bed, and she had missed him sorely. Some coldness and reserve remained between them, ever since the episode when she had discovered the marriage settlement. Yet he was never other than kind and courteous to her.

"You shall be the center of all eyes tonight," he said.

"Oh, I hope not!" she said involuntarily.

He smiled, and gently teased her. "Are you so shy then?"

"It is Henrietta's first presentation to the Prince. That is important," she said, turning slightly away. Leah held a golden velvet cloak for her to slip about her slim shoulders, and she was ready.

They descended the stairs together. The butler murmured that Lady Barnstable was already waiting for them in the drawing room. Sonia knew that Maurice and her sisters-in-law would be late—they always were.

"You have the box?" she whispered to the butler. He bowed, took the beautifully wrapped golden box from the table, and carried it for her into the drawing room.

"Good evening, good evening," cried Lady Barnstable. She was splendid in purple with her diamonds flashing. She raised her lorgnette critically to stare at Sonia. "Splendid, splendid! You look magnificent, and even more—beautiful!"

"Thank you very much." Sonia still felt ill at ease with the lady, kind as she had been. She took the box from the butler. "I wished to give you something to remember this occasion. If you will be so kind as to accept this from—from all of us —" And she set the box on a small table beside the lady.

"Indeed, indeed, you are most kind, you are more kind," said Lady Barnstable. She spoke in the slightly loud tones of one who was becoming deaf and refused to admit it. Neatly, she unwrapped the box, opened it, and stared inside. "Oh— my word—my word—whatever in the world—"

Sonia gazed at her anxiously. Would she like it? Would she

refuse it? She must know Sonia had created the little gem-like garden.

"What is it?" asked Alastair curiously, stepping closer to peer into the box.

"Take it out, Alastair, I might drop it," commanded Lady Barnstable. Alastair took it out with infinite care, seeing what it was, and set it on the table.

There it stood, the little gem-like flowers set in the rock crystal pot. Glittering in the firelight and the candlelight flashing, yet so beautiful and small and exquisite that the flowers seemed almost real. The lady put out her finger and touched them reverently, one after the other.

"I cannot believe it—I never saw anything like it—my dear gal, did you make it?" She turned abruptly on Sonia. Lady Barnstable's flashing dark blue eyes looked almost tearful.

Sonia nodded. "I hoped it would please you, my lady," she managed to say in her soft musical voice.

"Please me? Nothing could please me more!" she declared. "I shall set it on my bedside table, where I can see it night and day. How beautiful! Unusual! Never saw anything like it! Must have taken you months!"

It *had* taken much of her time for the past two months, but Sonia only smiled modestly without admitting that. She drew a deep breath of relief that it had been accepted. The others came in and exclaimed over the gift, looking at Sonia with awe that she could have created such a magnificent little flower pot of jeweled blooms.

Then it was time to go. There was only a few moments to admire everyone's clothing and jewels. Maurice wore ice blue velvet trimmed in gold, with his new gold studs. Edwina was in lilac silk, well suited to her gentle beauty, with sapphires in a small delicate tiara and a fragile necklace. Henrietta was in ivory satin as befitted a girl in her first season. Sonia had created a necklace of aquamarines and amethysts to set off her violet eyes. As they were chatting, and donning cloaks, she suddenly realized something.

All of them but herself were in blues and purples! She was the outsider, the odd one—in gold. Had it been on purpose?

No, no, she must not think so. But it did seem odd, the whole party matching and only Sonia looking different.

She swallowed her mean thoughts, concentrated on the thrills of the evening. They took two carriages to convey them to Carlton House. The lights of torches and the milling of carriages increased as they approached the Royal Crescent. Then they were being helped from the carriages by red-suited footmen, and walking up the broad stairs to the upper rooms. Sonia drew a deep breath. It could not be her, not Sonia Goldfine, going to dance and dine with the Prince!

Inside, all was confusion. Alastair took charge, and kept them together. Their cloaks given over to the maids, they proceeded into the reception line to meet lords and ladies, princes and princesses. Soon Sonia was sweeping a curtsey before the Prince himself.

She raised her eyes as she stood up, to find him gazing at her thoughtfully. He was heavier than she had thought, even after seeing unflattering cartoons of him. Yet there was kindness and courtesy in his heavy-set face, the thick jowls. He was splendidly dressed in velvet and silks, with diamonds on his hands. But it was the expression of his eyes that charmed her.

"Lord Fairley, where have you hidden your pretty wife?" asked the Prince, smiling at Alastair and indicating Sonia. "Why have I not seen her before?"

Alastair bowed, pleased, and begged to present his youngest sister, also. "This is is her first season, Your Royal Highness. She has been most anxious to have the privilege of meeting you."

The Prince smiled kindly at Henrietta, admonished her to enjoy her season. "Ah, to be so young and so lovely," he sighed. "Enjoy every moment, my dear. Youth is so fleeting!"

He had other cordial remarks for Maurice and Edwina before turning to other guests pressing up behind them.

"How nice and friendly he is," breathed Henrietta, stars in her violet eyes.

Their party moved on into the crowded rooms, and mingled with the guests. Alastair seemed to recognize them all, and was always bowing and introducing Sonia and Henrietta to them. Sir Frederick Toland came up and spoke to Sonia. "How pleasant to see you here, my lady," he said.

Edwina was soon asked to dance by Sir Philip Ryan. Sonia was surprised to see Alastair frown after them. She had thought Sir Philip one of his closest friends, but tonight they were rather cold to each other. Some tiff?

No one asked Sonia to dance. She stood stiffly, shyly, color burning her cheeks. She was conscious of the bright golden dress making her stand out. People was staring and whispering. Did they admire or disdain? She did not know, and dared not stare back at them.

Alastair asked her to dance, first making sure Henrietta was partnered. They moved into the stately pattern, making two of eight people in the set. She noted the ladies were staring at her again and she stiffened. The men bowed and moved her about. Soon she was back again with Alastair.

"Warm in here," said Alastair. "The usual crush." He sounded bored after the first flush of enthusiasm. She supposed he was quite used to such grand affairs.

He left her with Lady Barnstable at the side of the room, to go and procure some cool drinks for them from one of the footmen. Lady Barnstable made small chatter once they were alone, her bright eyes following first one and then another lady.

"Henrietta is doing nicely. A modest young miss," she said, with satisfaction. "I dislike brazen females intensely."

"Yes, so do I," murmured Sonia, thinking of Mrs. Daphne Porter with a shudder of distaste. She wondered how often Alastair went to her now.

"Edwina will make a fine wife. I must see about a young man for her. Anyone in the running?" asked Lady Barnstable.

"Why—I scarcely know," said Sonia, as Edwina did not confide in her.

"Must find out," muttered the lady to herself. "Ah, there is Mrs. Holm. Widow. Should be in gray. Suppose she's out to catch herself the next."

Sonia stood on one foot and then the other. Alastair took a long time to return to them. He seemed to be trapped in a gay circle of friends. Finally he managed to extricate himself, returned with a footman carrying a tray of glasses.

They stood and sipped the mild lemon-flavored drink. It was cooling and refreshing, and non-alcoholic. Sonia smiled and smiled at nothing, as Alastair and Lady Barnstable exchanged gossip about people they knew. She knew very few of them, she had nothing to offer in the way of small talk.

Then she did see someone she knew: Sir Jonathan Wiltshire, with whom she had danced the one other time she had gone to a ball with her uncle, on the memorable night when she had first met Alastair.

"Oh, isn't that, over there—isn't that Sir Jonathan—" She had not realized that in her eagerness to recognize someone her voice would carry.

The tall dignified soldier turned to see who spoke of him. He stared right at Sonia, then turned his shoulder and continued speaking to the gentleman he was addressing. Further, he took the gentleman's arm and went further away toward the door to the balcony. It was a direct cut.

Tears stung Sonia's eyes. She tried to blink them away. It might be a mistake . . . she was too sensitive. She gazed down at her gold-trimmed fan with the brilliant peacock design on it. She waved it slowly, pretending she had not spoken at all. She was sure Alastair had noticed, for his mouth tightened and his lips had lost their happy smile.

Lady Barnstable found an amiable companion, and they eagerly began to speak in penetrating whispers. Sonia and Alastair stood alone. "Another dance, my dear?" he asked gently, and replaced her glass on the tray. He put his arm about her. It was a slow dance she could follow, and they did not form a set.

When they stopped, no one she knew was in sight. Alastair bowed and smiled to those he knew, but few came near them. The guests spoke, nodded, went on. She and Alastair seemed to stand in a little circle apart from everyone else, no matter how crowded the floor was with dancers.

Alastair tried to make conversation. "At midnight, we all go downstairs for the collation," he said. "The table is spread with a plenitude of food—you will be amazed at the variety.

The Prince is noted for his hospitality. You may not recognize some of the foods—I do not myself."

She smiled, tried to answer. If he had come alone, she thought, he would be having a splendid time! She was the one who was causing the trouble, for no one would come near her. And yet the Prince himself had been kind and courteous.

The minutes seemed like hours. She shifted again from one sandaled foot to the other. Her smile seemed engraved on her lips. Alastair stopped another footman to get drinks for them both, with something strong in them this time. She merely sipped at hers. He drank his down with a savage gesture.

A lady smiled at him. Sonia said quickly, "Oh, do go and dance with her, if you wish, Alastair. I'll sit down near the window. My, isn't it warm in here."

Alastair looked grave. He took her arm without speaking, and led her to the window overlooking the balconies. He did not leave her, nor could he find her a chair—they were all occupied. She made an intense effort to think of something bright to say, her mind seemed fuzzy as wool.

Then she heard the clear malicious voice behind them. A woman was saying, "The Jewish-bride! Yes, that she is. And wearing some of her gold on her back!"

She stiffened, gasped. Alastair gave a furious look at someone over her shoulder. Sonia felt dizzy and faint. That someone should be so—so unkind. . . . When this very afternoon, the wealthy and important Nathan Rothschild had spoken to her as an equal. And the Prince himself had been kind!

Alastair put his arm about her. "It is too chilly here by the window, my darling, you will catch cold," he said protectively, leading her inside again. He kept his arm about her, he must have felt her shivering. She felt the tension in his warm body so close to hers. He was angry—protective. Yet she knew—she knew he was ashamed of her. The taste of it was gall in her mouth.

No one came near them. They saw Maurice at a distance, gaily dancing with one fair lady after another. Edwina was surrounded by beaus, fanning herself, laughing. Henrietta had gone back to Lady Barnstable, and was confiding something in her, her cheeks pink with excitement. The older lady was smiling indulgently.

Sonia gathered her courage in both hands. She gave Alastair a calm look. "I think I am spoiling the evening for you, Alastair. I beg you, call my carriage . . . let me go home. You can remain and make sure the girls are—are happy—"

His mouth set. "I am not happy here. I'll make sure Maurice and Lady Barnstable are looking after the girls. They may return home later. Wait here for me!"

He left her near the entrance to the room. The minutes dragged, yet he came back within five minutes by the gold clock near her. "I have called our carriage, it will be ready," he murmured.

The maid came with her cloak, and put it about her. Sonia lifted her head proudly and they descended the stairs, Alastair's hand under her elbow, holding her to him. At the carriage she tried again.

"I beg you, Alastair, return upstairs and rejoin the party. I do not wish to spoil your evening because of—of my headache." She invented it rapidly, to give him an out.

He did not take it. "I shall leave with you," he said curtly, his tanned face darker than usual, his blue eyes flashing. They entered the carriage and were driven away.

She could say nothing on the ride home. Her hands were clasped tightly together, her rings cutting into her palms. The humiliation of it! And it had been deliberate. They did not want Jewish people in their society, and they made it very evident. And she was spoiling it for Alastair.

At their home, she paused in the hallway. "Thank you, Alastair, for escorting me home. I pray you, do return to the ball, and dance with your sisters. They will be sorry if you do not."

He gave her a look. "Without you? No, thank you."

She bowed her head, and went up the stairs. Her feet dragged. She felt more weary than if she had danced all night. The shame of it dragged at her limbs, making them feel leaden. She felt him standing there, watching her go up to her apartment, but she could not turn and smile good night.

In her room, she began to undress. She removed the jewels, and set them away in the cases. Leah came, her face dark. Silently, she helped her mistress remove the gauzy over-dress and the topaz satin gown. When Sonia had put on her muslin nightdress and lace negligee, she sat at the dressing table and let Leah brush her hair over and over, soothingly.

She lay down to go to sleep. Leah exited, after blowing out the candles. Sonia's mind went round and round. What was best for her to do? Stay at home after this? Let Alastair go alone? Or would people whisper all the more? Should she have remained, kept her chin high, and forced them to accept her presence? But she could not endure that—the slights, the cold shoulders, the malice in their words. . . .

The door opened. She thought Leah had returned for a moment, and her head turned wearily on the lace-edged pil-lows. But the door was the one to Alastair's suite.

A dark-clad form came in, and the brightness of his blond hair caught the light from the window. He came over to the bed.

"My dear, I could not leave you alone tonight," he said simply, and moved into the bed with her. He turned to take her into his arms. A sob came into her throat. She stifled it proudly. She did not want pity!

But when he moved his hands on her, and pressed his kisses on her face and throat, passion arose in her. Her arms came up, to close fiercely about his neck, her fingers moving through his thick soft hair. He was stroking the long curls about her shoulders, whispering love words as he embraced her.

It had been so long—so long—and she had missed him. . . .

"My darling, my dear love," he said, and she could not re-sist that. Nor could she resist the gentle way he moved his fingers on her bared breasts, then put his mouth to her throat, kissing the pulse-beat there. She knew it was rapid, and it grew more rapid as his kisses deepened.

His passion grew, and so did hers. She did not care that he had removed her nightdress, and tossed it out of bed along with his. Their bared bodies met, joined. His arms held her tightly to him as he made love to her wildly. A soft cry came from her lips as he gave her pleasure.

"My lovely, my lovely," his murmured words were wooing and sweet. "My prettiest dear, my dove—how soft you are, so silky sweet—"

His lips pressed down over her shoulders, to her breasts again, down to her waist. Then he moved more rapidly, as though the touch of her excited him unbearably. And the pleasure between them was hotly honeyed as they struggled for fulfillment. She cried out again. He stifled her moan with his lips, their arms and legs entwined in the canopied bed.

He lay back, breathing rapidly, then once again he came to her, as though he could not get enough of her. She lay limply unresisting, thrilling again and again at his touch, at his movements. He nuzzled at her neck and shoulders, kissed her again and again, down over her breasts, taking the nipples in his lips and pulling at them. He gave her new passion, until again she cried out at his fierce possession of her body. She felt completely one with him, breathing with his breath, moving with his limbs, sighing with his sigh. She was shaking as with a chill when he was finally finished. Yet she did not feel cold, but hot, hot as fire.

He came down to rest, then, holding her closely to him, as though unable to let her go. And they slept, dark head close to blond on the pillow.

Chapter
11

‒•‒•‒•‒•‒•‒•‒•‒•‒•‒•‒•‒•‒•‒•‒•‒

SONIA did not go again to any big party. At Alastair's anxious urgings, she did attend a few smaller dinners, and, of course, she was hostess in their home. But she refused with one excuse or another to attend any large gathering.

She tossed her head proudly, her lips hard, when she thought of the slights and mockery, the malice in their whispers. They were jealous of her wealth, she thought. They were not too proud to go to her uncle for huge loans, but socially—no, they would not want to meet her socially! Well, she did not wish to meet them, either. She had enough to do —she had much work to keep her busy.

Soon, another event had her anxious and preoccupied. Her cousin's wife, Beryl, was expecting her baby. It was giving her much pain and illness. Sonia went daily to her; finally, when Beryl gave birth one night, Sonia was with her. Leah, too, was there, for she had much experience in these matters. It was a long painful experience for Beryl. When her baby son finally arrived, she was extremely weak and exhausted.

Sonia remained with her another day, until she was sure Beryl was out of danger, then returned home. She said little of it, knowing the others cared not at all for her relatives. She said, briefly, "My cousin's wife has had her child, and all is now well,"—and that was all she told them.

Alastair gazed at her thoughtfully, a slight frown on his face. "And you have been with her constantly? You must be weary," he said without expression.

"Very tired, thank you. I shall sleep for a while," and she went up to her room. She was glad to be in her own bed, retiring early to sleep into the next day until noon.

The season was almost over. She wondered what they would do this summer. Many in society had already left London, retiring to country homes.

She was dressed, with Leah brushing her hair, when Alastair entered her bedroom. He came over to the dressing table, looked at her in the mirror.

"You slept late today, Sonia."

She smiled faintly, not meeting his eyes. Edwina and Henrietta often slept until afternoon when they had been out at balls. Was Sonia now expected to get up early and work hard, as she normally did? She felt tired all over again, her temper only partially under control.

"Yes, and I have much work to do at the townhouse. I will go there presently."

His mouth had hardened. "I wish to speak to you about that," he said, picking up her small powder box and examining it idly, turning it about in his long fingers. She had made it of alabaster, with a small gold button on the top.

Leah, her face impassive, continued to brush Sonia's hair, then to braid it into its usual coronet about her head.

"Yes?" asked Sonia.

"The season is about over. The girls are weary. I should like for us to retire to the country before long. How are your commissions? Can you continue them in the country, or are they about finished?"

Surprise held her silent for a few moments. Her wide gray gaze met his blue in the mirror. He was looking intently at her, as though judging her reaction.

"Why—my work is at such a stage—I can leave it easily.

140

Most of the jewels were wanted for the season, and they are completed. No, I have nothing to hold me here," she added eagerly, wistfully. Could they really be going to Fairley?

"Good! Splendid! I shall ask the girls and Maurice to wind up their social life. We ought to be able to leave for Fairley within two weeks, say, by mid-June. Will that suit you?"

He had put his hand gently on her shoulder, as though wishing to touch her, and judge her feelings through the touch. She felt a wild thrill race through her body at the touch of his fingers. How responsive she felt toward him! How her blood seemed to sing when he was near her, her body trembled when he moved closer.

Beryl should be well on to recovery within two weeks. Sonia smiled and nodded. "It would suit me splendidly. I looked forward to going again to Fairley—it should be beautiful in the summer."

"Yes, Fairley is a beautiful place in all seasons," he said absently. That afternoon at tea, for which they were all present—a most unusual occurrence—he told the others.

Henrietta was a little reluctant, yet she knew the season was over. Edwina was relieved.

"Oh, I am so tired of being dressed up constantly! It shall be a relief to go and be comfortable," she sighed. There were shadows under her eyes.

Sonia glanced at her uneasily. Did she sigh for a young man? Did she lie awake because of unrequited love? Or was she simply tired of the round of the social life? Maurice did not care one way or another, for he amused himself wherever he went. In the country he could ride every day, and that would please him.

The next two weeks sped past. Sonia went daily to her work, finished two sets of jewels, and sent them to their purchasers. She refused several commissions against the winter, accepted two on which there was no time limit. She explained carefully that she was going to the country, and that she did not know when she could complete them.

Both ladies insisted they did not care, "Just so we have jewels by Lady Fairley," simpered one coyly. "She is so justly famous in London! How I admire the gems you designed for your sisters!" She had met Henrietta and Edwina, and had

141

examined their necklaces and tiaras as closely as possible. She wanted something designed just for herself.

The woman was foolish, but not malicious. Sonia managed to smile at her. "I shall design something especially for your own kind of beauty, with your reddish hair and green eyes. I think a green stone, with a delicate framework of silver—yes, a tiara that seems to float—"

They were delighted with her, and went away exclaiming it would be doubly pleasant to see her this fall, knowing she was designing for them. She packed up her sketchbooks, pencils, pads, locked away the remaining jewels, and sent word to her gem merchants that she might not see them again until the autumn. Meantime, would they watch for emeralds, fine topaz, more sapphires, and anything unusual in the way of gems?

It took five carriages to convey their party to Fairley, with their trunks, their maids, valets and footmen. The butler, housekeeper and a skeleton staff would remain in London, as usual. The housekeeper unwound so far as to assure Sonia that "My lady need not fret about the house in her absence. I assure you I shall take every care. The house shall be kept aired and ready for your return."

She was not nearly so cold and unfriendly as before, but came to Sonia for orders as she had formerly to Edwina. Sonia found some relief in that. Gradually she would win them over, and all would go smoothly for Alastair. That was all she cared about.

Sonia was much happier to see Mrs. Pendennis again. The good woman was waiting out in the graveled drive as the carriages rolled up after their journey of several days. She beamed, her cheeks red in the wind, and cried out, "Welcome, welcome! We have been ready these weeks for you!"

How pleasant to have such a joyous acceptance, after the chill of London and its society! Sonia took her hands, and said unsteadily, "It is wonderful to be here again. Thank you again. You are most good."

"Come in, my lady. That drive is a long chilly one. The fires are lit in all your rooms. And I have some Cornish pasties for supper with your tea!" She shooed them all before her like so many eager children, laughing happily as Maurice dared to give her a kiss on her pink cheek.

It was like coming home. Sonia slept soundly that night for the first time in weeks. She had no worries and humiliations to keep her awake. She wakened early the next morning, and went downstairs to confer with Mrs. Pendennis, to hear all that had happened in their absence, to make plans for the summer. Alastair soon came down and joined her for breakfast, dressed in his summer clothes of tweeds and wool jacket. His eyes seemed bluer than ever with the dark blue wool coat about his broad shoulders and his mouth ready to smile.

That first day, she wandered about in the gardens and, farther afield, into the apple orchards and out to the stables. She renewed acquaintance with the gentle mare she had ridden before, fed her an apple, and promised to come for a ride the next morning. Alastair had saddled up his huge stallion and had gone out eagerly to survey all his domain.

Edwina rose for luncheon; Henrietta still slept, she said. Edwina brooded over her meal, and gave Sonia little appealing looks. Sonia ignored them for a time, but finally Edwina came to her as she was sketching by the windows in the drawing room. The flowers were giving her inspiration for more designs.

"Sonia, may I talk to you a while?" Edwina appealed.

"Of course." Sonia set down her pad and pencil in surprise, and turned to the girl. Edwina looked younger today, in a simple lilac muslin, with blue ribbons tied under her slim young breasts. A scarf of white lace was thrown carelessly about her shoulders, and her beautiful blond curls were tied back loosely. How the young men of London would rave if they could see her beauty now, thought Sonia.

Edwina seemed to find it hard to begin, then words burst forth. She fiddled with the lace ends of her scarf, twirled the blue ribbons.

"How—how do you know when a man likes you, really likes you?" she blurted out. Her cheeks had gone crimson, and her soft blue eyes were distressed.

A fine question indeed, thought Sonia bitterly. How would she know? Then she pulled herself together. It was the first time Edwina had confided in her. She would not let her down. She thought of her cousin Jacob and his wife Beryl. They had the best, most devoted marriage she had ever seen.

"Why—when the man is kind, and thoughtful to you," she said finally. "When he thinks of your comfort first. When he works hard, not for a living, but to please you and make your home a—a nest for you and the—the children to come." She looked out at the beautiful well-kept lawns of Fairley. Her voice caught in her throat. She thought of Jacob, his face radiant and shining with pride and joy as he held the little baby son in his arms. As he bent over Beryl anxiously on her couch, and inquired if she was more at ease now. . . .

Edwina was heaving a great sigh. "Then Sir Philip Ryan does not love me!" she burst out, tears coming to her eyes. "He has neglected me, and forgotten to come to tea and—and I don't think he cares a fig for me!"

Sonia thought of the dashing red-haired young man. "Hmmm," she said. "I wonder—he is a friend of Alastair's. Perhaps Alastair knows of some—some prior commitment that Sir Philip has. Is he courting someone else?"

Edwina wiped her eyes with a small lace-embroidered handkerchief. "I have listened to gossip about him," she admitted, shamefaced. "Yet I could not bring myself to question Alastair further. I—I did ask him why Sir Philip did not come more often to the house. Alastair said he did not care for Sir Philip to come! Do you not think that is odd?"

Sonia frowned. It was odd, indeed. She had thought they were friends. "It may be that Alastair has discovered something—that Sir Philip is courting someone else, or that there is something. . . . I mean—it might be to his discredit. Alastair thinks the world of you and Henrietta and Maurice. I am sure he wishes to protect you and make a marriage that will do you honor as well as make you happy."

Edwina opened her blue eyes wide, and studied Sonia. "Do you know of something against Sir Philip?" she asked.

Sonia shook her head. "No, he seems pleasant enough. But sometimes men know each other, and hear things that ladies do not," she added wisely.

"Could you ask Alastair?" ventured Edwina.

"Oh, dear!" cried Sonia involuntarily. Edwina giggled, and her blue eyes lightened.

"I should not ask—forget that I did so, dear Sonia!" she begged charmingly. "Perhaps I should not know. Perhaps I should just accept that —that Philip does not care for me— for if he did he would come. Oh, I suppose there are other men in the world," she said with a toss of her head.

"There certainly are," said Sonia. "And some of them clustered about you at the balls as though they longed to be even nearer. Who was that older man with the smart military coat of blue, with the gold frogging? He had such a hawklike, interesting face—"

Edwina curled up beside her. With an animated face, she proceed to tell about him and about another beau, and on to other men and the times she had had. The words gushed out, confidingly, as though she had longed to have someone to listen with such interest. Sonia did listen. Putting in a diplomatic word or question at moments when Edwina flagged, she kept the girl talking. The brooding look was going from her face. Sir Philip had evidently hurt her, and it did her good to talk.

Henrietta wandered in, yawning, and opened her violet eyes in surprise to see her sister talking so to their sister-in-law. She soon curled up beside them, anxious to share in the reminiscences, telling of *her* beaus, the success of her season, and how much fun she had had. And how she looked forward to next season, and what clothes they would buy in the autumn.

It was quite the most pleasant afternoon Sonia had ever spent with them. When Maurice came in for tea, with Alastair soon following, looking weary but quietly happy, she was pleased to have them gathered close to the open fire, talking.

It was the first of many such pleasant summer days. The girls were more settled, Henrietta's presentation and first season behind them. Sonia was absorbed in her sketches, in the housekeeping, and in her new role as confidante to her sisters-in-law. Maurice enjoyed the riding and hunting, and even put his hand to some work under Alastair's direction. Alastair was busy as ever, setting the estate to rights, hearing complaints, hiring seasonal workers for the fields and for the harvest in the autumn.

They had visitors—the pastor of the church and his wife, the squire and his brood of children, several summer people down from London. On bright days, they could count on half a dozen or more visitors to tea and remaining for dinner. On rainy days, they were to themselves, and happy for it, sitting before the great roaring fire in the massive stone fireplace, talking of the day gone past.

Sonia had started making sketches for Edwina's and Henrietta's clothes for autumn. They were so eager and so lavish in their praises, she worked gladly for them. For Edwina, she chose simple designs to the girl's taste, in delicate fabrics that would not clash with the girl's gentle beauty. For Henrietta, she chose more daring designs, with great slashed sleeves of satin, and colors of tangerine and scarlet with brown braid. She thought about her jewelry designs also, and made a number of sketches for them, studying the flowers in the gardens for inspiration.

Wandering Jewish peddlers came often that summer, drawn by the news that a Jewish girl—one of their own—lived in the great house in Cornwall. Mrs. Pendennis usually fed them before sending them brusquely on their way.

Sonia found out, insisted that they should be greeted as guests, put up for the night or longer. And she should be informed when any came.

Reluctantly, Mrs. Pendennis would send a maid to tell her when any of the wandering peddlers came. Sonia would go down to the great kitchens and greet them in Hebrew or German or Polish.

They would sit down at a kitchen table and talk. The peddlers were usually new to the country, knowing little English. With their black beards and hair, their unkempt appearance, their old clothes and foreign accents, they were viewed with great suspicion by the staff. Some, taking them for gypsies, wanted to lock up the silver.

Sonia would ask them for news. "How is it in Vienna?" she asked one from Austria.

"Bad, very bad," he answered in German, shaking his head sorrowfully. "Until that madman Napoleon is defeated,

146

there will be no peace. He is worse than the rest, he and his soldiers, poking here and there and trying to find out money and paintings. Some say his men have carried off half the treasures of Europe."

They would sit and talk in a foreign language. The cooks and maids would eye them fearfully, wonderingly, hearing their mistress talk in those strange tongues. Sonia would see to it that the Jews would have plenty of food to eat, and more to take along with them. If they were shabby, she got clothes for them.

When one was robbed and beaten on the highway, she took him in and kept him for the summer. He had a room over the stable. Often in the twilight as he was recovering they would hear his plaintive violin, sobbing like the cry of a lost soul.

"They make me shiver," whispered Edwina, involuntarily hugging herself. "Those men, in such dark clothes, and walking everywhere. Why do they come here? What do they want?"

They were seated before the fire on a rainy night. Sonia glanced up from her sketches, to see Edwina's troubled look. Edwina was genuinely afraid of the strange men.

"Let me explain," she said gently, laying aside her work. Maurice and Alastair put aside their gazettes, listening also. "Many places in Europe persecute the Jews. They have nowhere to hide. We send money to them, to help them come to England, where they have a better chance to remain alive, to make a living decently. Yet many cannot speak English. The first thing they must do is to learn English, and to speak it well. Next, they must learn to make a living. So, we provided them with goods such as the country wives need, and send them out to peddle in the country."

"It seems cruel," said Henrietta. "Listen to him play!" They all paused in their talking as the faint sounds of the violin came to them. "He is talented. Why must he wander the countryside?"

"He will learn English," said Sonia patiently. "Later he will be set up in a shop, taught the trade, sponsored. If he wishes to send for his wife or mother or some other relative, the Jewish congregations will aid him. We help each other. As they helped me when I first came to London."

"You!" exclaimed Maurice, looking at her, in her expensive velvet dress, the gray velvet like satin in the firelight, the trim of golden braid about her slim throat. "But why should you have needed help?"

"Because I inherited money?" she smiled faintly, and shook her dark head. "I was a girl of eleven. My mother had died—"

"Oh, wait, wait, start at the beginning!" urged Henrietta eagerly. "You never talk about yourself!"

Seeing they were genuinely interested, Sonia began again. She told about life in the Viennese ghetto. About her mother, and her tragic death at the hands of a drunken mob. About her father and his grief—how he had brought her to London, to her Uncle Meyer. "He did not live long, only long enough to see me here. He had no wish to live, once Mama was gone," she added in a low tone, tears brimming in her eyes.

They listened, as though to a fairy story of some strange world. And indeed, it was a new world to them—this one of violence, suffering, hunger, and cruel death. She told them how good her uncle had been to her, how he had advised her, strengthened her. He had hired Leah to be her abigail, to teach and help her. Her cousins had been good to her. She had been taken in and become part of their family.

"Uncle wants only my good," she said, with a little unconscious sigh, recalling to herself how he had arranged her marriage for money. "He has his own ways of arranging things, that is true. But I know he is a very wise man, and he looks far into the future. After my father died, my uncle was as my own father to me."

They listened and questioned her, and she answered patiently. Then Edwina returned to the subject of the peddlers. "Well, I can see how they need help. But they look so—so ominous—I can't help shuddering—"

"They do not look English," said Sonia sadly. "One must look beyond that, into their eyes. You will see their sadness, their grief at leaving homes, families, friends, all they held dear, to come to a strange country and begin all over again. They are to be pitied and helped, not feared."

"Sonia is right," said Alastair, who had been listening in silence. Over his pipe smoke, he added, "We will take in all who wish to come here, my dear. I shall give orders that even when we are not in residence the peddlers are to be given food and shelter here, to stay as long as they wish. I will speak also to the parson, and see that he understands the situation. How much cruelty is done when we do not understand!"

His gaze met hers, and she knew he meant this for an apology to her, for all that had been said and done in her hearing, for all the malice that had been shown. She bent her head, wondering. How kind he could be, how gentle.

Alastair had been coming sometimes to her bedroom. She loved to be in his arms, but some cool reserve sometimes kept her from full response. That night when he came, she felt closer to him. He was beginning to comprehend her nature, her background, why she was the way she was.

He caressed her so carefully, so sweetly, that sometimes she shivered with delight. She wondered sometimes about a child. She was not pregnant. Could she become pregnant by him . . . would she have his child? And what would happen to a child of theirs?

She wanted a child . . . she adored Beryl's little new son. She had held the mite in her arms, wondering at the perfection of his body, the exquisite little head, the tiny fingers, the warm clinging body. To have a child by Alastair! It would be so wonderful, no matter what pain she had to go through.

Yet—could she endure the insults her half-Jewish son would inevitably receive in his life? He would be a marquess, as his father had been, assuming one of Alastair's other titles while young. He would be the eldest son, inheriting the titles, the estates, all that Alastair had. But—he would be half Jewish. Alastair did not bother to sit in the House of Lords. Would his Jewish heir be allowed to do so? Could they keep him out?

When she thought of the difficulties ahead, she could have groaned and flung out her arms in rebellion. It was too much to expect of her, that she could manage all this!

If she had only known, she would have refused to marry Alastair. And yet—she would have missed this—the warmth of his family now they had come to like her—the grand life of society, even though she felt outside it. And Alastair himself, making love to her, treating her with honor and respect as his wife, helping her adjust smoothly to the many duties she had. And being in his arms—she would never have known the ecstasy he gave her.

She sighed and turned closer into his arms, snuggling her face against his bare chest. There was a deep V of curly blond hair down to below his waist. She put her hand timidly on it, then stroked down to his thighs daringly. He gasped with pleasure. "Oh, darling," he murmured, and clasped her more closely. His kisses fell on her smooth shoulders, and he grew more passionate.

As he moved over her, she put her hands on his shoulders, so broad and wide and winged over her. She stroked her hands over his smooth skin, fingered the scar on one shoulder where he had been hurt in battle. If the saber had gone more deeply, she would never have known him, never known him. . . . The thought seemed unbearably sad.

He put his lips on her eyelids, felt the wetness there. "What is it, my dove, my dear?" he whispered anxiously.

"If we had never met—had never come to know each other—" she managed to say.

"Fate has strange ways of ordering us about," he said against her cheek. He moved his lips to her earlobe and down below it in a tingling sensation. "Are you sorry?"

"No—no matter what—I am not sorry. . . . Are you?"

He only laughed, and gathered her more closely. Afterwards, she remembered that he had not answered in words.

Chapter
12

━●━●━●━●━●━●━●━●━●━●━●━●━●━●━●━●━●━

IN mid-July of that year of 1810, Meyer Goldfine sent a messenger to Sonia. He brought a letter, and had instructions to escort her back to London. She read the letter as he sat in the kitchen, taking some food and drink after his long hard journey.

Dearest Sonia,
I beg you to proceed at once to London. There is something urgent to be done, I cannot put it in a letter. I beg you not to inform anyone of the matter. Tell your husband it is some business or other, you will think of something. I pray you to be here by July 14 if you can make it.

> Your loving uncle, Meyer Goldfine

It was brusque, hurried, and she could tell by his hen-track penmanship that he had written in great haste. She wondered at it, frowning over the missive.

She spoke in German to the messenger. He shrugged, for either he knew no more than she did or would not speak of it. She folded the letter and went up to her room to tell Leah.

She ordered the abigail to pack for them both, then sent word to the coachman. She sat down to think what she would say to Alastair.

She had received several letters from Beryl and from Uncle Meyer, also from some merchants who had fabrics and gems from the Orient to offer her. She must think of some convincing reason to go with such haste to London.

Alastair returned before she had her story ready. He came up to her bedroom.

"Sonia? One of the grooms told me that a stranger had come with a message for you. What is it?" His face was concerned.

"Why—it is from Uncle Meyer," she said, turning her face from him. Leah was continuing to pack, setting garments into the two small trunks near the great wardrobe. He glanced at the abigail, frowned, turned back to Sonia.

"Where are you going?" he asked abruptly. He was tired, his boots muddy. He had been attending to a drainage ditch which had overflowed after a heavy rain. That he came to her room in such disarray showed his concern.

"I must go to London, Alastair," she finally said, simply. "Uncle asked me to come. Beryl is not well, and neither is he. I am very worried. I must go."

"Wait a few days, and I will go with you. I can instruct the men what to do. Maurice will take charge."

It was already the eleventh of July. She could not wait, she had to leave immediately to be there by the fourteenth.

She managed a smile. "You must not leave your work for me, Alastair," she said calmly. "Leah will accompany me, and Uncle's servant. My own coachman shall drive me. You must not trouble yourself. I shall be back within a short time, I feel sure."

He was not satisfied. "But why must you go in such haste? Surely his sons will see to his comfort—"

"I have always been close to him," she said, feeling guilty. Meyer was not ill, at least he had not said so.

"Sonia, be reasonable! I will go with you when I can, within a short time—"

She shook her head, turning from him. "No, Alastair. I will go early tomorrow morning, as soon as the servant is rested. I pray you, do not stop me. I have also some business to attend to—there are merchants to see. That is not of much interest to you, I feel sure." She smiled, and tried to say it playfully, but he scowled, wanting to argue about it.

It was delaying her, to soothe and divert him. Leah must be helped to pack, the coachman told. She finally spoke a little sharply and Alastair took his leave to his rooms.

Leah went down to speak to the coachman, and ordered some food prepared against the journey. They would not stop except to change horses. Word would be sent ahead to arrange that. It made others curious, this unexpected trip made in such haste.

Alastair was angry with her, and the girls very puzzled, when Sonia departed early the next morning. Alastair had risen early, too, to see her off. His grim face was the last one she saw as the carriage rolled down the driveway to the open road.

She leaned back into the comfortable squabs with a sigh of relief and dejection. She would have a time, soothing his ruffled feelings when she returned. But when her uncle called her so urgently, she had to go.

They made a long day of it, changed horses, proceeded through the night. They rolled into London at about midnight of the second day, going directly to see Meyer Goldfine at Sonia's townhouse.

He was still up, unusual for him, and was waiting for her in his dark red robe and his little skullcap to keep him warm. He pressed her hands—his fingers were cold.

"Uncle, you must be ill!" she exclaimed, holding his hands in her warm ones, and surveying his drawn face anxiously.

He shook his head. "No, no, I am not ill. Tomorrow, Sonia, you will go to the home of your cousin Jacob, to see the baby. From there, Jacob will take you to see—a friend. You must go, I beg of you."

"Alone?" asked Sonia.

Leah spoke up quickly. "I shall be with you!" and she glared at Mr. Goldfine.

He tried to protest, but was too weary. Sonia retired, as did Leah, and rose at about eight the next morning. She washed, dressed in a demure summer gown of pale green muslin, donned her cloak after eating, and was ready to depart.

At about ten o'clock she arrived at the house of Jacob, and was greeted with such relief by her cousin that she thought surely Beryl must be ill.

But no, Beryl was sitting up in the drawing room. At her side was a basket in which lay the baby, cooing and kicking up his heels. Her cloak was taken, she was greeted, then allowed to bend over the basket and admire the son and heir.

"What a lovely boy, what a darling!" she exclaimed, and no praise was too extravagant for the proud parents. They agreed to it all. She sat down to talk, still wondering.

Beryl was not well, for she did lean back much, and seemed much fatigued. Jacob was always putting cushions at her back, or bringing a hot drink, or inquiring anxiously if she should not lie down.

"No, no, I am quite well, quite well, Jacob," she said finally, but then burst into tears.

Sonia and Jacob both tried to calm her, but finally her abigail took her off to bed.

"What is it, Jacob?" Sonia asked anxiously.

Her handsome cousin, pulling at his beard, shrugged and said, "She is disappointed, yet relieved, and she is fond of you. Come, we must be off, our appointment is at twelve."

Puzzled all the more by his cryptic words, Sonia and Leah went with him in his carriage. They were driven down one street and up another, until the carriage came to a halt at a modest yet handsome house.

Jacob got down, and helped Sonia from the coach. He would have left Leah, but the woman got down firmly and went with them. He said, mildly but firmly, "You will not be allowed to hear the conversation, Mrs. Stein."

She frowned. "And why not?" she demanded. Jacob gave a sigh, and led them to the door. The door was opened before he could knock, and a butler showed them in.

Mrs. Leah Stein was put in another room to wait, to her

great disgust. Jacob and Sonia were shown to a drawing room, where a heavy-featured stout man rose to greet them. Nathan Rothschild!

Sonia caught her breath. He greeted them, bowed them to chairs, and pulled at his sagging lower lip thoughtfully.

"She knows nothing of the matter?" he asked Jacob. Jacob shook his handsome dark head. "Good, good." His accent was very thick at times. When he lapsed into German, Sonia felt relieved, for it was much better than his English.

"Lady Fairley," said Mr. Rothschild. "I have told you a little, in confidence, about our procedure for getting the soldiers' pay to Viscount Wellington in the Peninsula." He shot her a sharp look. She nodded, feeling rather numb.

He seemed to muse a moment, then continued.

"Sometimes our couriers are stopped. We have had to change couriers frequently of late. Now I have another plan, and I was going to use our friend and your cousin, Jacob, and his good wife. However, Mrs. Goldfine is quite ill, her child's birth left her exhausted. The trip can be difficult and tiring. I have decided it would be cruel to expect her to go. She says she could go, and she was much distressed when I told her I would ask you to go in her place. She thought it was too much to ask of you."

His words explained much. Sonia bent her head, and by an effort of will kept her fingers still in her lap. "How—would we go, sir?" she asked.

"By coach to an obscure port. Then across the Channel on a ship of mine. By another coach—you will be met. Then, you and Jacob are on your own. You shall be a Frenchwoman—for you speak the language like a native—you are a widow. Your husband died recently. You are taking his ashes home to your former domain in the South of France. You will travel by day, wearing black cloak and black bonnet. Jacob will be your brother, patiently caring for you."

Sonia was so shocked she could scarcely speak. Jacob spoke up keenly.

"And the gold, Mr. Rothschild? Or do we take bank notes this trip?" Jacob inquired.

"Both," said the financier. "Gold will be in the floorboards of your coach. It will be transported in the ship. The man who meets you will assist you in storing it safely under the floor of the coach. I have obtained many notes in Spanish, Maltese, and other currencies, also, for they are lighter in weight. The sum will do much toward meeting the debts of the military in Lisbon. The soldiers will not fight without their pay, and in truth they are sometimes in pitiable condition," his voice softened from its brusque tone. "Officers are forced to sell some of their cloaks, even, to buy their food. Their men are worse off."

"When—do we go?" asked Sonia faintly.

"I will send you word. You will remain at your townhouse tonight and tomorrow. What did you tell your husband?" he shot at her suddenly.

"That—that Uncle Meyer and Beryl were ill. Also that I must see my merchants from the Orient."

"Good. Good. From here, proceed to my warehouses. There you will meet two of your merchants—who are also selling me some gold they have collected. Jacob will go with you. Talk with them, purchase what fabrics you wish. Jacob will bring the gold to my counting house."

He proceeded to tell them more of his plans: whom they would meet, how they would travel by day in France, by night in Spain, what couriers they might encounter, the passwords.

Then he turned to Sonia. "You have been quiet, Lady Fairley. I have not your promise as yet that you will go on this very difficult and hazardous journey."

She did not hesitate. She knew the importance of the journey. It was crucial to Wellington, to the armies, to England, her beloved adopted country. Her own safety was of little importance—the gold and specie must go through. Mr. Rothschild thought she could do the job. She must try.

"I will go, sir, and I am grateful for your trust in me."

He smiled, his rare gentle smile. "You are a lady of courage and intelligence," he said. "May the Lord be with you, support you—and see you safely after this mission back home again."

"Thank you, sir."

He spoke a little longer with them, then they were on their way. Leah was silent, fuming and indignant that she did not

156

know what was going on, and very suspicious of what was happening to her charge.

At the warehouses, Sonia spoke with her merchants, bought some fine fabrics, and ordered them delivered to her townhouse. Two lengths pleased her especially—a lilac one for Henrietta, a silvery pink for Edwina. Jacob counted the gold the men had brought, gave them Mr. Rothschild's receipt. The cousins returned to Sonia's townhouse.

At the last moment in the carriage, Jacob said, "Sonia, you will pack one small trunk and a valise, be ready to depart at any moment. When I come, we must leave at once, day or night. You understand?"

"No, I do not!" cried Leah indignantly.

Sonia hushed her gently. "Yes, I shall be ready, Jacob. Pray, give Beryl my kindest regards, and kiss your son for me."

He pressed her hand and got out of the carriage. He helped her out, then Leah, and waited until they had entered the house before going on his way.

At the door, behind the butler, Alastair appeared! His face was flushed, his eyes blazing.

He had seen her from the windows of the drawing room as he waited impatiently for her. He was tired—he had traveled by horseback, with only a change of clothing in his saddlebags. He had arrived at his townhouse to find the housekeeper knew nothing of Sonia's arrival. Now at her own home, he found her dallying at the door with her handsome dark cousin!

"Sonia, what the devil is going on!" he demanded, as she entered the house.

She stopped, shocked and amazed. "Alastair!" she gasped. "What—are you—doing in London?"

"Following you!" he snapped. He pulled her into the drawing room, and shut the door in Leah's face. "Now! Tell me what you are doing, why you were not at home with your 'sick' uncle, who has gone off to his counting house? And where have you been all this morning?"

"Alastair—good heavens—how can I answer all your questions at once?" Frantically she tried to think. She had not dreamed he would follow her to London, and so quickly! She

157

must be getting ready to go on her dangerous adventure. And had he come after her—or was some other business drawing him here? Such as a longing for Mrs. Daphne Porter?

She took off her bonnet, shook back her hair. She was too weary and excited to think straight. Alastair folded his arms, looking like a judge with a wilting victim before him.

"And why did you not go to our home, instead of here?" he added harshly. "Don't you consider my house yours?" He flung his hand about to indicate the room, smaller than his, though as richly furnished. "Well! Answer me!"

Chapter
13

ALASTAIR would not be fobbed off with foolish stories. Sonia sat down in her cloak and bonnet, surveyed him anxiously. She ought to be planning her journey, arranging to purchase or rent mourning garments, and so on. But first he must be appeased or sent back to Fairley.

How ever could she do this?

"Alastair," she finally began. "I must—must go off by myself for a time. I wish—a holiday. I have much to think about. I beg you to trust me for a time—"

"Trust you for a time—while you go off on a holiday!" His face was flushed, his tone rose. He ran his hands through his unruly blond hair and began to pace the small room so that it seemed even smaller. "Sonia, you are mad! Tell me the truth! Why did you come to London?"

She closed her eyes. "My uncle was ill. He is better. Beryl is still ill—after having had her baby last month."

"The truth!" he demanded scornfully. "What does all that have to do with your going on a holiday—alone?"

"I must get away. I am weary."

"Alone?!" he repeated. "If you are weary, I shall go on holiday with you. You know that no respectable woman goes away alone. What has possessed you? Tell me what is wrong . . . why are you weary? I know you were weary when we left London, for you were white and drawn," and his voice became unbearably gentle. He flung himself down on the settee beside her and took her hands strongly in his. "Tell me, Sonia."

"I—I have much to think about," she said weakly. Oh, it was so lovely to feel his concern! But she must not think about that, she must fix her mind on going on this mission. It was so important—to England, to her countrymen, to Alastair himself. How would he feel if his comrades died in battle against the French, when she might have been able to prevent such a catastrophe by taking money to them?

He would never know about it, but she would know.

"We can go off to some seaside resort," he said eagerly, his fingers pressing hers. "We could be alone—is that what you wish? Have I piled too many duties onto you, Sonia? You are weary of the continuing presence of my brother and sisters? I know they confide in you and they must be worrisome to you."

"No, no, it is not true, that is not a burden but a joy," she said hurriedly. "I enjoy—their confidence, their trust. No, that is not it—"

"What then? Is it me?" he asked, more sternly, gazing down keenly into her face. "Do I come to you too often, have I been brutal to you?"

Warmth came up into her face, she turned from him shyly. "No, Alastair, that is not it. I have come—to enjoy—I mean —I wish to do my duty. And you are not—too—I mean—I like it when you come to my bed!" she finished desperately, flushing wildly.

"Well, then," and his voice went down coaxingly. "Why not let me take you on a holiday? We could go away for a week, a month. I will send word to Maurice to manage matters for us. Come, Sonia, do let us go away together—"

It was so tempting. She closed her eyes against the pleasure she felt. She must not listen, she must resist. But the picture of them together, in some quiet cottage on a seashore, alone together, with just the two of them—wandering the beach, clasping hands, his concern over her. . . .

"I cannot," she whispered. "I must go away—*alone.*"

He flung her hands from him in temper, rising and pacing the room again. "I fail to understand you!" he cried, his blue eyes flashing with rage and pain. "Why must you be alone? Where are you going? I saw you with your handsome cousin —yes, he is the only one besides your uncle who attended your wedding! He sat alone, and I thought he wept! Did he regret your wedding so much? Had he longed to marry you himself? Did family keep you apart, forbidding the marriage of first cousins? Have you loved him long?"

She sat, silent and amazed, before his attack. It was so unexpected and alarming.

He flung round on her. "You do not answer! Have I hit on the truth? He married another because he could not marry his first cousin! Is that the answer?"

She shook her head. He paid no attention, off on this tack.

"That must be it, he is devoted to you. My God, do you think to go off with him? This Jacob Goldfine, one of your own faith and beliefs, a dear cousin, a man with whom you grew up—"

"I beg you, Alastair, say no more!"

"I have hit on it, I am convinced!" he raged. "Well, I forbid you to go off with him! He shall be nothing to you! You shall go home to Fairley with me and stay there. I was a fool not to see this before."

"It is not true," she managed to say in a gasp.

He frowned down at her, imperiously. "Well, that is over. You must forget him! Sonia, think of your future, think of our future together! No good can come of mourning the past! Forget him! We will go off together, and become closer—"

She put her hand to her head. "I must go—and lie down," she said faintly. This was all such a new attack, she could not fend it off. She must have time to think.

He saw she felt really ill and bewildered, and let her go. She went to her room, and Leah helped her remove her shoes and lie down. She lay for a time in the darkness. But her brain was thinking, thinking.

There must be a way out. Alastair seemed to show such true feeling for her. Surely he must be coming to love her. Life, which had seemed so bleak, was turning rosy and beautiful. She had promised to go on this mission—but what if she could find someone to take her place?

She did not want to jeopardize Alastair's feelings for her. What if there was promise for the future? He did seem anxious and upset over her. It was not just her reputation he thought about. He seemed truly concerned about her, about their lives together. Was he coming to love her? Could it be true?

Yet—yet she must be planning to leave. There were the black mourning clothes—bonnets—packing—some gold of her own—and being ready to meet Jacob—there was no one else to go—Beryl could not go. She might go if Sonia did not, and she might die—gentle Beryl, with her new splendid little son. . . .

What if Jacob and Beryl were caught, imprisoned, even killed? Their baby son an orphan even before he had scarcely opened his beautiful dark eyes!

No, no, she could not do that to them. . . .

The house seemed quiet. Leah stole into her room.

"Where is—Alastair?" she asked faintly of the abigail.

"He is gone off to his townhouse. There were letters to open, he said, my lady," said Leah, coldly, clearly disapproving of all these events of which she was being kept ignorant.

"Ask for my carriage to be brought around," said Sonia, and got up. She put on her shoes, her bonnet and cloak. She said firmly to Leah, "No, you may not come with me. I shall return shortly."

"My lady, I don't like all these comings and goings!" cried Leah.

Sonia did not either, but it had to be done. Deaf to Leah's warnings and pleadings, she went off alone in the carriage, directing her coachman to a shop where she knew she might rent widow's weeds.

She found what she wanted, and took three dresses, a large black bonnet with black ribbons, a black veil to cover her face, and black gloves. She had black boots and slippers already.

Wearily she climbed back into the carriage; she put the packages at her feet. She directed the man to drive her back to the Fairley townhouse. Perhaps Alastair would be home. If so, she would have the packages carried in by the back entrance, and so up to her room.

She was gazing idly from the window, sheltered by the broad brim of her straw bonnet, when she saw Alastair's carriage. It was unmistakable—the smart town carriage, with the panels emblazoned with his coat of arms. She sat up straight, stared wide-eyed at the vehicle.

Her coachman knew all about London, he was London-born and -bred.

"Who lives at that house?" she demanded, pointing.

The man looked idly at the house, his eyes widening when he saw the carriage. He hesitated, and slowed the horses. "That, ma'am? Why, this is a smart building of apartments, for some rich gentry," he said.

"Do you know who lives there, any names?"

He kept his head rigidly forward, and clucked to the horses.

She repeated her question. He finally answered reluctantly. "A certain Mrs. Porter, ma'am, does live there. Mrs. Daphne Porter," he said, then cursed to himself when someone crossed his path recklessly.

She sank back into the seat, and put her hand to her face. So—this was why Alastair had come! He had chased her to London, but it was probably just an excuse to see about his— his mistress! And Sonia had thought he was concerned about her, his wife. She could have laughed bitterly, but a sob caught in her throat instead. So much for his concern!

She was silent as they drove home. At the townhouse, she had the coachman bring the packages to her room. Alastair was out, she would not have to risk another confrontation. She might not be able to guard her tongue, so angry and hurt was she.

Her small trunk and valise were empty. Leah was hovering about. She sent her away, curtly. The maid departed, sniffing.

Sonia stuffed the two dresses into the trunk, put in some undergarments and a sack of gold for her own use, if needed. She fairly tore about the room, packing what she must have.

Then she changed her clothes, putting on the one black dress which came to her toes. She had on traveling boots, comfortable thick clothing for the Channel crossing, which could be cold even in July. She felt stifled, her breathing came hard, but she worked on.

Then, dressed and ready, she called for a footman. How his jaw dropped when he saw her, in black dress and bonnet, with the trunk and valise ready! They went down to the waiting carriage, and were off. She felt badly about not saying goodbye to Leah and her uncle—but she must take advantage of Alastair's absence. And he was with his mistress. His mistress!

Her teeth clenched, her jaw ached by the time she reached Jacob's house. She had her things carried in. Jacob was standing there, an anxious look on his dark face.

She dismissed the coachman and her carriage, and turned to Jacob. "Lord Fairley followed me to London. I must leave at once," she said briefly.

Jacob nodded. "Yes, it is best if we leave soon, anyway. Beryl is weeping and carrying on. I cannot remain, or she will sicken. It is best if we leave at once." He called his carriage, and put Sonia and her bags inside. Then, with his own small trunk and valise added, he jumped in, and they were off to the coast.

It was a long hard journey, through the night. Sonia and Jacob were both silent, thinking of those they had left behind with widely differing thoughts. Jacob's were tender, anxious. . . .

Sonia had felt bitterly furious and angry. Then, her rage had subsided into a sort of numb acceptance. It was better this way. Perhaps she would be killed. Alastair would have the money, and could marry his mistress if he chose without having to sneak behind his wife's back to go to Daphne Porter.

Anger rose in her, and she clenched her fists until the fingernails bit into her palm. That he should cheat on her like this while wooing her with false words! And all the time he did not really care. . . .

But he had not promised to care for her, he had not said he would love her. She sighed and turned her face blindly to the darkness outside. No, Alastair had never said he loved her. He had not sworn false.

How her heart longed for him! If only he had loved her—but that was not to be. She felt numb by morning, worn by the long journey in which she had not slept, by her emotions, by her despair.

At dawn, they arrived at a quiet port. A schooner with folded sails rocked in the harbor. It was misty, but the sun was coming through the morning clouds, casting a rosy glitter across the blue-green waters. Sonia thought it looked beautiful. Jacob looked more anxious.

"It could storm before nightfall," he muttered, shaking his head. Sonia did not care—at that moment.

The schooner was ready for them. Jacob and the red-faced bearded captain conferred in low tones. All was in readiness —the gold and specie were stacked in small boxes, locked in the main cabin. They could set off almost at once, the tide going out about eleven o'clock that morning.

So they decided. The coachman was told to wait for them, no matter how many weeks they were gone.

Weeks! thought Sonia, shocked into awareness. Would it be weeks that they would be gone? Yes, it could very well be weeks—oh, what would Alastair think? But did it matter?

No, nothing mattered.

They went on board, and Sonia was given the main cabin, locked in with the gold and specie. She eyed the boxes. That such small innocuous-looking boxes could be so important! They could help win a battle! She mused for a time on the curious ways of men. They went at each other with fists and guns, killed and maimed each other, all in blind obedience to some higher powers of their government that said they should kill for strange reasons. And why, why? When they might live in peace, and love, and be happy.

Wars were strange things. Peculiar, when one thought about it, thought Sonia, lying back in relief on the narrow bunk.

Why did men kill each other? Why were they so ordered? What strange motives did men like Napoleon Buonaparte have, that he wanted more and more countries added to his string of conquests? Why should that little man who had been a corporal want to conquer more countries than he could possibly rule? Why not let others live in peace? Why did he have to march his armies and sail his navies across oceans, all to make the guns flame and men fall in sprawling blood and death?

Then the boat began to sway and lurch from side to side, and she forgot all her philosophical thoughts. She tried desperately to keep from being ill as the schooner slid out further into the rough English Channel across to France. She pressed her handkerchief to her lips, and tried to think of pleasant matters . . . .

She groaned in the narrow cot as the schooner plunged on and on. Jacob knocked, but she could not get up. He called out anxiously to her. She finally forced herself to her feet, fell across the floor toward the door, managed to unlock it.

He carried a tray of food. She almost got sick at the sight of it. "Sonia, you must eat!" he said gravely. "It will help you—have you been ill?" He was flushed from the wind and rain, and his thick hair and beard were soaked with salt water.

"Not—yet," she managed to gasp. "Take it away—I cannot eat—"

"You must eat something. Here, have some tea and bread. Then I'll take you up on deck. The fresh air will make you more the thing."

With his hearty encouragement, she managed to drink some tea, eat half a slice of bread. Then, on his arm, she struggled up on deck. The wind and rain lashed at them. Jacob found her a corner where she might sit on a low chair and watch the rolling sea. Strangely, she did feel better, out in the elements.

"It was fortunate," Jacob shouted above the wind. "We are in a storm—not many ships out in this! We won't be noticed, with luck. We'll land in France tonight, about midnight, when the tide goes in on the French coast."

She nodded, not risking speech. He paced the deck with the lieutenant, they glanced at her occasionally to make sure she was all right. She noted the small insignia on the sleeve of the lieutenant, the same as was on the lifeboats lashed to the gunwales of the schooner. They all carried the insignia of

House of Rothschild. So this was the property of Mr. Nathan Rothschild himself! His own ship—no wonder he felt confident of carrying gold to France! Another captain who had been hired might betray him—but not his own men. . . .

Jacob brought her some cushions as the rain let up. "You can sleep here," he said kindly. "We might not get much sleep tonight."

She was left alone. Curled up in the cushions, she did at least fall asleep. She had felt so tired, so depressed, that she had not slept well for nights. Now she could sleep, and she did, with the feeling that no matter what happened it did not matter.

How could it matter? Alastair did not love her. He had gone to his mistress even after quarreling with Sonia about her leaving alone! She wondered that he had followed her to London. Why had he bothered? His pride, or his curiosity, she supposed, and turned to sigh against the pillow, brushing her handkerchief to her eyelids. She would not weep for him —he was not worth it.

If only she could stop caring about him! If only she could stop loving him!

She started when a hand shook her shoulder. "We are near the coast," Jacob said quietly in her ear. She sat up with a jerk, having forgotten where she was. Dusk had fallen, mists and clouds hid moon and stars. It was a perfectly dark night, with rain lashing again at the small schooner and the men who were lowering two small boats into the black waters below.

The lieutenant went ashore with two sturdy seamen. Waiting in the darkness, her black bonnet over her face, Sonia peered toward the shore. It seemed so far away to be ventured to in such small boats! They all watched intently, anxiously, until the signal came. A lantern, with a hand swinging before it.

"All well. The coach must be there," muttered the captain. He shook their hands heartily, wished them well, and helped lower them into the boats. A brawny sailor carried Sonia down the rope ladder. She did not think she could have managed alone in her heavy skirts.

In the small boat, she clutched the sides with a fervent silent prayer that they might not upset. She watched the small boxes being sent down the side: nine, ten, eleven, twelve, thirteen—that was all.

They rowed ashore. The seamen seemed to be all muscle as they plied the heavy oars silently, then stepped out into the surf, practically dragging the boats up on the sand. A carriage was waiting for them, a huge barouche.

The floorboards of the barouche had been taken off. Now the small boxes were stuffed carefully under where the boards would go. They were packed so that there was no space between them. Cloths were packed between the boxes so they would make no sound of jostling when the carriage moved. Boxes of gold were balanced front and back, the specie in between.

The floorboards were then hammered back into place, cloths covering the hammers muffling the sound. Then the small trunks were loaded and the two valises, and then Sonia. Now they put a handsome little urn of black and gold into the seat before her, fastened it into place.

"What is that?" she whispered curiously.

"The ashes of a dead Frenchman—your husband," grinned Jacob, patting the urn. "Genuine, trust them for that! His name was François. I've told you your name and age and all that."

She nodded, trying to stifle a shudder. She would be traveling all the way with the ashes of a dead man! It was necessary, but it made her shiver. It seemed like a bad omen, such disrespect for the dead.

Farewells were said quietly, and good wishes for their safe journey. Then the barouche doors were shut and fastened, and Sonia sat alone in the huge carriage with only the ashes for company. And the gold and specie, she reminded herself, with an attempt at humor. She drew her thick black cloak about herself. It was of velvet, and had belonged to her uncle.

Jacob climbed up onto the open coachman's seat above her, clucked to the two horses, and they were off. She saw briefly the faces of the seamen as they gazed curiously after them. The last friendly faces for a long time, she thought.

And so they were started on their desperate adventure.

Chapter
14

DAY followed day and night followed night in wearisome routine. Sonia held a loaded pistol on her lap or beside her when she slept. Jacob kept the horses to gravel-strewn or dirt side-roads. They sometimes had glimpses of the Atlantic Ocean on their right.

Jacob was driving through the countryside, avoiding towns and villages. As the days passed and they avoided trouble, they were tempted to become careless. But always they sternly kept in mind the importance of their mission, took every precaution.

Jacob would find a farm and leave the barouche with Sonia guarding it. He would walk to the farmhouse, plead for milk, bread, cooked meat, and cheese. He paid for it cautiously, like a Frenchman, bargaining for it, but paying enough so that they would not complain.

Then he would come back and they would eat and drink, with the horses turned loose on the rich grass. After a hasty meal and a brief rest for themselves and the horses, they would go on again.

169

The first several days, they traveled through the night, pausing only to rest the horses, letting them browse sleepily on the green grass of the roadside.

On the fourth day, they saw a cloud of dust in the distance down the road. Jacob found a thick wood, and drew the barouche to a halt, hidden in the trees. Then he walked to the edge of the wood and peered out to study the situation.

His caution was worth it—the "cloud" turned into a squadron of French cavalry, pounding along, looking everywhere with keen eyes. They waited more than two hours to make sure the troopers were gone before they ventured on the road again.

They had traveled for a week when really bad weather hit. They had been fortunate, for no more than a few mild showers had fallen those July days.

This was a real thunderstorm, building up in the West, then coming in from the ocean. Jacob had been watching it worriedly, and began to look for shelter as the afternoon wore on.

He found a series of caves carved in crude limestone in a deserted section of the countryside. They drove the horses into one cave, with the barouche barring their exit. First they gathered great armfuls of thick grasses and brush for the horses to eat. Then they sought their own comfort, spreading blankets in another cave.

Soon the rain began to pour down. Thunder and lightning roared and rumbled among the hills. Sonia watched, fascinated, as the giant bolts of lightning struck a tree near them, crashing it to the ground. One of Jove's thunderbolts, she thought.

It rained all the night, soaking the ground. Jacob collected rain water in a bucket, so they had fresh water to drink that night. He dared to light a small fire in the rear of the cave. Over it, he rigged some forked branches. From them he swung the bucket. Sonia managed to cook their smoked meat with some greens. They had a good hot meal for the first time since leaving the schooner.

The rain continued. She would waken, turn over under her velvet cloak, and peer outside to see the rain lashing at their cave. Jacob would get up and go out to make sure the horses were still there and the barouche in no danger of rolling away. Some of the stones and rocks had gone slithering down the hillside in the deluge.

He came back. "All well," he reported briefly, and returned to his blanket. He seemed not overly concerned about Sonia, and she smiled ruefully in the darkness.

He would have been wildly worried about Beryl if she had gone with him. It would have risked their lives. He might have insisted on going to a village, putting up at farms, chancing discovery. With Sonia, the girl he knew from childhood, his cousin, he was not one-tenth so concerned.

And Sonia was wondering how Alastair would have acted if he had been in Jacob's situation. Alastair! Sonia curled her hand under her cheek, and turned over on the rough blanket. Her eyes opened to the flashing lightning, she thought of her husband, regretfully, wonderingly. What was he thinking now? What had he said when he found she was missing? At least Leah could tell him nothing. Her abigail woman would not hesitate to say she had been left out of the confidence of her long-time mistress.

Alastair. If anything happened to her on this journey, when would he know? What would he think? Would they tell him why she had gone? She thought not, for state secrets were too important. Alastair might be left to conclude that she and her cousin had run off together on a romantic interlude. Her mouth twisted in anguish.

She loved him so dearly, but it was not working out. How could she explain this when she returned? Would she be allowed to tell him of the mission, once it was successful? Or would he turn away from her in disgust?

Sonia fell asleep and dreamed of Alastair. He was holding her in his arms, tenderly, her cheek brushing his rough cheek. He was murmuring to her, "Sonia, I love you dearly, I love you madly. You are my dove, my dear, my love——"

She wakened, smiling, gazing about herself in bewilderment. She had forgotten for a time where she was. Then she remembered. Alastair was not here, and he did not love her. Jacob returned to the cave.

"Sonia? Are you awake? I called you for a while, but you were sleeping heavily, so I went to see to the horses." He crouched down close to the reddish embers of the fire and blew on them.

She struggled up. So it was Jacob's voice she had heard in her dreams, not Alastair's. She pushed back her heavy hair, reaching for her brush to braid it up. So much for dreams.

Jacob stood up, having built up the fire again. "We'll have to stay another day. I hate to take the time, but another storm is following hard on this one." He spoke in French, as they had been told to do all the time they were in France, no matter if they thought themselves alone.

"I shall wash out some garments then," said Sonia practically, getting up and feeling every bone aching from the hard ground. She moved about, swinging her arms until she felt better. After a breakfast of cold meat, hot coffee and some stale bread, she felt even better, more cheerful. They were alive, and deep into France.

She rinsed out some undergarments, and spread them across wet rocks. Later when they were traveling she would spread them out in the coach, should there be sunlight. She washed some socks and other garments for Jacob. He thanked her absently. He too was remembering home and family, she thought, as he stared into the fire. How hard it must be for him to leave his adored wife and their fascinating infant son.

Two days were spent in the cave. Then, finally, the rains and storms had spent their fury. The hill roads were dangerous, for rocks slid down with small avalanches tumbling onto the dirt roads. But they had to go on. They hitched up the horses. Sonia stood well back while Jacob drove the barouche down to the road.

She followed, helping him pack up their trunks and valises once more.

"The boxes?" she asked in a low tone. "They are all right, the ones with the paper?"

"Covered with oil-slicked cloth," he murmured, nodding.

They proceeded. She hung out the laundry, changing the pieces as each dried in the sun and wind. Her lips turned up in a smile, for it looked funny to see her undergarments hanging over the somber black doors of the barouche.

They went on and on. Jacob kept a sharp lookout for dust on the roads. But, about a week later, as they were nearing the south of France, he was fooled.

A troop of cavalry galloped out of the grassy hills, and just

172

into their path on the road. Jacob pulled the horses to a stop, called down softly to Sonia. "French cavalry. Make sure your face is powdered and lined."

"All right," she called back. She had seen them coming. Reaching hastily for her valise, she powdered her face with the graying powder, added some to her hair where it showed below the bonnet. Now she took a black charcoal pencil and underlined her eyes lightly, and drew small lines about her mouth and chin. It made an incredible difference, aging her by twenty years. She let her shoulders slump. The fact that she was tired from the journey helped.

The French lieutenant ordered Jacob down from the driver's seat. Some troopers came to peer in the windows.

"It is my sister," she heard Jacob explaining respectfully. "This is her paper, this is mine. She goes to bury her husband—"

"Bury her husband!" came the incredulous words. "How can that be?"

Someone flung open the door of the barouche. Sonia gazed at them with narrowed eyes, her black bonnet firmly in place. A soldier reached in.

"You come out, ma'am," he said curtly, but with courtesy. He helped her out. She staggered a little as she came down the steps, and he caught her arm. "There you are, ma'am. What is your name? Why are you on the roads?"

She quavered. "I am Madame Lestair, Madame François Lestair. My husband—my poor dear husband—" She caught her breath, put her handkerchief to her face, and continued. "He is dead. He is dead!"

"Calm yourself, my dear sister," said Jacob, moving nearer to her, anxiety on his face. He also wore somber black. "They will understand our mission."

"You should not be on the roads without a permit," said the lieutenant sharply.

"We have a permit here," and Jacob began to fumble in his pockets, as though permits were far from his mind. "Ah—in this pocket—I believe. No—here," and he produced it and gave it over.

The lieutenant examined it keenly, dubiously. "Ah—to the south of France, you say? For what reason?"

"To bury her husband. She has set her heart on burying

173

him in the cemetery where our parents are buried," said Jacob, in a low tone, glancing furtively at his "sister" with the handkerchief to her face. "So upset was she—"

"But carrying a body through France! It is not permitted!" said the lieutenant, snapping the words importantly. "It is against the law! It can cause disease!"

"No—no— " said Jacob, and waved vaguely to the coach. "He is there, in that urn—"

"Urn?" The lieutenant went to the coach, stared at the small black and gold urn.

"Yes, it is François," said Sonia, her voice breaking. "All that remains of my dear, dear François! To transport him to our cemetery it was necessary to burn his beautiful body. How I wept! But no one would listen. I carry his ashes—all that remains of my beautiful François—" and she began to sob as though actually in earnest.

Through her wails, she heard Jacob explaining hastily and apologetically to the guard. "It was the only way they would allow us to transport his—his remains. My sister was much upset—she still weeps about it. I pray you, do not set her off again, it has been difficult enough for her—" And he gave a heartfelt sigh.

The troopers still insisted on peering into the coach to see the contents of the trunks. They pawed through the black garments, but missed the gold concealed in the linings. One muttered that he wanted to lift the lid of the urn. The lieutenant, turning pale, finally did so, sniffed, sneezed, and set it back hastily. He sealed it with a red wax bearing his insignia.

Sonia wept through it all, quietly but steadily. All she had to do to make herself weep was to think, what if Alastair was in that urn? And she could weep as though her heart were breaking. Jacob kept patting her shoulder, murmuring to her soothingly—while keeping an anxious eye on the troopers poking about the coach.

They were finally allowed to continue. Jacob was shaking on the coach seat. Sonia felt rather faint herself. In the distance, they could see the mountains of the south of France, toward the border with Spain. But they were miles off yet.

Now Jacob began to consult a ciphered map he had in his pocket, drawn on oiled paper. He watched sharply for landmarks. They traveled only at night. In the daytime, they drew up the coach in deep woods or into small caves fronting on the ocean.

The end of the fourth week came, and Sonia was becoming weary and desolate. Alastair must be raging—or worse, indifferent. She had never dreamed it would take so long.

Then they were in the mountains. The night closed in about them, but did not hide them from the eyes of the shrewd and wary Basques to whom the mountains were home. Jacob was stopped on the road by some burly shepherds in thick wooly coats, with their sheep baaing about their heels.

"Where do you go? Who are you?" They kept asking sharp questions in accented French and Spanish.

Jacob said something. They relaxed, said they would take him across the mountains. Sonia could only suppose they were enemies of the French.

They rode again by night. By day, they hid in the crude homes of Basque shepherds. They crossed the mountains, some with snow on them. She gazed at the white powder in amazement. When they got out of the barouche to rest the horses for a time, she walked about in the cold snow, picking some up in her hands. She did not often see snow now. In her childhood, she had seen it in the mountains of Austria. She remembered one joyful holiday when she and her parents had gone to Salzburg and walked through a snow field. It made tears come to her eyes, remembering that far-off time.

Did her parents look down from heaven on the doings of their beloved young daughter with amazement and fear? Perhaps they kept watch over her, and protected her. She prayed a little that night, thinking of them. In her prayers she remembered to include Alastair, to find him comfort—if he was at all concerned about her. For her own safety, she cared little. Her future seemed dim. But the gold and specie must get through. She did care about that.

Then they were over the mountains and down into green lush valleys. The soil was red, yet the fields grew thick with green and golden wheat. The Basques left them. Soon Jacob met some Spaniards. They were darkened by the sun, and Sonia thought they had fierce cruel eyes. They stared at her indifferently, for she was made up all the time now, with grayed powder and black lines on her face. They thought her wizened and elderly, there in the hot sunlight in her crumpled black dress and thick black bonnet.

"Yes, we take you. You have money?" they asked.

"No, but I must get my sister to safety. Her husband is dead, and she wishes to bury his ashes in their home cemetery west of Madrid—" Jacob deftly altered the story according to the territory. His Spanish was as good as her own. The Spaniards helped them through, warning them of the vicious dogs of French soldiers who had ravaged their land.

August had slipped past, and it was now September. Jacob began to seem worried. They traveled only at night, and only on deserted country lanes—mere dirt ruts. They heard of battles in the distance. The Spanish folk were angry and sullen.

A band of Spanish guerrillas caught up with them. Jacob told them they hoped to escape the horrible French. The guerrillas helped them on to another band, and to another. The barouche rolled its ponderous way across the north of Spain, down the coast, and finally, one great night, they crossed the border into Portugal.

Their most recent Spanish guerrilla protectors had told them of the Portuguese armies and the Ordenanza. These were Portuguese peasants who wore no uniforms but fought like devils, said the Spanish admiringly. The Spaniards worked secretly with these former enemies, for they were united in a common cause—the expulsion of the hated French troops of Napoleon from their peninsula.

The Portuguese men wore woolen caps, breeches, and short brown cloaks. They carried few firearms, but did have pikes, knives—any weapons that came to hand. When the French caught them, they ruled they were "out of uniform," hanging them in spite of General Wellington's protests.

Jacob drove on, and soon they encountered their first band of these Ordenanza. They swarmed about the barouche, demanded to see their papers, and broke out in excited language when they saw they were in French. Sonia came out of the barouche, and began to talk to them in Portuguese. They stared at her.

"What is a lady such as yourself doing in Portugal?" they asked her sharply, again and again.

Disregarding Jacob's quick rebuke, she said simply, "We

have an important message for the great General Wellington. We have come far to find and talk with him. Can you take us to him?"

They muttered among themselves, and gave Sonia and Jacob dark suspicious looks. Finally their leader, a young man of more noble appearance, whom Sonia suspected of being more than a peasant, came to them.

"We have decided to trust you. We will take you to Wellington. But the trip is long and dangerous."

Sonia smiled faintly. "We have come a long way," she said. "The best part of our journey is yet to come."

He gave her a keen look and nodded. "I comprehend," he said, and she thought he did. He might know of these secret missions that brought gold and specie down to Wellington. Perhaps he had helped the money get through before. "The General is at Gouveia. We take you there."

They did as much, and Sonia was intensely grateful to them. These rough peasants and their more aristocratic leader certainly knew the countryside. They took them through rough passes, barely scars in the mountains, across rivers, including the Douro, of which the dispatches and gazettes had been full after the battle there in May, 1809.

Always guarded and surrounded by the Portuguese, Sonia and Jacob rode in comfort in the carriage, letting their rude escort conduct them South. They came to Gouveia. Sonia was about to get out of the carriage when the leader stopped her.

"I think Wellington is not here now," he said quietly. "I will find out where he is."

Disappointment clouded her features. She sank back and gazed at Jacob. He nodded reassuringly. "The generals are always moving on and we must catch up," was all he said.

Would they ever reach Wellington and his army? Sonia felt as though their goal was like a distant horizon, ever receding from them. She bit her lips and tried to keep fears from overwhelming her. She was intensely weary from weeks of tension and keeping on guard. She had been sleeping poorly, and when she did sleep, would dream of Alastair. She would waken with tears on her cheeks.

She was thinner than ever, as was Jacob, his cheeks sunken

under his beard. They had not eaten a decent meal since the schooner. They both felt their energies dissipating. Yet, they must keep going, they must go on. They could not fail with their goal finally within reach.

The Portuguese leader returned, seeming satisfied. "We shall go on. He is at Bussaco, I have heard." He seemed more than pleased; he seemed eager and excited, under his contained cool manner. Sonia wondered. Could they really trust him?

Jacob leaned forward. "Where are the French?"

At his sharp voice, the leader smiled, a grim satisfied smile. "Not far," he said. "If we are in luck, we shall be in time for the battle. The old fox, General Masséna, against the leopard, Wellington. A great battle, eh?"

"My Lord in Heaven," muttered Jacob, putting his hand to his face. The leader laughed and shut the door of the barouche. He swung up on the seat, to cluck at the weary horses.

They were off again. "What did he mean?" whispered Sonia fearfully.

Jacob said shortly, for his temper was wearing thin, "It seems we are going to be in time for the confrontation between Napoleon's favorite general and England's!"

Sonia gazed at him, her gray eyes wide. "A battle?"

They drove on, day and night, halting only to refresh the horses. The Portuguese escort had obtained horses and kept up with them. By means of their own, they had armed themselves with ancient blunderbusses and a few muskets. Sonia wondered. Jacob whispered, "French-made—they must have met sentries or advance pickets somewhere." Sonia shuddered.

The carriage began to climb uphill; it seemed a long painful climb. Sonia would glance outside and shiver at the fearful sight; sheer cliffs all about them, rose-red rocks. At one point she saw a seering perpendicular cliff of gray granite until the road twisted. She saw it again later. They seemed to be climbing up behind that cliff.

Finally, the barouche rolled to a halt. Voices shouted the challenge—in English!

Jacob poked his head out, then got out of the carriage hurriedly. "Good day, good day!" he said excitedly, with respect.

A cool deep voice responded to him. "Mr. Goldfine, it is very good to see you. I hope you bring me good news?"

"The best of good news," said Jacob, a choke in his voice. He turned to the barouche, and helped Sonia down. The Portuguese were beaming proudly. They had brought welcome visitors to the great general, and now were seeing him themselves. This was a great day!

Sonia was looking at a very tall handsome man, plainly attired in a hat without plume and a dark gray cloak. He stared at her, then smiled and took her hand gently.

"You are most welcome. Come in—we are quartered here in the convent in some comfort." Holding the great general's hand, Sonia was escorted through whitewashed walls into a small room furnished with a table and some chairs. Maps were spread on the table. The general ordered them removed, and tea and hot food brought.

He and Jacob conversed in low tones. Presently, the boxes were brought in. Sonia counted them automatically, even as she drank the scaldingly hot tea. Twelve, thirteen—yes, they were all there. Those precious, terrifying boxes . . .

Then Sonia remembered the Portuguese men and started up. She went to her valise, removed a small bag of gold coins concealed in the lining, and said, "I must speak to the men who brought us here."

Jacob was busy, the general merely nodded absently. Sonia went out, her bonnet removed, her face so weary and lined that the soldiers merely glanced incuriously at her. She found the Portuguese strolling about, looking everywhere. Their leader stood near the barouche, watching as the floorboards were being pounded back into place.

He turned with a gentle smile for her. His gaze sharpened as he saw her face. He bowed. "You have arrived and are happy, madam?" he asked.

"Very happy. I am most grateful. Please—will you accept our gratitude and this little money—for your men," she added hastily, as his head went up proudly.

He bowed gracefully. She thought again, this was no peasant. "For my men—I accept," he said with a smile. "And you, madam? What do you do?"

"I do not know. It is in the hands of the Lord," she said.

"As all things are," he answered. He slipped the bag of gold into his coat pocket, and stood watching her as she returned to the small room of the convent.

Jacob Goldfine and General Wellington were counting the boxes with satisfaction. "And there is more on the way?" asked the general, anxiously.

He caught their looks. "You see, my soldiers' pay is in arrears," he said simply. "They cannot live and fight on the land. Until your—contact—arranged it, the money did not get through and my poor fellows were in a bad way. I am very thankful that he is so clever. I will thank him personally when I return at last to England."

"More is on the way," said Jacob. "In what way and manner I do not know, but it is coming. Always. You may be sure of it."

General Wellington drew a deep sigh. His voice was quietly thankful. "That is good, that is very good. Now we can fight. But first, what may I do for you? Which way will you go?"

Jacob stared at him. "Do you know—I thought so hard about how to get here that I never considered how we would return?"

The men laughed. Sonia managed a smile. She was so tired she could have cried, and every bone in her body ached. But they had arrived, they had done it, they had delivered the gold.

"For now, you must rest," said Wellington, and gave orders for their comfort. That night Sonia slept in a bed. For the first time since mid-July, she was alone in a room by herself. She stretched out gratefully. She did not know what the morrow would bring, or how they would get home. But she knew some satisfaction—the mission was completed.

In the morning, she was awakened abruptly to the sounds of shouts and distant firing. She sat up, completely awake, listening.

She did not know then, but she soon learned, that the Battle of Bussaco had begun that twenty-seventh of September.

Chapter
15

SONIA dressed hastily and went out to the main room. Jacob stood there, bending over a map with one of Wellington's aides. He turned as she came in.

"Madam, you must be ready to leave at once; the battle has been joined!" the aide said.

"I am—ready," she said faintly, looking at Jacob.

He nodded. "I have maps and some food. Come, I will take your trunk and valise to the barouche. The horses are standing."

There was no time to wash or eat. She ran out to the great coach and a soldier helped her inside. There was much firing now, though dawn had scarcely broken, and a thick white mist seemed to swirl about the heights of the gray cliff. Wellington came to see them off. He wore his usual plumeless cocked hat and a gray great-coat.

"Good luck, goodbye, and thank you a million times," he said, taking her hand gently in his. "You have my letters and instructions to the men at Lisbon. They will see you aboard one of our transports, to return to England as soon as possible."

They thanked him hastily, and were off. The horses were rested, and had eaten. Jacob drove down the narrow winding road to meet the road to Coimbra.

Even as they rode, the firing increased. Great blasts of cannon burst on their ears and Sonia put her hands over her own to dull the sounds. Still they pounded, pounded, mingled with the lighter crack-crack of musket fire and small arms.

The barouche jolted down the steep incline which finally became the main road. It seemed to go behind the great gray cliff, gaunt and stiff beside them. Over the top of the cliffs they saw men crawling.

Jacob drove more slowly, Sonia peering out to see what was happening. Then she saw the men, bloody, maimed, calling out to each other, hands held up beseechingly. They were falling down over the rocks, down to the road. Jacob's caution was understood. The wounded horses were falling into the road, and so were the men. One horse, maddened by its wounds and the cracking of muskets, pounded past them, foaming at the mouth, its eyes wildly rolling. From the saddle hung the limp form of a man in uniform, his head bouncing on the road. Sonia drew back, putting her handkerchief to her face in horror.

Still the shouts and the shots went on, and on, and on, deafeningly. The barouche slowed to a crawl. Sonia heard men and women shouting, children crying. She had to look out again. As they neared Coimbra, whole families were joining in the mad torrent to escape the battle. Poor, wealthy, middle-class, beggars, farmers, finely dressed women—they were all pushing baggage carts or riding horseback, clutching the few possessions they had managed to save.

Jacob shouted down, "Lock the doors, Sonia! Show your pistol at the window! Do not let any enter!"

Horrified, she saw hands clutching at the doors of the barouche and faces held up piteously. She heard them begging for a ride to get them away from the battle zone. At first she wanted to help—but the shouts of Jacob deterred her. She showed the pistol and yelled at them as he had directed.

He whipped up the horses and sped them past the first wave of terrified people.

In a quiet place on the road further on, he paused to let the horses breathe. He jumped down to make sure Sonia was all right.

"I could not let them in. They would have tossed us out and taken the coach," he explained breathlessly, his face white behind the black beard. "People do not reason in times like this, the feeling for rescuing one's self is too strong. They would have killed us both."

He glanced back over the road, and said, "Eat something as we ride, there is no more time to stop." He got up again into the driver's seat, and they went on, just ahead of the refugees, until they entered into Coimbra.

Behind them thundered the guns of battle—ahead of them the screams and shouts of people who had lingered too long in the safety of their homes, thinking the battle would never touch them. Now they fled, with anything they could carry.

Jacob fought off men with his whip, and grimly pushed the horses on through the crowded streets. Sonia gulped back nausea as she saw the scenes. There were wounded French prisoners of war, their blood as red as their uniforms, lying in the streets, to be spat at and walked over—Portuguese men in their rough brown cloaks—British soldiers, eyes wild, plundering the houses, some even before their frightened inhabitants had fled. . . .

They went on, making it through the town. People were streaming down the road toward Lisbon. Some paused to rest in the fields, eyes vacant, terror on their faces.

Before the day was over, more joined that frightened throng. Sonia saw more and more British soldiers, whole units marching together. She wondered what had happened, and how long they could keep on with their horses tiring.

Then she saw him. . . .

"Jacob! Stop!" she shouted and pounded on the roof of the carriage.

"I cannot—you are mad!" he shouted back.

"No—there are our friends who took us to Wellington— stop—stop!" Sonia screamed at Jacob frantically. She had recognized the face of the leader of the peasants—he was leaning on the shoulders of his comrades, his foot bound in bloody rags, his head bare, his face full of suffering.

Jacob pulled the barouche to a halt and Sonia opened the door. As a dozen people tried to get in, she called over their heads frantically to the Portuguese ordenanza, "Come, come, you who helped us before!"

The leader lifted his head, gazed at her, then barked orders at the two men holding him up. They pushed through the crowd, using words in Portuguese that Sonia had never learned. Then the wounded man was pushed into the carriage opposite Sonia. Another man followed him in, slamming shut the door and locking it, shouting obscene insults at the mob. A thud on the seat above them—the other man had joined Jacob on the driving seat.

"Well," said the leader, and a slow wry smile lit his darkened smoke-blackened face. "It is your turn to rescue us, eh?"

She managed to smile back at him. "I hope so, sir, the turmoil is terrifying. You were—in the battle?"

"Yes, last night it began about the hour before dawn. Our part did not last long," and he grimaced. "I think I stick now to my former role of carrying messages."

He moved his bandaged foot, and the pain seemed to shoot through him. The man beside him had a bullet in one shoulder and another in his hip, but he set his teeth and said little. Jacob yelled above them, and used his whip, and the man with him shouted insults at the crowd.

The aristocratic leader of the Portuguese peasants said mildly, "I think they will manage. But the horses tire. We will halt at a place I know about two miles down the road. There we can hold off the rabble. . . . They should have evacuated Coimbra as ordered and not waited until the last minute."

"Did—did General Wellington know there would be a battle?" asked Sonia naively.

He smiled a little, kindly. "All the earth knew it, madam. Wellington gave orders to scorch the earth before him, so the French could not live off the land. Up to now, it has worked. The general planned this site at Bussaco for a stand against the French. Now the battle comes. If only those fools of Coimbra had obeyed his orders and left, burning the stores of grain and foods also, all might have been well. Now, they choke the roads in their flights, and it will be a bad time."

He leaned forward to gaze from the window of the barouche.

"We come close—" And he shouted up to Jacob. "Take the road to the right, and go a half-mile to the small farm. There we will stop for the night!"

Jacob obeyed, turning off. Presently the carriage drawn by the weary horses pulled to a halt in a farmyard. It was empty. No one was in the farmhouse.

"I pray to God the owners left early and not joined this mad flight," muttered the Portuguese man.

He hobbled down, his man there to give a devoted anxious arm to him. Ignoring him, the leader turned to give Sonia a hand out of the carriage. He gave her his little wry grin.

"Madam, I think you are somewhat younger than you would have us believe," he said, gazing at her face. She had forgotten the gray powder and black lines in her anxiety to be off.

Jacob had slid down from his seat, and came up to them hastily, his worried look on Sonia. "This is my sister," he began gruffly.

Sonia lifted her hand. "He deserves the truth from us now," she said in rebuke. "We have saved each other's lives, I believe. I am Sonia Goldfine Charlton, Lady Fairley, of England. This is my cousin, Jacob Goldfine."

The man stared, losing his smile. "Lady Fairley? You are married then." He glanced at her hand, ringless. "Your husband permits you to make this mad journey?"

Jacob stiffened. "It was necessary," he said curtly. "And your name, sir?"

The man bowed, a strange sight in that modest farmyard —it was more suited to a ballroom, with glittering candles and the perfume of grand ladies. "Paulo de Mondego, at your service, Lady Fairley."

Sonia offered her hand. He carried it to his lips and touched it lightly. Then he let it go gently.

"Now—for some water, hot food and bait for the horses. Carlo, Juan—you watch for a time, then I will watch."

The men obeyed him instantly, taking their weapons in grip, one facing the road, the other the fields behind them. Jacob went to unhitch the horses. Paulo helped him, limping noticeably. Sonia went to the well, and drew up the bucket of water.

She carried the bucket into the kitchen, and there stared around amazed. The owners must have fled in great haste, for the table was still set for breakfast, the food cooked on the stove, done almost to burning. She rescued the hot pan using the thick pad nearby. Jacob came in, followed by Paulo de Mondego.

"They must have gone in much haste," she told them. They nodded, glancing about. Paulo limped into the adjoining room. She heard him moving about.

"Do not confide too much, Sonia," growled Jacob in a low tone. "We are strangers here. Best to say little."

She nodded, her mouth compressed. Her impulse was to feel safe with Paulo, but who could know? Nevertheless, she realized she had felt better these last two days than she had felt in two months. They were with friends.

She served the forgotten breakfast. Jacob and Paulo ate, then went out on guard while Carlo and Juan came in for their meal. They seemed shy with her, keeping their faces averted while they ate hastily.

Paulo returned after his men had left. "There is a bedroom on the second floor where sheets are still on the bed. All is in order there, Lady Fairley," he said formally. "I think you had better rest while you can."

"I was preparing some food against tomorrow," she said, indicating the table and stove. She was cooking some meat while rolling out the bread dough which had been rising all day.

"A good idea. If you prepare enough for three days, we will probably arrive at my house in Lisbon before the food is gone," he said with a smile. He added, "So you can cook, also?"

"Yes, sir . . . it was necessary in the old days."

He sat down, propping up his injured foot, and began to

clean some vegetables he had gathered from the small garden outside the window. He was deft with a knife, and meticulous in washing the vegetables. Jacob came in as they worked, looked anxiously from one to the other, but seemed relieved that they were contentedly working at their tasks.

He helped pack up the vegetables, and said, "You go off to sleep, Sonia. We will pack up the meat and bread in the morning."

"The bread is not yet baked," she protested, glancing toward the brick oven door.

"We will take it out when it is finished," promised Paulo. "The room is the first at the top of the stairs."

"Thank you, then. Good night."

She went up to the room and was grateful to find her trunk there. She opened her valise, looked about for water, and found a full jug and a clean basin on a small table near the window. Paulo had provided well. She smiled, removed her clothes, and washed for the first time in weeks. It felt so good. She rinsed out a couple of things, hung them near the window to dry, and went thankfully to bed.

It was the last sleep she was to have for four more nights. When they started off again in the morning, it was to find the roads clogged with refugees, making yesterday's journey seem like a pleasant excursion. They were thankful again and again for the presence of Paulo and his two men—burly, scowling peasants who kept the carriage from being overturned as the hysterical fleeing residents of Coimbra and the countryside fled toward Lisbon and farther for safety.

Sonia found time to say to Paulo, "Whatever is it? Why are they so maddened? I thought you said that Wellington was winning the battle?"

"So he is. The French are defeated. We heard it on the road today," he said wearily. She thought his foot gave him much pain, but he would not speak of it. "Yet still he has ordered retreat. I do not know why. I pray God he knows why!"

The next day, they heard that Wellington's soldiers were indeed retreating. The roads were now clogged with soldiers as well as civilians. From Coimbra, the prisoners in jails and the insane in asylums screamed to be let out, for the town was on fire and they feared being burned alive. Wellington gave orders, and the British soldiers freed them, to escape as best they could. So murderers and madmen joined the wild flight down the Lisbon road.

Once Paulo said sharply, while gazing out the window, "Do not look, I pray you."

But he was too late. Sonia had seen the man strung up on the tree. Near him, grotesquely, was a mirror in which his swinging body was reflected, swaying gently in the wind. She put her hand to her mouth.

"Why—why?" she managed to choke out.

"Probably for looting," said Paulo. He turned her about so she did not look again. "The mirror was gilded and much prized, no doubt." There was irony and sadness in his voice. "One thinks of foolish things in the midst of the fight for life."

He leaned back, and did not speak for a time. The horses were toiling uphill. Paulo leaned out to gaze, keenly, intently.

"Ah—so that is it! The leopard has outfoxed the fox!" he muttered.

Later, he explained. He saw fortifications, which later were called the Lines of Torres Vedras—three lines of fortifications which Wellington had ordered prepared in secret. The secret amazingly had been kept for a year. The British had retreated into the mountains, not toward the sea, where the French might have flung them from the Peninsula. As the French advanced, their fate was being sealed.

They drove on through the hills, pausing only to rest the horses, bait them, and feed themselves. Then they drove on and on. Over the mountain passes, where grim cannon lay concealed behind the lines of Wellington. Down into the valleys, toward Lisbon . . .

Finally, one night at dusk, they drove into the city. It was amazing to see lights, to hear music and laughter.

Paulo smiled at their surprise. "Yes, Lisbon still dances, on and on," he said wearily. "Some do not even know we fight. Thank God enough know that they are prepared to defend our country. We have been invaded enough—we ought to know how to act!"

He took them to his townhouse. Then indeed Sonia and

Jacob knew they were dealing with a nobleman. For the house was a grand one on one of the main avenues. His servants came running to bid the party welcome. A doctor came to tend to the injuries. Soon they all were comfortable.

Sonia slept deeply, indeed it seemed she would never sleep enough. And she was so hot. . . . The doctor felt her forehead anxiously. "A fever," he muttered to Jacob, and gave her some medicines.

Nightmare followed nightmare. She thought someone fed her from a porcelain cup of white and purple. She saw Jacob's bearded anxious face as in a haze, with white mist swirling about him. Paulo came, peered down at her, and shook his head. "Shock," he said. "It is too much for the delicate lady."

She wanted to protest that she was not delicate, that she could endure, as much as any man. But her tongue was thick and she could not utter the words.

When the haze finally lifted, she was so weak she could not sit up. But the fever was gone. She was so cool and comfortable she wanted never to move. She gazed about her bedroom wonderingly, for she had never seen such quiet splendor, even in the finest rooms of London. There were crimson silk draperies about the bed, paintings on the walls, cool blue-green tiles in intricate designs half-way up the walls of the bathroom. An elegant balcony was strewn with tangled vines of crimson and white flowers, which gave off perfumes day and night.

Jacob was anxious to leave. It was the second week of October. They could take ship soon—some transports with Wellington's injured soldiers were leaving from the port of Lisbon in two days. One ship had cabins for them—Jacob had paid high to get them. Along with the letter from Wellington, it had sufficed.

Paulo did not want her to leave. "You can go later," he urged. "Let your cousin go without you."

Jacob scowled. Sonia shook her head. "I must return—home," she said. "You are—most kind."

"You are too weak to travel!" said the gentleman vehemently. "And what kind of husband do you have to allow you to make this dreadful journey?"

Her mouth quirked in wry humor. "He did not know, for I left when his back was turned. I have yet to face him!"

"Por Deus!" She had to laugh at his shock.

But it was a weak laugh. She felt languid and disinclined to move. But she had to go with Jacob. She had to go home and face Alastair's wrath, his questions, and perhaps his cold dislike. He might even—leave her. He might be done with her forever.

She stifled a sigh, and told the kindly Portuguese maid what to pack for her. Her clothes had been cleaned, ironed, washed, mended, and were all in order for her. Her trunk was packed, her valise prepared.

Paulo de Mondego took them down to the ship in his grand carriage. He would keep the barouche against the day when someone might send for it he said. "In case it is needed again," he added, "because my poor country still has need of your gallant soldiers."

He left Sonia at the ship with evident regret, kissing her hand again and again. The look in his eyes told her she might stay and be welcome forever. But she could not stay, much as she appreciated his unquestioning gallantry.

"You are a brave and a good woman. If your husband does not appreciate you," he said, half-jokingly, "return again to Lisbon and send me but word!"

Jacob did not like this, and said so to Sonia later, very positively. But she let the matter pass, for she was feeling ill again, and took to her bed in the tiny cabin next to his.

The journey seemed a very rough one to her. The large vessel swayed alarmingly from side to side, sending her baggage across the floor, only to have it slide back again, again, and again. She felt too ill and too weak to stand. Jacob brought her food, water, hot tea, and cared for her anxiously.

The soldiers were in a worse way—crammed into the holds with only a few of their comrades and a doctor or surgeon to look after their wounds. Some died quietly or with a protesting cry, and were buried at sea.

The Atlantic pounded at them in one last futile effort to destroy them where the French had failed. The convoy groaned and pressed its way northward, toward safety and the English shore.

By the time they reached port, Sonia was practically unconscious. She was thin as a bird; her hands were so white that one could see the bones through the flesh. Jacob wrapped her in a blanket and carried her ashore to the nearest inn. There he sent a messenger to the small port where his carriage and his faithful coachman waited these three months. It was almost the end of October.

The coachman came with the carriage. Jacob conveyed her to London, and deposited her at her townhouse. Leah came running from the house, out into the foggy evening, with cries and sobs of dismay as Sonia was carried in by two sturdy footmen. Jacob was almost as exhausted. He did not even wait to speak to his father beyond a word of greeting.

Leah got Sonia to bed, this woman who could not even open her eyes. Leah said, staring down at her sternly, "And where have you been these months? Your husband has been crazed with anxiety, and is after me at all times to learn what I know. I promised him I would send for him at once, and so I shall!"

"Not—tonight—I beg—you—" murmured Sonia, and turned her head to the pillow.

But Leah did send for Alastair, and he came at once, storming into the house. Leah hushed him, showing him Sonia, sleeping the sleep of complete exhaustion, white as her pillow.

"My God, what happened to her?" he whispered, and would not leave her for a time, gazing down at the thin body, the wasted face and hands. "I cannot believe this. What could have happened?"

"She is home at last," said Leah, with some satisfaction. "Now, we will not let her leave again!"

Chapter
16

ALASTAIR moved into Sonia's townhouse. She was unconscious most of the time for the next few days. He hovered over her, worried about her, incredulous at the wasted form he saw. What could have happened to her?

He longed to question Jacob, but her cousin was at his own home, closed in with his wife and baby son. He questioned Meyer Goldfine, who shrugged and said, "How could I know what has happened?"

Alastair thought the uncle knew more than he was telling, but he knew also Meyer could keep his silence. It would be easier to find out from Sonia when she had recovered.

He had never known such fury, such frantic anxiety as in these past three months. Sonia gone, never a word from her, her maid as furious and anxious as himself. . . . People asked after her, and all he could do was say brusquely, "She has gone to the country for a holiday," and that was all.

Edwina questioned him shyly, but quieted when he turned on them all angrily. "I do not know where she is! If I knew, I would go after her and haul her back, and whip her in the bargain! Defying me like this, shaming me—and gone without a word! I'll be damned if she can play me such a trick!"

So his brother and sisters shook their heads and told polite lies to society. They had all returned from Fairley when it seemed evident that something unusual had happened.

Alastair had gone to see Jacob's wife, but Beryl seemed to know nothing. He was amazed to learn that Jacob was gone. Had he deserted his own wife and baby son? It seemed incredible.

Alastair hated the opening of the season. All stared at him, or seemed to, when he went out. He stayed home more often, gazing vacantly at the walls, trying to read or occupy himself. He took more care of the books, brought accounts up to date, drove his secretary frantic with conflicting orders about his engagements.

Maurice escorted Edwina and Henrietta about, Alastair being coldly uninterested in anything to do with Vauxhall, the opera, plays, or balls. Henrietta shook her head over him. "If this is what happens in marriage, I think I shall be a spinster," she told Edwina gravely. "Why, Alastair does not even wish to dance!"

Edwina sighed. She took a graver view of the matter, worrying quietly about whether Alastair and Sonia had quarrelled. Sonia was so quiet, but she had a temper, and a determined will of her own, and such pride! As much pride as Alastair, if not more! Whatever could have happened?

Then finally Sonia had returned, and Alastair hung over her. He waited anxiously for her to open her eyes, to speak. She finally did, on an early day in November, when she saw him there, at her bedside.

"Why—Alastair," she said, and her voice had a glad ring. "It is—you?"

He squeezed her thin fingers carefully. "It is I. And who is this, my little thin bird?" he said caressingly. "Can it be my Sonia?"

Her fingers were still hot and feverish, but her gray eyes were clear. She smiled weakly. "It is—Sonia. I thought I would never . . . Oh, my, am I home at last?"

"At your townhouse in London, my dear. But as soon as

you can be moved, I shall take you to my house," he said with firmness. "That is where you belong!"

She sighed and went to sleep again, her fingers clinging to his. He worried over her, scowling at Leah as she moved about the room.

"Where can she have been?" he asked abruptly.

Leah said, "I do not know, but she is home, and that is all that matters!"

It was not all, but he could do nothing about that now. He brooded over her thin form, ordered broth and sops for her, and fed her himself whenever she wakened. Leah suggested strengthening cold puddings and milk custards. She finally ate some of those also that week, seeming to gain strength each day.

Finally the time came when she could sit up. The doctor came, a silent, bearded man who felt her pulse and said, "Now, the fever is gone. That is good. You must be easy for a time, madam."

"I'll take her home," said Alastair.

"To Fairley?" murmured Sonia.

The doctor shook his head. "No long journeys for a while," he said.

Alastair followed the black-bearded doctor from the room. In the hallway he urged, "Where could my wife have picked up this fever, Doctor?"

The doctor gazed at him with half-closed eyes. "Anywhere that she traveled, my lord," he said abruptly, then went on down the stairs.

Damn it! Was everyone in some conspiracy to deceive him? He went back to Sonia's room, scowling. She was propped up against the pillows, and had picked up a hand mirror. She studied herself with troubled eyes.

"I look terrible!" she said as Alastair came in.

He smiled, in spite of his worry. "Now, you are recovering! How feminine you sound!" he teased. "Actually you look much better than you did. Such a thin wisp of a thing!"

He sat down on the edge of the bed, took away the mirror; and bent to kiss her. She responded with unexpected passion, her hands on his shoulders, and a pink coming up in her cheeks. He kissed her again.

"Do you know how much I missed you?" he murmured into her ear, kissing it and then the bit of white throat below it.

"How much?" she said, her gray eyes shining and sparkling. How animated she looked, now that the life in her had started to return! He had noted before how expressive her large gray eyes were, how they showed her moods. When she was happy, they shone with beautiful lights. When she was depressed, they seemed a dull gray. And when she felt insulted, he had seen her with eyes like cold gray marble.

"I missed you bitterly. All life was dull for me—and I shouted at Maurice and the girls until they fled from me."

"Oh, Alastair!" she reproached.

"Where did you go?" he asked abruptly, holding her so he could see her face. The dark curly lashes drooped over her eyes.

"I cannot tell you," she said simply.

"Don't you know?" A trace of harshness came into his voice. His fingers tightened on the frail shoulders.

"Oh, Alastair, do not question me, I pray you. I cannot tell you anything. I—I went for a holiday—"

"And came back looking as though you had been in a battle!" he said furiously.

The lashes opened wide, she gazed at him for a startled moment. Then she laughed feebly. "That is a jest, indeed," she said.

"I'll ask Jacob!"

"He cannot tell you. I beg you, Alastair, do not ask us. We did nothing to be ashamed of," she said quietly, a catch in her voice. "One day I may be able to tell you. But I cannot tell you now, I cannot."

With that she would say no more. Her obstinacy vied with his jealousy and curiosity. She was too weak to be pushed. He satisfied himself with bundling her up and taking her back to his townhouse.

Edwina welcomed her with great relief, the others with delight and pleasure. "Oh, to see you again! But you are so thin and wan," exclaimed Edwina compassionately.

Edwina saw her up to her apartment, shooed Henrietta away when the younger girl would have chatted. Sonia was weary from the move, Alastair saw, and he ordered her left alone to recover.

The housekeeper *would* insist on going to Sonia for orders so soon after such a serious illness. Alastair was cross. "You managed with Edwina . . . keep on doing so!"

"Oh, but my lord—my lady knows so much about matters," said the difficult woman, bowing and leaving.

Alastair smiled and sighed. In the few months she had been his wife, Sonia had managed to win their hearts, no matter what they had thought of her in the beginning. And she had impressed him with her wisdom and experience in household matters. She was a darling girl, and he had missed her so much. Now he felt happier and could relax, stretching out his feet to the fire. Even with her all the way upstairs in her own room he felt her presence in the house and was satisfied. Her long absence had been a horrible worry, a torment.

At night, he slept with the doors opened between their apartments, fuming that another room was between them. He felt rather uneasy for he had sent Leah to her own quarters and said he would take care of Sonia should she waken. The abigail had not liked that, but Alastair did not want someone always about.

He wakened with a great start when he heard Sonia cry out in the night. Leah had said her mistress had been having nightmares, and that that was one reason she had not wanted to leave her alone. Alastair grabbed his robe and sped to her room. She was sitting up. He lit the candle at the bedside, and sat down beside her.

Her eyes were shut, she was grabbing at empty space. "Oh, the faces—my God, the faces," she was moaning. "No—no, you cannot come into the carriage. No, no! Go away or I will shoot! I warn you, I will shoot! Oh, the faces, the bloody faces! There is blood on my hands—"

He was deeply alarmed. He took her shaking hands, and held them tenderly. They were chilled, the fingers stiff. He pressed them to his warm body. "Sonia," he said quietly. "Sonia, you are home with me. My dearest Sonia, it is only a nightmare. Wake up!"

She was moaning, saying words in another language. He

197

did not know what it was but it was soft and sibilant. He shook her slightly, and held her to him.

"Alastair?" Her voice came muffled against his chest.

"Yes, my dear. You were dreaming."

He brushed back her hair. Her forehead was damp with perspiration. She was shuddering deeply. "I dreamed—I was still back there. . . . Oh, Alastair, am I home? In my dream I was going home, but I also dreamed of waking to the cruel reality—"

He soothed her, tender and anxious. But he was the more deeply puzzled about her. It was certain she had gone on no holiday or romantic entanglement. No matter that Jacob had gone with her. Either something had gone badly wrong, or they had shared some desperate venture. What could it have been?

She finally calmed and lay back. "I am awake. Forgive me, Alastair, I did not mean to waken you."

But her hands clung reluctantly to his sleeve. He smiled down at her, and took off his robe. "I am going to remain with you tonight, doctor or no doctor," he said firmly. "I will hold you when you dream, and you will know you are safe."

Her eyes brightened. "But you—you might catch the fever—"

"No matter." He crawled into bed with her, blew out the candle and drew her into his arms. How slim and frail she seemed. He stroked his hand lightly over her bare arm. "There, now, love, my dove, sleep and be calm."

"Thank you, you are so good—to me—so good—" She turned and curled up against him like a child. But her body was not that of a child. He felt heat racing through his veins. He repressed all desire sternly, for she was not nearly strong enough for any passion. He held her closely to him and continued stroking her arm and shoulder, for it seemed to soothe and comfort her.

He slept with her every night after that. She continued to have some nightmares, but he would waken as they began, for she would stir and moan and sometimes cry out. He could soothe her before they got a grip on her. She seemed better for his presence.

Sonia continued to improve, and more rapidly now, and

soon she could walk slowly downstairs and sit in the smaller drawing room for a time. Then the others clustered around. Edwina was eager to tell her about a new beau, Henrietta wanted advice about some dresses for the winter. Maurice came and went, flitting from one girl to another, but always in high spirits. And Alastair was happy to sit with Sonia, contentedly smoking his pipe with his feet stretched out to the fire, like a country bumpkin, as Maurice teased him.

Alastair would not be drawn. "I have done all my running about," he said. "I am an old married man now. Besides, Sonia will do too much if I don't stop her!"

So he remained with her much of the evenings. During the day he came and went, discharging the business of the estate at Fairley by post, or sometimes attending the sessions of Parliament in which he had recently begun to take an interest. He did not speak of these to Sonia, as he was not sure she was interested. She never questioned where he went, and she did not seem to take much notice of what went on for a time.

Finally, he saw her with her sketch pad, and realized she was drawing again, some jewelry designs. He was pleased, for it meant she was becoming herself once more.

Edwina was urging her to go out with them. "You have not gone to anything this season, and truly it is a gay time," she told Sonia one evening. "Do come with us to Sir Frederick Toland's ball. It promises to be quite the thing! And you could wear your new silvery dress. Alastair, have you seen Sonia's silver gown?"

"No, I have not. When shall I see it, Sonia?" he asked lazily.

She smiled shyly. He enjoyed watching that flash of animation come into her pale cheeks. "It is in the new Greek design, Alastair," she said. "The gown is of silver, with a deeper silver Greek key design on the hem and sleeves, and the whole covered with chiffon. Edwina is delighted with it. She will have one of delphinium blue, and Henrietta one of rose."

"Charming," said Alastair. "And when shall we go out again? Do you wish to attend Sir Frederick's affair?"

"Well—I do feel stronger," she hesitated, her finger on her lip in her usual gesture of consideration.

"Oh, do let us all go!" urged Henrietta, sitting up on her deep cushions before the fire. "Everyone has been asking about Sonia, and saying where is she, and how is she recovering. She must come out, and let people see her and how well she is."

Alastair sent out their promise to attend, and was amused at how eagerly the girls prepared. He decided to wear his blue velvet trimmed with silver to match Sonia's silver, and his blue sapphire ring, of which he was very fond. He went to see Sonia when she was dressed and her maid was doing her hair.

"Exquisite," he breathed when he saw her before the mirror. She looked almost ethereal, as though a puff of wind would blow her away. There were silvery draperies about her, and the chiffon over the silk, and Leah was setting a silver tiara on her head with the loveliest of vivid blue sapphires on it in a delicate arrangement. "I am almost afraid to touch you, my dear! Are you sure you are real, or are you a fairy queen?"

She laughed and blushed at his compliments. Leah gave him a pleasant look of approval and said, "Does she not look a very princess? And all designed by herself, if you will!"

He raised Sonia's wrist to study the delicate silver and sapphire bracelet, so fine it looked as though it could be crushed by a finger. She wore a ring of one sapphire and small ear-bobs in her delicate ears. She gave a swift look at him, shyly, approving his blue and silver, and noting that he wore the star sapphire. He held out his hand, with a smile.

"My lucky ring, my dear," he said caressingly.

"I am so glad that it pleases you," she said simply.

She stood up, and he caught his breath again. The silver silk clung to her slender body, showing the slim waist, the rounded soft breasts, the smooth hips, and the long legs. Beneath the silver chiffon overdress, the silver Greek key design of the hem and sleeves shone through in a dim glimmer. Such a dress a Titania might have worn, flitting through a green forest glade.

He escorted her proudly down the stairs to the hallway.

The girls were in good time, Edwina radiant in blue velvet cloak with a glimpse of her lighter blue chiffon and silk gown beneath. Henrietta wore her rose velvet cloak over a rose gown. Maurice ran down the stairs to stop and stare.

"A bevy of goddesses," he said so solemnly that they all had to laugh. That started them out in a gay happy mood, and the beaming butler aided them into their carriages.

Alastair was proud as he took Sonia in on his arm. Everyone was turning to stare at her, to whisper and wonder at her ethereal beauty tonight. She was exquisitely gowned and coiffed, and her jewels outshone anyone else's, he thought. They might wear their heavy diamonds and emeralds, but no one had such perfectly designed gems as his wife. And her gown—it moved with her, whispering about her delicate silver-shod feet.

Sir Philip Ryan came up to them soon, giving Edwina a longing look. Alastair was cold but correct. He knew the young fellow was still seeing Daphne Porter. He was no man for Edwina. Thank goodness Edwina had found another beau, a man she liked better. The beau, Ralph Hastings, soon discovered her and took her off to dance. He had no title, but Alastair had come to know and like him. He was self-made, in the City, a shrewd broker with much commonsense. Edwina could do worse, for he had a good heart and came from a fine family in the country.

Alastair clasped Sonia about the waist, and led her into a set. Several guests spoke to her warmly. "Where have you been? You have been ill? All the summer? How sad. How fine it is that you have returned. You still look a bit wan. Was it the fever?"

Sonia met their looks and words with quiet composure, and answered very briefly. She gave herself earnestly to the set, following the steps agilely. Afte the dance, Alastair anxiously took her off to a corner near the dowagers.

"Now, you are not to get weary, or you shan't come again for a time," he said, bringing her a glass of cold punch. She thanked him with a glowing look.

"I am fine, Alastair. I shall not overtire myself." Then she glanced past him, and her face seemed to set. He looked around casually after a moment.

Daphne Porter was coming toward them. She was in a sensuously clinging gown of crimson satin, her green eyes mocking them.

"Alastair, my dear," she cooed, when she came to them. Alastair eyed her dispassionately. How overblown and coarse she looked, next to the delicacy of Sonia. Had she gained much weight, or lost her looks, or had he never seen her so clearly? "I have not seen you for a week!"

"It has been much longer than that," said Alastair curtly.

"It seems like that!" she agreed, with a trill of a laugh.

Sonia's eyes had gone cold and gray like a marble statue. Alastair felt her stiffness and stillness next to him. Daphne turned to her.

"And you have been ill, one hears! All the long summer and autumn! How curious! What kind of fever was it?" Her shrill voice seemed to penetrate the warm perfumed air. Several dowagers, in their blacks and purples, turned to listen, their heads forward and their eyes alert.

"The doctor did not say," said Sonia warily. "But I am quite recovered now."

"Splendid! Then you can work on a commission for me, can you not? I wish to order some jewelry. It will have to be done quickly, you know, for I wish it for a ball with the Prince Regent!" Her loud insolent tones were those of a lady with a tradesman. Sonia's face went even more pale.

"I regret I have no time for more commissions," said Sonia. And she looked past the woman as though she did not see her any longer. Her face was set, her mouth had lost its sweet curve and seemed bitter. And Alastair noted her eyes, how gray and cold they looked.

Daphne seemed inclined to argue. "But this would take you no time at all! A gentleman friend has found some splendid emeralds for me, and I wish them made into a long necklace." She glanced coyly at Alastair, and said in a softer tone, "Gentlemen can be so very—kind—can't they?"

The implication was that Alastair had given her the jewels. Alastair stirred, angry with her, yet he could not show it. He was furious with her, and with himself for having had anything to do with this greedy female.

He said in a chilly tone, "Lady Fairley has no time to take

on any commissions, Mrs. Porter. I advise you to go else-where."

The thin reddish eyebrows raised. He noted she had colored them. Her very blond hair—had she dyed it, or had it always been that brassy hue? "Well, if you are going to be difficult," she pouted. "I can tell you, Lady Fairley, you won't get much business if you are so rude to your patrons!"

Sonia looked past her, as though she had already left them. Alastair took her arm, and moved her away from Mrs. Porter. The woman stared after them, a malicious smile on her lips. She had shot some poisoned darts into vulnerable places, she thought.

Edwina came up to them, radiantly lovely, clinging to the arm of Ralph Hastings. As they were introduced, Sonia did not regain her color or her smile. Edwina looked at her with anxiety.

"Are you too weary, my dear Sonia?" she whispered. "It is such a crush here."

"We will leave early," said Alastair. "A few more turns about the room, then I will take Sonia home," He held her possessively to him. He felt she had moved a distance from him, and he resented it bitterly.

Ralph Hastings bowed to her. "May I have the pleasure of a dance first, my lady?"

He was so nice, so calmly understanding, that her mouth relaxed and she nodded. Alastair gazed after them, as they moved into the set.

Edwina took his arm. "Don't worry, Alastair. When she is tired, she will say so, she is a sensible girl. Now, do say how much you like Mr. Hastings! Isn't he a dear?"

Chapter
17

••◦••◦••◦••◦••◦••◦••◦••◦••◦••◦••◦••◦••◦••◦

As Sonia grew stronger, the puzzle of where she had gone haunted Alastair all the more. Her cousin Jacob and his wife Beryl came to call. They seemed devoted to each other. Alastair watched jealously for any signs of special closeness between Sonia and Jacob, and thought he could find them.

"My dear cousin, how are you?" Jacob greeted her affectionately, holding her hands. He kissed her cheek.

"Well, thank you, Jacob. And you?" Her gaze seemed to search his face anxiously. Jacob did seem thinner, and his cheeks seemed rather sunken.

Where on earth had they gone together? They seemed to have no sense of shame about it! Yet, Beryl was warm and loving to Sonia. She kissed Sonia's cheek, squeezed her by the waist, and spoke of her child.

"You must come and see us soon. You will not know the baby! How he grows! And he is the image of Jacob!" Beryl was glowing, plump and motherly-looking now with her hair tied up in a chignon and a bonnet set back on her head. She was short, dark, not nearly so lovely as Sonia, thought Alastair. Had her husband left her openly for Sonia, for a time of three months? No, he knew these people—they were devoutly religious and moral. He had spoken to them, listened to them, become more acquainted with them. What had happened, he could not imagine.

Meyer Goldfine had come that evening, unusual for him. He was wrapped in a black velvet cloak as he entered, shivering against the early December cold. Mist and fog swirled outside the windows and came into the hallway whenever the big doors were opened.

It was a family evening, and Sonia's face glowed pink with excitement. Maurice was there, and Edwina and Henrietta, a little quiet and shyly interested in their Jewish guests. Sonia had arranged the meal. Alastair was not certain if the foods were special or the usual fare. They had talked and chatted over the meal, of events in the city, of cousins of Sonia newly arrived from Vienna, of the gazettes and their reporting of political events.

Jacob and Meyer seemed as keen as Sonia about national and international affairs. Alastair found himself arguing with Jacob, in a good-natured way, about the outcome of the war on the Peninsula.

If General Wellington had really won the battle of Bussaco, why had he retreated before the French? And why did he not engage them in battle if his forces were superior? What kept him inert there in the mountains?

Meyer finally said mildly, "I am sure the general has his reasons." His German accent was strong tonight. "We do not know all that goes on down there . . . it is far away."

"Two friends of mine, from my former regiment, have returned to London," Alastair said, frowning slightly. They had both been wounded. He had gone to visit them, and had come away sickened and vowing to aid them in any way he could. One had lost a leg and was still feverish. The other had lost an arm up to the shoulder, and had an immense red scar across his formerly handsome young face. The tragedy of war! How it brought home to him the foolish ways of men with each other.

"Oh, yes, Alastair, you were going to tell me how they are

getting on. Shall I send a footman with more delicacies? And has my doctor been to them?" Sonia's quick sympathy had gone out to the two young officers she had never met.

Alastair nodded. "All is being done that can be. Ah—but we were talking of the war. I do not understand why Wellington does not move against the French."

"He is a brilliant man, well-versed in warfare, and he knows the French," said Jacob, his dark eyes sparkling with interest. "I am sure he has motive for what he does."

"You speak as though you had met him," said Maurice idly, with a smile. "He has made his mistakes, he was recalled—"

"He has his enemies and detractors," said Jacob sharply. "But I am sure we could have no more splendid general there."

Sonia gently turned the conversation to a play that had opened. Jacob and Beryl had attended, and had something to say of the acting and the movement of the plot.

When they were thus engaged, Alastair moved over to sit beside Meyer Goldfine. "I have been wishing to speak to you," he said in a low tone.

The mild dark eyes studied his. The aging hand reached up to stroke his gray beard thoughtfully. "Yes, my son?"

It gave Alastair a curious pleasure to be called that. Even his father had not—he had been stern and harsh of temper, expecting all to bow meekly to him. His rebellious older son had not, and there had been many a scene between them.

He spoke quietly. "I have tried to discover from Sonia where she went those three months. She refuses to tell me. She says she might be able to tell some day, but not now. I am growing weary of her excuses. Can you tell me now where she went?"

The dark eyes narrowed, still studying him. "My dear Alastair, I cannot. You must be patient. I have told you, she is a good girl, a noble girl, with much courage and devotion to duty. Is that not enough? There must be trust between you . . . I have told Sonia that."

Alastair frowned. "Trust between us? She has no cause to mistrust me," he said sharply. "But what about those three months?"

"Since she said she will tell you when she can, you must wait and believe her. Patience! Young people have no patience. The years drift by, and I am old. Still, I remember how hot-headed I was as a youth. Time could not move swiftly enough for me! And here I am near sixty, and time has sped," he said with a smile and a sigh.

His shoulders were stooped, and he seemed frail in the big chair. Alastair drew back. The man would not tell him, and he could not push him. His angry look went to Jacob. The man was laughing, animated. Beryl looked up at him proudly, with a slight happy smile on her pink lips.

The evening went swiftly by. Maurice had threatened Alastair that he would leave when he became bored, but he did not go. He was enjoying his arguments with Jacob, for they could jest and laugh together in spite of their differing upbringing and beliefs.

Edwina and Beryl seemed to have much to discuss. Alastair saw his sister's blond head bent close to the dark one, and they were murmuring seriously. He caught the words, "Husband—babies—devotion—prayers—" and he smiled a little. Edwina was becoming quite serious about her Mr. Hastings by the looks of it! She seemed to have matured a great deal this past year.

Henrietta sometimes listened to them, sometimes turned to Sonia, asking her for an opinion. Sonia answered with a smile, her patient look gentle on Henrietta's young head. Even Henrietta did not seem so silly and flighty as she had been. Having Sonia to confide in had been good for her also. As Alastair watched, Henrietta tossed her head, and Sonia laughed softly. Her face was bright, her gray eyes were luminous and sparkling. He enjoyed looking at her oval face, the red mouth. How much better she was now! He still shuddered when he remembered how pale and wasted she had been on her return from the "holiday" trip.

The clock chimed eleven. Meyer looked up at it. "Eleven o'clock! I must go home. I am always in bed earlier," he said, mildly concerned.

"You say you are in bed earlier. But when I look into your room, I find the lamps burning while you are still absorbed in a book," said Jacob, scolding him with a smile. "I know you. You pick up a book and forget the time!"

"You are wicked to give me away," said Meyer with a boyish grin. He managed to get to his feet. Alastair sprang to assist him with a hand under the old man's arm. "Come now, I must go. Call my carriage, if you will. You have been too entertaining, and I have quite forgot myself."

"We must go also," said Beryl firmly. "The baby will be wakening soon." She blushed charmingly. "I still feed him," she confided softly to Edwina.

"You do? You do not have a wet nurse for him?" asked Edwina. She seemed to hang on the answer.

Beryl shook her head. "No, I love to feed him, and it is no trouble. I will not have a wet nurse for him. Some are careless and given to drink."

Alastair saw them all to the door, saw the affectionate kisses between them and Sonia. Certainly Beryl had only respect and love for her husband's cousin. It was all the more puzzling.

Edwina and Henrietta went up to bed. Maurice decided to remain home for a change, and picked up a book to study for an answer to an argument he had had with Jacob. Sonia glanced about the room, straightened a drape automatically, then smiled good night to the two brothers.

"Wait, I will come up with you, Sonia," said Alastair, catching her up at the foot of the broad stairs. The butler and two footmen were extinguishing the torches at the door and the candles in the front drawing room. Maurice continued to read by the light of the fire. His valet would wait up for him.

Sonia felt light on his arm, but not so fragile as she had been. "It was a fine evening, was it not?" she asked as they ascended.

"Splendid. It went very well," he said absently. "Jacob seems to follow the gazettes closely."

"Yes, he does, and so does Uncle," she admitted. "It is our country, as well, you know. We are deeply concerned about —matters, and how the war goes."

She sounded slightly defensive. He smiled down at her. "Of course, it is your country," he said, and then remembered an argument in the House of Lords about admitting

Jews to the Bar. The few wishing to do so had been over-whelmed by the opposition. He frowned slightly. Until he had begun going to the sessions, he had not dreamed there was such prejudice against Jews in Parliament itself. Royalty received Jews privately; some dukes and other titled persons patronized Jews as musicians and artists, or went to Jewish money-lenders. But they could not accept them as doctors, lawyers, generals, or friends. How much they missed, thought Alastair, thinking of the conversation this evening, and the good sense and thought of Sonia's relatives.

"I like your people," he said abruptly, following the train of thought.

"I am glad." Her face glowed as he went into her bedroom with her. The candles were burning. Leah was seated in a straight-backed chair, her feet planted firmly before her, waiting for her mistress. "Good night, Alastair. Thank you—for being so kind to Uncle and my cousins."

"I shall come in later," he said calmly, smiling down at her. "I don't want you having nightmares!" He was pleased by her blush. She was sensitive to him, and he enjoyed making her more aware of himself. He was humming off-key as he went into his bedroom where his valet waited.

He dressed, waited a bit, then went to Sonia's room. It was in darkness save for a candle near the bed. She was sitting up, a sketch pad in hand, drawing. Her dark head was bent intently over her work, and he saw how the white lawn of her delicate nightdress showed the curves of her breasts and the creamy whiteness of her shoulders and arms. How lovely she was.

She raised her head. The gray eyes were absent, then focused on him. "Oh—Alastair—" she said, on a breath.

"Working—so late?" he teased. She grimaced and set aside the pad.

"I promised two sets of jewelry, and have done little on them," she said, simply, lying back on the pillows. "I must really do some work tomorrow. Perhaps I should go over to my house."

"This is your house, Sonia," he said decidedly, climbing into bed beside her. "If you wish, bring your gear over here and work. I shall be better pleased if you are here and can lie down when you tire. I know—I shall have Edwina keep an eye on you. She won't let you do too much, if I ask her to guard you. Leah lets you do too much, she has no will power to withstand you!"

"Now, Alastair," she rebuked gently. He took her into his arms and lay back, feeling her slight rounded form against his. "You know she has my welfare at heart."

"Yes, but you bully her," he said, laughing softly against her throat.

"I do not bully her!"

"Yes, you do. You have a very obstinate will, my dear!"

"Oh, how can you say that—"

He ran his hand over her shoulder, down to her arm, then to her rounded breast, cupping it in his palm. All desire to tease fell away from him. Passion was rising in him, it had been so long since he had loved her.

"Sonia," he said, against her ear. She went still as a mouse. "Umm?"

"I want you tonight. Are you—you aren't feeling ill, or anything? I was going to wait until you were stronger—" The urgency in his voice did not seem to alarm her. Her arms went up and about his neck.

"Oh, it has been such a time, my dear," she said simply. She was generous in her loving, she always had been. He bent over her, his mouth going hungrily to her lips.

Her mouth parted, the soft pink well-shaped lips opened before his onslaught. He tried to be gentle and slow, but passion was rising so swiftly in him. He forced himself to go carefully. She had been ill such a long time. . . .

He nibbled at her shoulder, teased at her arm, moved his lips over her chin, down to her throat, and then to her breast. He remained there for at time, his lips moving over her bared breasts, feeling her hands threading tenderly through his hair, caressing the back of his neck. Her slim sensitive fingers went to his back, and moved slowly over the muscles there, thrilling him. Oh, she was so delightful, so full of delight, he thought hazily.

He drew up the hem of her nightdress, and stroked his hand over her thighs. His lips continued to tease at her breasts, pulling at the small pink rosebuds of the nipples. She caught her breath and her arms went more closely about his body, pulling him down to her. He moved his hand to her slim back, down to her hips, stroking up and down, rousing her. Then to her thighs again, and she was ready for him, moving under his body.

He swung over her more fully. He caught his breath, said, "If it is too much for you, I will try to stop, my darling."

"No—no, don't stop—oh, don't stop—" She was moving under his body, showing her rising passion, her hands clutching at his waist, one hand went to his hips. He brought the two of them together, as carefully as he could, feeling a surge of delicious pleasure at the long-awaited meeting.

He lingered long over her, drawing it out, with wonderful results. For she met his passion with her own shy longings. They came together, again, again, and he knew the delight of having her cry out with pleasure at the end. When he could, he slid off her naked body, and drew her into his arms. Their nightgowns had been discarded, flung wildly over his head to the floor. Now he was able to enjoy the feel of her warm slim body against his own, length to length.

"Oh, you are my darling," he whispered. "You are so beautiful, my dove, my dear."

She was weary, and soon slept on his shoulder. He lay awake, worrying a little that it might have been too much for her. However, in the morning, she seemed radiant and full of energy. He felt satisfied, and was pleased with their relationship. He loved her now, he knew. He had never before known what love was.

But he loved Sonia. Loving her, he had discovered the meaning of love. Love was when one desired the good of the loved one more than one's own. Love was a total meeting of mind and body, of heart and soul, drawing so close there was no room between them for dissension. Love was a craving when the beloved was away, a delight when she returned. Love was a quick defense, being hurt when the other was hurt—being happy when the other was happy.

He blinked at the morning light, amazed at his thoughts. He had married for money, thinking bitterly never to find happiness in this life. But not seeking his own happiness had brought him more joy than he had ever believed possible to find. What a paradox that was!

The days went on, and the nights, and they slept together often. There was but one flaw in his paradise. Sonia would not tell him where she had been those three months. He became angry at times, almost violent with her. She grew pale, but shook her head, her mouth drooping in sadness.

"I cannot tell you, Alastair. I beg you, do not ask again."

He could not refrain from asking. He knew he hurt her, as he would not allow anyone else to hurt her. Yet he must ask, again and again, for her trust and her belief in him. It seemed to violate everything they felt that she should not trust him in this matter.

His passion vied with his anger, and he took her again and again in those cold December nights. She met his passion with her own. In this she gave freely.

And the days went on to Christmas. Alastair had gone out shopping with Edwina and Maurice, trying to find something appropriate for Sonia. She was not ready yet for the long drive to Fairley. Her strength did not equal her will. Often she had to lie down on the couch in the afternoon when no visitors came. So they would have to spend Christmas in London, though Sonia spoke wistfully of Fairley.

She had completed the jewelry commissions. He had taken Edwina into his confidence. She had gone daily with Sonia whenever she had to go to her own house to work on jewelry or meet with customers.

Sonia had not agreed to set up a workroom in his townhouse. That also made him uneasy. She had not broken all her ties with her old life. She still spoke of it as "my own townhouse," not seeming aware that she hurt him. When he was gone all the day she did not ask where he went. He was not sure if she was not interested, or if she did not care.

He sighed sometimes in the dull sessions of the House of Lords. Sometimes the speakers did drone on so. He would think about Sonia and their problems, and wonder what might happen to their marriage.

Christmas came. The house was decorated beautifully on the ground and the first floors. They had two trees, one in the huge drawing room and one in the servants' quarters. He had the pleasure of giving his gifts to Sonia, and seeing her eyes sparkle with pleasure.

His gifts were simple, but had taken much thought. Edwina had led him to a fine dressmaker, newly fled from France. The clever modiste had made up a beautiful dress of English wool in a wheat color trimmed in gold braid. Matching it was a thick woolen cloak of the same colors and a beautiful bonnet. Sonia simply had to put on the cloak and the bonnet at once, parading for them, her cheeks pink with pleasure.

Alastair had seen that the jewelry she liked best was simple yet well-designed. He had gone also to a jeweler and ordered gold bracelets in Greek design, with a matching pendant and slim gold chain. These, too, she liked very much.

Sonia had designed and had made up several dresses for the girls—in feminine fragile shades of blue for Edwina, flashing gold and touches of scarlet for Henrietta, and one gown of fragile violet for Henrietta in which she would look like a fairy. Maurice was the proud recipient of a stunning set of rubies—studs and cufflinks of Sonia's design.

For Alastair, she had made more studs and cufflinks of star sapphires, which matched his ring.

"My dear, you must have been working too hard," he rebuked her gently, coming over to thank her with a kiss.

Her face glowed and her eyes were luminous as when she was very happy. "I enjoyed it so much, Alastair," she said simply. "You are all my family now."

He liked it that the girls had exchanged loving gifts. Edwina had given Sonia a charming sewing basket of wicker covered with rose silk frills, fitted out with all sorts of golden thimbles, measures, pins and needles and a box of colored silk threads. Henrietta's gift to her sister-in-law was a glittering jewel box, of tortoiseshell trimmed in gold.

It was altogether a happy occasion. Alastair went with Sonia to visit her uncle and take some gifts to him. Meyer had some uncut gems for her—and a bundle of extravagant lengths of silk fabrics for "the girls," as Meyer said with a twinkle in his eye. Alastair lingered to talk with the old gentleman, discussing philosophy and the differences in holidays between religions, while Sonia took gifts to the servants and transient guests in her house. They still took in Jewish emigrants—peddlers, old women with bewildered eyes, young women in head scarves, and little children with sober looks and thin legs and arms. They seem to come and go. Alastair was sure he never saw the same ones twice.

He had a lingering wonder—perhaps this was where she had gone on the mysterious "holiday." Could she have gone back to her old country, to Vienna, to get some relatives or friends out and to safety? But surely, if that was so, she would admit it.

So the pinprick of doubt that was larger by the week still bothered him; it remained to remind him that though he and Sonia had grown close in many ways, there was still this lack of trust between them.

It did boil down to that. She wanted him to believe blindly in her, and he could not. Not when he thought of the fond looks she gave Jacob and the way Jacob kissed her cheek when they met. He had to know the truth about that one day, as soon as he could. Their marriage could not be complete without trust.

Chapter
18

●●○●○●○●○●○●○●○●○●○●○●○●○●○●

Sonia hugged her secret to herself, one that made a little dreamy smile come to her lips often. She was going to have a baby! Alastair's child! How happy she was! She hoped so much that he would be happy also.

Did he want her child? He came to her often, without reluctance. He was fond of her, she knew that. He was anxious for her comfort, and his family liked and confided in her.

But a child? Did he want her child? The heir to his estates? If she had a son, would they accept the half-Jewish child?

She put off telling him for a time, until she was certain. She had thought by Christmas that the child was on the way. Now she was fairly sure of it.

Leah knew also, instinctively. Sonia knew that her abigail realized it by her extra anxious care of her. She must not reach high in the wardrobe for a bonnet—Leah jumped to do it for her. Sonia must not work long during the day—Leah scolded her into coming home by mid-afternoon.

Yet she put off telling Alastair. She was not sure of his reaction. Some little warning, some fear troubled her. She scolded herself, but could not be calm about it.

Everything seemed to happen at once. It was toward the end of January—a bitterly cold January, with fogs and mists that enveloped London and with ice on the cobblestones that made Sonia afraid to go out.

Sir Frederick Toland gave a dinner party in his townhouse. Alastair insisted on their going. When Sonia tried to refuse, fearing to be out in the cold and ice, Alastair looked hurt.

"I want you to know my friends better, and come to like them as I do," he said sternly. "You have avoided them, I know. They ask after you. No one could have been kinder than Lady Barnstable in your illness last fall. She often sent flowers and fruit from her greenhouses."

"I know—I have written—" Sonia hesitated anxiously. "She is to come on Saturday?"

"Yes, she will be there, and many others whom you have met. Do say you will come, Sonia. Wear the new rose gown with the gold braid—that is so charming."

When he coaxed, she could not resist, and she smiled, and let herself be persuaded. She dressed for the evening, as he had asked, in the new rose velvet dress with the gold braid about the hem and sleeves. She wore Alastair's gifts of gold bracelets and earrings, and he was pleased.

They arrived when the party was in full swing. Sonia hated to be early, and to endure long empty conversations with looks darted at her. She kept her chin up, and her eyes wary as they entered the large drawing room.

Lady Barnstable swept up to them, trim as a pocket ship in full purple sail. "My dearest Sonia, you are looking beautiful tonight!" she said, and kissed her on both cheeks. Sonia smiled with restraint. Alastair had probably asked her to be kind.

"Good evening, Lady Barnstable, how pleasant to see you again."

"I longed to call on you, but Alastair refused me. He said you must become fully well again. You look blooming!" The keen eyes took in her appearance, lingered on her breast and waist, then back significantly to her eyes. But she said nothing, for which Sonia was thankful.

"Thank you, you are very kind. May I express again my appreciation for your gifts of fruit and flowers. I especially enjoyed the violets—how fragrant they were!"

Lady Barnstable looked gratified, though she waved the thanks away with her diamond-ringed hands. Her purple turban tossed. She took Sonia by the arm and led her about the room, introducing her, clinging to her, as though determined to launch her into society. Whatever had Alastair said to her, Sonia wondered, even as she smiled into faces, shook hands, said the polite things required.

As some other latecomers arrived, there was laughter in the hallway. Sonia stiffened. Could that voice be . . . ? She managed to turn around casually, just in time to see her husband greet the couple that had just come in.

The gentleman was Sir Philip Ryan, red-haired and dashing in a green suit and violently golden waistcoat, and the lady with him was Mrs. Daphne Porter. Mrs. Porter's hair was more red than before, with golden lights in it, and she wore a crimson velvet gown cut very low, and a strand of huge emeralds set in gold about her throat.

Lady Barnstable's hand tightened on Sonia's. "That—that female," she growled under her breath. "How dare she! She becomes more arrogant by the minute!"

Alastair's smile seemed stiff. He greeted Sir Philip, raised Daphne's hand to his lips. Everyone was staring at them, and whispering. Sonia felt overcome with fury. How dare Alastair parade his mistress before her? Was this why he wanted her to be there? How could he be so cruel? It was not like him—if she knew him. She wondered if she did know him.

They went in to dinner. Sonia was on the arm of a gentleman she knew by sight. He was elderly and polite—an earl. She was supposed to be honored by that, she told herself bitterly. Alastair had taken in Lady Barnstable, but he was seated where he could see and talk with Daphne Porter across the table from him, and admire her stunning beauty.

The earl rambled on about hunting and shooting, then onto politics. Sonia listened politely, contributed enough words to encourage him to go on, then turned to her partner on the other side. She knew him only slightly, and they did not have much in common. He devoted himself to his dinner, as though his stout frame had to be heavily stoked for him to continue with this life.

The dinner seemed never-ending. She was nauseated by the huge servings and the heavy starches. Sir Frederick was a bachelor, and a widowed sister was his hostess. She was lively, judging by the sound of laughter coming from her end of the table. Sir Frederick was exchanging animated talk with Sir Philip and the others around him. There must be fully twenty at the table, thought Sonia, and counted—yes, twenty. She was about in the center, and could not see Alastair's face, for he was near the hostess on Sonia's side of the table.

To her relief, the hostess finally rose. The ladies went with her to the green drawing room. The gentlemen lingered over brandy and port, and some were the worse for it when they joined the ladies. Sonia was relieved that Alastair stood upright, moving under his own steam. She wondered when they might be able to leave.

But Daphne Porter soon had him by the arm, and was whispering to him. Sonia turned from the sight, and talked to Lady Barnstable and the hostess about fashions, the latest play, the possibility that a Regency Bill would soon be passed, giving Prince George command of the government.

"I understand that Lord Fairley has been talking in the House of Lords for passage of the bill," said Lady Barnstable approvingly.

Sonia stared. "He has?" she murmured. She had not known that Alastair ever took his seat there.

"Yes, does he not say so? I thought he must confide everyting in you, my dear, you are so intelligent, and so knowledgeable about events," said Lady Barnstable encouragingly. She waited for a reply.

Sonia's gaze sought Alastair's, but he was bending to hear what Mrs. Porter said. Her mouth tightened and she turned back. "Not everything, my lady," she said, unable to conceal her bitterness.

The lady's hand caught her arm and she squeezed it comfortingly—then changed the subject. She knew also, thought Sonia. The evening was becoming interminable. If only she might go home—if only she had remained at home! It was bitter enough, imagining Alastair with his mistress. To see them, side by side, his blond head bent to her reddish-blond hair, his face laughing down into her charming one. . . . Sonia felt suddenly ill, and put her handkerchief to her face. The spasm finally passed. She breathed deeply and it went.

Alastair returned to Sonia's side, looking a little uneasily at her. She seemed stiff, her face drained of color. "Are you feeling weary, my dear?" he murmured anxiously.

"Yes, I thought I might go home in the carriage. It can return for you," she said curtly.

He felt chilled. She did not look at him, she seemed bored and ill-at-ease, not like the way she was with her cousins. Well, she must learn to like his friends, he thought testily. They were not all her weight intellectually, but they were good fellows, and the ladies were splendid, some of them.

"Only another hour, and we will both depart," he said, as curtly as she had spoken. "It would be insulting to be the first to leave."

He straightened abruptly, and stood with his hands behind his back. Daphne came up to them, moving alluringly in the crimson velvet, her great green eyes fixed on him.

"Alastair," she said, and slid her hand into his arm. Unwillingly, he recalled how infatuated he had been with her, the nights and days she had lain in his arms. He had been unable to leave her at times, for she had been so willing, so passionate. . . .

But greedy and difficult, also, he reminded himself.

"Daphne, you do look splendid," he said, for something to say.

She gave a sly downward look toward his wife, sitting so primly on the sofa next to Lady Barnstable. She laughed a little, whispered loudly enough for them both to hear, "Darling, Sir Philip is having a party at his hunting lodge in Scotland. He has invited us both. It would be such fun. . . . Do say you will come!"

"Hunting? At this time of year?" he asked, amused.

"Who said anything about hunting—animals?" she murmured, and giggled up at him, her green eyes sparkling.

"There are several of us going. Do say you can get away! You need a holiday, darling, you have stuck so close to home and work!" And she gave a little malicious side-swing of her body, pressing against his.

He caught Lady Barnstable's frosted look. He felt rebellious. Sonia was cold and haughty tonight. At least Daphne was friendly. . . .

"I don't see how I can get away," he said mildly. "Much work to do—"

"Leave it to Maurice! You have before!" she urged. She pressed her fingers on his hand, the great emerald gleaming. He thought, Sir Philip is coming up to scratch—or does she have yet another lover? She was becoming very promiscuous. It might be amusing to see if he could take her away from them. . . .

But no, he loved Sonia. He did not want to leave her.

"Impossible at this time," he said suavely.

"Oh, dear!" she pouted. Sir Philip came up to them, swaying on his feet, his face almost as red as his carrot-colored hair.

"Daphne, did you t-tell him our p-plan?" he stuttered.

"Great idea, eh? Hunting lodge out of season?" He began to laugh. "Should be cosy and happy, eh? Lots of hunting going on!"

Sir Frederick Toland overheard and strolled over. "What are you up to now, Philip? Eh? Shouldn't talk so before the ladies!" But he did not lower his voice. Alastair saw Sir Frederick's sister frowning and hastened to change the subject.

"Do you think the Regency Bill will pass?" he managed to say. The new topic roused feelings, and kept them going for quite fifteen minutes. Some thought the Regent would be worse than having a mad King, for he was frivolous, had some bad advisors, and he might go either way, Conservative or Liberal. And what about the war in the Peninsula—would he support it or order Wellington home?

Daphne grew bored, and moved away to speak to some other friends. Alastair saw Sonia with tight-clenched fists in her lap and took pity on her. She wasn't used to such company, or late nights either.

He bent to her. "I'll order our carriage," he said, low.

"Thank you."

She was cold, and formal, turning to speak to Lady Barn-stable, before rising to join Alastair. She thanked the hostess, smiled frostily at Sir Frederick, ignored Sir Philip. No, she didn't care much for his friends, thought Alastair, irritated and on the defensive. She probably did not know of his attachment to Daphne Porter, but she might suspect as much.

However, she had much to explain of her own conduct! Fumes of wine in his brain, Alastair vowed to himself he would have it out with her tomorrow. He was tired of beating about the bush. Sonia was quite well now. He would tell her he had to know the truth—or else! She was his wife, and she had to make a clean breast of the matter!

He was angry when they arrived home to find Leah sitting up for her. "You don't need to sit up," snapped Alastair. "I will take care of my wife."

"Leah will stay in my room tonight," said Sonia, careful not to look at him. "It is late, and you will want your sleep."

It was a dismissal. In his own bedroom, he fumed and roared at his valet. He did not want to admit the evening had been a dismal failure, boring for him as well as Sonia. His friends were charming and amusing, or at least they used to be. The repetition of the same views over and over had ceased to entertain him, but stubbornly he thought they were splendid fellows for all that.

He slept late the next morning, and was further annoyed to find that Sonia had risen early and gone to her townhouse to work—taking Leah but not Edwina.

"She was in a strange mood; she would not have me," said Edwina simply. "Do—do you think she does not really like me, Alastair? Truly, I thought she did—" She seemed close to tears.

"Nonsense. She loves you, I am sure of it," growled Alastair. He paced his study, wondering whether to go after her or wait until she arrived home for tea. She usually came by then.

After luncheon, the butler brought the post to him. It was a motley lot of letters. He flipped through them without interest, then came on one with a strange franking.

He turned it over in his fingers, about to open it curiously, when he caught sight of the address on the envelope.

Sonia, Lady Fairley, it read. And it was from a chap in Portugal! Alastair stared. Did she know someone in Portugal? Usually she received her letters at her own townhouse and said nothing of them.

He hesitated, studying the address with growing suspicion. The return was that of some titled fellow—Marquis—something or other—Paulo de Mondego.

That settled it. Sonia was not going to exchange flirtatious letters with some foreigner without telling her own husband! Alastair ripped open the envelope.

With growing alarm and incredulity, he read the handsome black handwriting.

My dearest Lady Fairley,

I have thought of you day and night since last we parted. When I gaze at the portraits of my house, I see only your beautiful face. Forgive me for writing, you said that you were married. However, you said also that you had not informed your husband of your voyage. That gives me courage to hope that there is some future for me.

My charming lady Sonia, I think of you so often. How courageous you are, so intelligent, so beautiful. No other lady of my acquaintance can equal you, and I long to see you again. Perhaps you have left your husband?

May I come to London and seek you out? I have waited months, fighting with myself. But I shall leave all, my duties here, my family, my responsibilities, to come and see you, if you will but give me leave. If you are now free, then I may pursue my courtship!

My foot is healed at last, I can do more than hobble about. I eagerly await your word . . . pray give me a favorable response. You need not commit yourself; do but let me come and gaze into your lovely glowing eyes, as we did in the carriage—speak honestly and bravely—as we did then.

I eagerly await your permission to come.

Your
Paulo de Mondego

"My God!" whispered Alastair. He read the letter again, taking in the firm handwriting, the crest on the notepaper. "What has she done? My God!"

His doubts and suspicions had all focused on Jacob, her cousin. Now—now—here was another fellow—member of the nobility of Portugal! She had been to *Portugal* . . . he spoke of her being in his house there! Alastair turned cold with shock and fright. His beautiful, his modest, his highly moral wife—what had she done?

She must have been swept off her feet. To go to her lover in Portugal—surely someone she had known before—to go to him, make her cousin take her to him—stay with him for three months. . . .

Alastair took out his handkerchief and wiped his face. It was damp with sweat. He longed to throw the letter into the purging fire. But he would not—he would confront her with it—he would have her answer now!

He sat there for a long time, staring into the fire, then lifting the hated pages to read them again, over and over, until the words were imprinted on his brain.

He heard the carriage, finally. He jumped up and went to the hallway. He saw Sonia come in with Leah behind her, like a gray shadow, the faithful retainer—who had not gone on this journey with her! No, Leah, like himself, had been left behind on this journey. She had left Leah, who adored her mistress, and had gone off for three months. . . .

Sonia smiled wanly when she saw him, for she was weary. He had no compassion, the anger burned so furiously in him.

"Come in here, Sonia," he said curtly. Leah frowned at him disapprovingly.

"She is weary," said Leah.

"Come in," he ordered, and stamped off into the drawing room. Sonia followed him and he slammed shut the door after her.

Her great gray eyes questioned him. Her face seemed so innocent, so calm, with the slight tinge of grayness that showed her weariness, even after the cold ride in the carriage.

"I have received a letter—meant for you," he said icily.

"A letter?" She seemed to turn even more pale, glancing at the pages in his hand. "But I never receive—I mean—"

"Yes, he probably writes to your *own* house?" sneered Alastair. "Well, I have it now. Your love letter from Paulo de Mondego!"

"What?" she whispered. Her hand had gone to her throat.

"I said—your love letter—from Paulo de Mondego! A marquis of Portugal, I believe, by his crest—" He held out the letter to her. She took it automatically, gazing at his face rather than the script.

"Paulo is only a friend," she said quietly. "He helped us— he should not have written—"

"Indeed!" Alastair began to stride about the room, so furious that only activity would soothe him. "A friend, eh? A friend, indeed! He asks if you have left your husband yet! He asks to come and gaze into your beautiful eyes, as you did in the carriage—"

"Oh no!" she breathed. She glanced in a dazed manner at the writing but did not read it. "Oh, Alastair, he does not mean it. He knows I am married. There is nothing between Paulo and me . . . I swear it!"

"Do you swear it? Do you? You will perjure yourself!" he raged. He swung around to her. "Tell me what happened on that journey! You went to Portugal—I know that much—"

"I cannot—tell—you. I beg of you, Alastair! You are not yourself, you are not calm—"

He could have struck her. He raised his hand, and she cringed from him. "I could hit you, you bitch! Looking so honest and turning up your nose at my friends! I could strike you—"

"No—Alastair—do not!" She sat down uncertainly on the edge of a chair, and pushed back her bonnet. "I have meant to tell you—I must tell you now—no matter how angry you are with me—I am to have a child. I pray you—do not strike me."

A child! He stared at her, at the bent head. A child! If only she had said so, before that hateful letter had arrived!

"Whose child is it? Jacob's—or your Paulo's?" he sneered furiously. "Whose child is it? Did you think to palm it off as mine?"

226

"Alastair!" The great gray eyes were in agony, but he refused to see that. She put out her hand in pleading, and he turned from her.

"I am going to Scotland!" he said harshly. "With Mrs. Porter and the others! When I return, you can inform me what you wish to do. Send for your lover, Paulo, if you wish. You might as well live openly with him—and his child!"

He strode toward the door.

"Yes, go to your mistress!" she cried after him, her voice breaking. "Go to Mrs. Porter! She has been your mistress these years. Now you may live with *her* openly. And when you marry her, your sisters may be more willing to receive her—"

He slammed the door on her words. He went up to his rooms, and ordered his valet to pack—three trunks of heavy winter clothing, his hunting boots, his guns. The valet, startled, packed for him, and had the further task of having to order his carriage for that very night.

Alastair stormed out without seeing Sonia again. He was so angry with her that he did not trust himself. He would take that white throat in his hands . . . he would strangle her! Having her lover's child, deceiving him—all those months— all the year! God, he was sick with it, with his fury. The coachman did not dare to speak to him, so they drove on until the horses were so tired they were on the verge of foundering.

The valet had been peering out into the cold January night. "There is a fine inn coming up, my lord. We are almost to it . . . if I might recommend—"

Alastair's first fury had worn off, and he was half asleep and cold in the great coach.

"Yes, yes, we will stop for the night to rest the horses," he said wearily.

They stopped, but he could not sleep. He roused early the next day and they pressed on. He knew where Sir Philip Ryan's hunting lodge was in Scotland. He might arrive before them, but he would be sure of a welcome. Some shooting and living in the glens might clear his brain, he thought.

He brooded, staring out the window at the cold gray hills,

227

the gray skies, as the horses trotted cautiously over the icy roads to the north.

He could not think . . . his brain seemed numb. He had trusted Sonia . . . he had married her in good faith. She had been a virgin when they married, he would have staked his life on that. She had been so shy, but willing, and even passionate when she had learned how to match his ardor.

And that they had come to this! That letter from her lover —Paulo de Mondego! He clenched his fists, and muttered angrily to himself. His valet glanced at him apprehensively. His master had been given to whims, but this was the wildest yet.

They crossed the border into Scotland and wound through the hills going north. Day followed day, and Alastair finally calmed. The wild beautiful country soothed him, making him better able to think again. The very monotony of day after day of travel, the jingle of the harness, the inns they stayed in, the varying foods, the quiet, with little talk. . . .

The journey encouraged thinking, as journeys will. He began to see things in more perspective, as his first anger cooled. Paulo de Mondego had not said he was her lover— nothing in the words had said so. Rather he had been eager to woo her; he had asked if she was still with her husband. What if Sonia had not given in to him? What if some other urgent task had taken her to Portugal? And why Portugal, for God's sake! They were at war with the French, for that was why Wellington was down there. And what about the man's injured foot? Why injured? In a hunting accident, or something of more importance?

Too many questions. He cursed his impulsiveness. Finally one morning, brooding over his breakfast tea, he came to a decision.

When he and his valet went out to the carriage, to find fresh horses ready, Alastair said curtly, "We will turn back. To London."

His valet, shuddering in his cloak from the Scottish cold, was relieved. "Yes, sir, my lord!" and he gave orders to turn back.

Alastair brooded in his corner of the coach, shifting restlessly from time to time. Days wasted. He could have had the truth from Sonia by this time. He would get it from her, by

God, or he would go to Jacob and wring his neck! Yes, that was it, he would threaten Jacob with bodily harm, if Sonia did not tell the truth. She was fond of her cousin, she must tell him!

Too many mysteries. That strange disappearance must be accounted for!

And he must have the truth about the child. He began to count. Sonia had not returned until late October. Now she told him in late January that she was to have a child. He had noticed nothing, but if she had been pregnant on her journey, she would have been well along by this time, at least three months or more. He frowned. He wished he knew more about the matter. It could be his child—but if she had had Paulo as a lover—or her cousin Jacob . . .

He wished the horses would go faster, but they could not for slick ice covered the ground and snow swirled about the huge coach. It would be dangerous to go more rapidly. It had been foolish to start out in the winter. . . . He must be patient now until he reached home. Then he would have the truth at last!

Chapter
19

SONIA did not know if she were more coldly furious or more hurt. Alastair's words rang in her brain.

"Whose child is it? Jacob's or your Paulo's?"

That Alastair could think so badly of her! That he could insult her so!

She heard the noise of his leave-taking—no one in that great house could miss it! The slamming of doors, his shouts, his furious orders to valet and coachman. The protesting whinnies of the horses being hitched up on the icy cobbles near the stables. Edwina's tears and pleading, Henrietta's scolding, Maurice's bewildered questions.

Noise, fury, anger—she had never experienced such. Her life with Uncle Meyer had been placid, calm, a life of the mind. It seemed that her calm was gone forever here in this household!

She wakened early the next morning and was promptly sick at her stomach. She was reminded again that she expected Alastair's child—and that he had gone to Scotland to be with his mistress!

She drank some hot tea, which settled her stomach. Then she ordered Leah to pack.

Leah tried to dissuade her. "Now, my lady, you will be sensible," she pleaded. "It is enough that my lord has gone off in a tizzy. You must be calm—for the sake of the child!"

"If you do not pack for me, I will!" And Sonia began to tear down dresses recklessly from the wardrobe racks—heavy woolen dresses, cloaks, and bonnets. . . .

Leah cried out, taking the garments from her. "Be calm, please be calm," she pleaded, but Sonia would not be calm. She had been grossly insulted, deserted. Why should she be the only calm person in the world?

She had thought about it in the wakeful hours of the night and she had decided. She would leave Alastair, he would divorce her, he could keep the money. That was all he wanted. He could keep the hateful money—and she would keep his child. He would not want her child.

She knew exactly where she would go. Not to Uncle Meyer, for he had betrayed her in this marriage to Alastair. Not to Jacob, not to any relative or friend.

She would go to the country, into retreat. Nobody would find her now.

Edwina came to see her as she heard the sounds of Sonia's movements from below. Sonia greeted her coldly, turning from Edwina's tear-stained face.

"Sonia, you are not leaving also! You cannot! Alastair has a terrible temper! He will recover it and return, you will see!"

"No, I will not see!" cried Sonia passionately. "I will be gone from this house where I never was welcome! He may return or not, as he pleases."

She was cramming books into a valise, with Leah vainly attempting to stop her. Trunks stood nearby, filled with dresses and undergarments. Edwina sighed deeply, and went looking for Henrietta. Henrietta had great charm and persuasion when she chose.

Henrietta came to Sonia's room, sat on the bed and gazed

thoughtfully at Sonia. "I always thought you had such a good sensible mind," she murmured hopefully.

"It shows how mistaken one can be!" snapped Sonia.

She crammed in two more books, added her sketching pads and a bundle of pencils.

"Do you go to your townhouse?" asked Henrietta. "And may we come and visit?"

"I shall not see you," said Sonia ominously.

Edwina tried again. "But dearest Sonia, we need you here. You know that Ralph and I—that Mr. Hastings and I—may announce our engagement soon—" And she blushed charmingly.

"I will be sorry to see it," said Sonia bitterly. "Marriage is a fool's game. No woman truly knows a man until she marries him, and then it is too late. He shows his true nature, becomes a devil—a very demon!"

"Oh, Sonia!" Edwina began to weep again, gentle tears falling from her beautiful blue eyes. Sonia turned her back, and swept several miniatures from her dresser recklessly into her next valise.

"I cannot pack them all," she muttered. "Edwina—I should say *Lady* Edwina—will you kindly order all my other possessions packed and sent to my townhouse? I am sure my lord will not wish to be burdened with clearing out these rooms."

Henrietta looked at Leah, pleading silently. Leah flung up her hands, palms upward, invoking heaven.

"When he comes back, he will be so upset," murmured Edwina, wiping her eyes.

"No, he will not. He will be glad!" said Sonia. "He will get a divorce from me, and marry that—that mistress of his, Mrs. Porter. And you will have the pleasure of getting along with that brazen woman. I am sure you will enjoy her company!"

Maurice had come into the room in time to hear this last. "Come, now, Sonia, do show your usual good reason—"

She glared at him. Edwina was weeping again, and Henrietta looked on the verge of tears. Maurice came to Sonia and slid his arm coaxingly about her waist.

"Now, my dearest sister, do be calm. Let your abigail put

you to bed and get some rest. You are overwrought. I don't blame you, for Alastair is a beast when he gets in such a devilish pucker—"

"So he is. Well, from now on, he can take out his ill humors on his—his next wife!" said Sonia, her mouth snapping on the words. "See if she hangs on him then!"

There was no calming her. Packed, she called for her coachman and private carriage, a huge barouche in which they stacked the many trunks and valises and two hatboxes. She was off within the hour, leaving the girls weeping and Maurice shaking his head.

"Can't blame her," said Maurice sadly. "Devil a time when I ever marry! It is a cursed state, turns people mad enough for Bedlam."

Edwina burst into further tears, and ran from the hallway. Henrietta gave her brother a reproachful look and said, "You'd best send for Alastair, or Ralph Hastings, perhaps. He is sensible enough."

Meantime, Sonia was traveling west. Two footmen on horseback were escorting the carriage solemnly. She allowed this as far as the edge of London, then curtly dismissed them, as the barouche turned onto the road to Cornwall.

She wished no outriders to report her true destination to anyone at all.

Leah looked relieved after they had turned onto the Cornwall road. "There, now, we'll be happy in Fairley, and able to relax," she said, patting Sonia's gloved hand. Sonia did not reply, staring from the windows into the gloomy January dusk, paying no attention when the horses skidded dangerously on the icy road.

Sonia felt in a daze, once her first fury had passed. She felt rather ill from her fit of temper, and wondered if it would affect the child. She sighed deeply from time to time, and made no objection when Leah insisted on stopping early at an inn.

They rested the night, and continued through the next day. The road to Cornwall was dearly familiar to Sonia now. She saw the landmarks through tears. Leah chattered a little about their welcome at Fairley.

"Mrs. Pendennis will be that glad to see us. She says as

how the winters be lonely," remarked Leah. "I never thought to like a Christian so much!"

"She is a good woman," agreed Sonia dully. "I hope she will continue to be kind to the Jewish peddlers."

Leah gave her a curious look. "Whyever not? She has her orders from you, my lady!"

Sonia brushed away tears. She felt as icy as the churning streams beside the road, flooded by the rains and snows of winter. So cold, she thought she would never be warm again, in spite of the thick blue-green cloak in which she huddled. Alastair's gift to her! She had forgotten that . . . she had reached instinctively for her warmest cloak, and it had been this one of Scottish wool. Her hand caressed the fabric.

The third day they began to approach Cornwall, through the lovely Devon countryside, browned now after the autumn chill and winter's heavy hand. A few snowflakes began to fall, and then more, swirling down in ever-thickening clouds.

"We'll be home by evening," encouraged Leah, looking out at the snow apprehensively.

After stopping for luncheon, Sonia said to the coachman, quietly, as he helped her into the carriage, "We will come to a fork in the road soon. Do not take the road to Fairley— take the southern fork, to the left."

He stared at her, his grave face crinkling with worry. "But my lady—"

"The *left* fork," she said firmly. He sighed, and looked at Leah.

"Now, my lady, wherever will we be going?" asked Leah, reproachfully, her dreams of a warm bed fast fading.

"You will see," said Sonia.

They took the left fork, and began following the coast road. On their left, the seas roared against black rocks, across the sands, sending up their billows of spume into the snowy air, until one could scarce tell where the ocean waves left off and the snows began. The skies seemed to open up and pour out the fleecy white flakes, huge flakes that foretold a heavy snow.

"It's going to be a bad storm," murmured Leah, glancing hopefully at her mistress.

"We'll be there by dark," said Sonia, staring out at the sea.

How dark it looked, how menacing. How much better it would have been if she had gone down in that sailing vessel which had brought her back to England! Yet—yet she had had a few more months with Alastair before . . .

They began to come to a few small villages perched precariously on the rocks—stone houses where a few fishermen spread out nets, with a few small boats resting on skids against the time when men could go out for the catch. They passed one village after another. Sonia began to watch carefully from the window.

Finally, just after passing one village more desolate than the others, she called out to the coachman. "Take the lane to the right!"

He turned off obediently. The horses had a hard time tugging the great coach along the frozen ruts of mud. The barouche lurched from side to side, then came to a halt.

"We are stuck!" said Leah. It was the final blow to her.

Sonia tugged at the handle. The coachman got down, opened the door for her, and lowered the steps. Sonia got out to see the lights of the nearby cottage as its door was flung open.

"Well, it's Miss Sonia!" cried a friendly voice. Sonia ran up the few steps to be enveloped in the arms of Rosa Bartel. "My dearest child, whatever are you doing here?"

Sonia held her off, to beam down at the rosy cheeks, the bright eyes, the white hair of her former nanny. "Oh, dearest Rosa, I had to come to you," she said simply.

"Come in, come in, all of you," called out Rosa. " 'Tis a small place, but there is room for you all!" She blessed them as they came in, recognizing Leah. "Dearest Mrs. Stein, how good to see you! And you have brought me my baby girl safely!"

Sonia sighed with relief to be taken to a tiny room up the narrow stairs that wound to the second floor. The simple bed was just what she needed, along with the sound of the sea from the windows. When she had seen the cottage years ago, it had been rose-covered. The birds had been singing in the trees, and the sea had been blue and friendly. But the cottage had been by the sea—it knew bad times as well as good—the creaking of its boards against the winds, the smoke from the

236

chimney billowing into the rooms when the snow gusted. . . . .

And she was alone here, with only her two dearest friends who would not betray her. Here she would wait for her child in peace and quiet, away from the bellowing and fury of Alastair and his horrible accusations.

Many years ago, after Sonia had grown too big for a nurse, she had bought for her the home Rosa wanted—a cottage on the coast of her native Cornwall. Now it would be Sonia's refuge.

Alastair returned home to London on a cold rain-lashed day in mid-February. He entered the house to be met by the news that Sonia had departed.

Edwina told him hopefully, "The footmen who escorted her part of the way told me she took the road to Cornwall. I think she has gone to Fairley."

His scowl cleared. "Yes, yes, good. I will follow her. She has always liked Fairley. We shall clear up our differences there."

He paused only for a change of clothes, an overnight stay, and a change of horses. Then was off again. But three days later, at Fairley, he was aghast when Mrs. Pendennis told him Sonia was not there, and had not been there at all.

"But where can she have gone?" he asked.

He fumed, returned to London, and went straight to Meyer Goldfine. The elderly man was nodding before his fire when Alastair was shown in. He started awake.

"Dear me, dear me, how pleasant to see you," beamed Meyer. "And do you bring Sonia with you?"

The innocuous question loosed a storm on his head. "She has left my house and home!" roared Alastair. "And I mean to find her and haul her home again! How dare she leave me!"

"Leave you?" Meyer's frail face turned even more pale. "Oh, no, she would not leave you!"

Alastair had to look through the whole house before he was convinced that Sonia was not there. Edwina had wisely not obeyed her sister-in-law's commands to remove her possessions from Alastair's home. Sonia's own apartment still contained her unused drawing board, dried paints, a canvas tacked to a frame, untouched for months.

Alastair ran his hands through his hair, settled his hat once more, and was off to confront Jacob Goldfine. Jacob had heard rumors about Sonia, and was as coldly angry as Alastair was hotly furious.

"No, I do not know where Sonia is," he said for the hundredth time, planted solidly before Alastair. "No, you shall not search my house. Sonia is not here. I wish she were, for I should protect her from you. I was against this marriage from the first—I knew it would not work!"

"Oh, you did, did you!" roared Alastair, quite frightening Beryl, who was nervously trying to sew. "You have gall enough for a legion! Is she hiding in this house? Haul her out, I say!"

"She is not here, my lord, I assure you," Beryl said quietly. She stood up, put her hand gently on Alastair's arm. "She is not here. We do not know where she has gone. We have asked around, discreetly. None of her relatives and friends have seen her. I am so worried about her."

Alastair reluctantly believed her, and turned on Jacob again. "I mean to have the truth about your little jaunt with her, though," he said threateningly. "If I have to call you out —I will know!"

"And if I have to knock you down and throw you out of my house, you shall not know!" bellowed Jacob, his cheeks red with rage, his black beard bristling.

"Jacob—my lord! I beg you, do not quarrel! It will not bring Sonia back!" cried the distressed Beryl.

Alastair, fuming, left the house. During the next days and weeks, he questioned everyone who might know about Sonia. Disregarding the gossip, the snickers, or the real concern of Lady Barnstable and others who respected Sonia, he stormed about London, trying to find out where Sonia was hiding. No one knew, or would tell him.

He was quite distracted, and he grew thin and even more bitterly touchy. Edwina tried to comfort him, Henrietta did not. His younger sister said, "If you had not flaunted your mistress before her eyes, she would not have left! How could you, Alastair? If any man treated me so, I should scratch his face!"

He flushed, swore, but she faced him out. "She is not my mistress," he finally admitted sullenly. "She has gone with Sir Philip Ryan, and I wish him well of her! A more greedy bitch I never met. I have not . . . been . . . with her since —well, my marriage."

"Does Sonia know?" asked Henrietta practically, to Edwina's well-bred horror. Ladies did not discuss such matters.

"She should know! I have been faithful to her—"

"I think you had better tell her straight out," said the admirably prosaic Henrietta. "I don't think she does know. She said you meant to divorce her and marry Mrs. Porter. Of course, she was very angry. She has as bad a temper as you do, Alastair."

That did not help. He raged off to his study, to cross off his mental list the last of the names of those he thought might be hiding Sonia. Then he returned to Meyer Goldfine's house to see if the uncle had had any word of her.

"She is not found?" asked her uncle. He seemed even more frail that March day, huddling under his velvet robes. "Dear me. Where could the girl have gone? She was always so obedient. I well recall how mature she seemed when she first came to us. She entered the house, leading her father by the hand, a child of under ten, saying, 'Here, Papa, here is your brother. He will take care of you,' and she put his hand in mine. My poor brother, his mind was almost gone, he was so distracted. Sonia, she had to think for them both, getting them out of Vienna. We smuggled them to London—"

"Where—is—she—now?" Many other times, Alastair had been fascinated to listen. Now, he wanted only to find his wife. And to know the truth about her . . .

"I do not know, my lord," said Meyer, leaning back, eyes closed. "I do not know. My poor dear Sonia."

The maid, unasked, brought in a tea tray. The motherly woman poured it in silence, served a cup to Alastair and to Meyer. The fragrant brew soothed Alastair, calmed him a little.

"I must know where Sonia went those three months," he said finally. "I am almost out of my mind with it. We have quarreled over it again and again. Then that letter from the Portuguese man—that did it. I could have struck her!"

Meyer looked more alert. "She—had a letter from someone—in Portugal?" he asked. He frowned.

"Yes, a bold arrogant letter," said Alastair, growing hot just thinking of it. "She was furious that I had read it. He asked her if she had yet left her husband! If she went to him —" He clenched his fists, wondering how soon he could take ship for Portugal.

Meyer moved his thin hand over his face. "No, no, she would not. I felt sure the marriage would be well," he said sadly. "You seemed so well suited. She is of such an intelligence, my Sonia, and of such beauty, grace, and integrity. I knew you would come to love and admire her."

"I do," said Alastair, and his shoulders sagged. "I do love her, I do admire her. But, my God, how much must a man endure? She will not tell me the truth about that three months' absence. And she has left me!"

"She will return," said Meyer hopefully.

"She told me she was expecting my child. I asked her if it was that of another man. I asked her whose child it was!" cried Alastair, angry again, his blue eyes flashing.

"You did not!" gasped Meyer. "You said that to Sonia— the soul of honesty and virtue—"

The words stung. Alastair raged, "Then if she has such honesty, why will she not tell me where she went? You know —Jacob knows—why can't *I* know?"

"And she is to have a child," murmured Meyer, his eyes glowing. "She must return!" He seemed to meditate deeply. "Alastair—my lord—you must go to Nathan Rothschild."

"She is involved with another man?" asked Alastair, aghast.

Meyer managed a feeble chuckle. "No, no, but he knows the truth. Only he can tell you. Wait, I will write a brief note and send it to him by your hand." He struggled to get up. Alastair stopped him, and brought pen, ink, and paper to him.

Meyer scrawled a few words, folded the paper, and put the address on it. "There, take that to Mr. Rothschild. See him privately, using my name. Then, tell him the situation, and see if he will tell you the story. I cannot, for my lips are sealed."

The coachman did stare when Alastair directed him to the counting house of Nathan Rothschild. He did not think his master was in the suds again. He had not been near a gaming house these months. Still . . . He set the horses in motion, and they went into the City.

Alastair had to cool his heels in the outer room of the Rothschild house for a good half-hour, which did not improve his temper. Finally he was admitted to see the man Meyer had sent him to.

He found a plump, shrewd man with red hair, a sagging lower lip, a bulbous nose, and sharp eyes. The man nodded briefly to a chair, not bothering to rise from his desk. He continued to scribble. A clerk took the message away, and shut the door. Mr. Rothschild leaned back in his chair.

"Well, my lord?"

Alastair handed him the note. "From Mr. Meyer Goldfine," he said, and watched the man's face anxiously. This man held the secret, but what could that be?

"I can tell you nothing," said Mr. Rothschild brusquely, waving him away.

"Indeed, sir, you damn well better tell me the whole story," said Alastair, his chin going up. "I have hunted all over London for my wife, and Cornwall as well. I have asked a hundred people where she is, and no one will even inform me where she went those three months last summer. I will know the truth before I leave this office!"

Mr. Nathan Rothschild studied the firm chin and blazing blue eyes of the man before him. "Hmmm," he said. "And why do you wish to know? You do not trust Sonia Goldfine? Hmmm?"

Alastair bit his lips, and now he looked more like a troubled, haunted young man. "We have not trusted each other," he admitted. "She believes I have continued an affair with—another woman. I have not. I believe she is too fond of her cousin, Jacob. Her uncle swears by her virtue. My God, what can I believe, especially when she is to have a child and has disappeared?"

The older man frowned, stared down at his desk. "You

have a service record, I believe," he said, abruptly, after a silence.

Stranger and stranger. Alastair patiently told his rank and regiment, his years of service.

"Hmmm. And you love your country, and would not betray her?"

"You need not ask, sir!"

"No, I believe not. Well, your wife, Lady Fairley, also loves and honors her adopted country, England. She has done what she believed best to help her, in a noble and courageous way."

Alastair stared. This was not at all what he had expected. "I—do not follow you, sir! What do you mean?"

The blue good-humored eyes finally softened their shrewdness. He looked more kindly at Alastair. "Well, well, I see I must tell you the story. Only, it must go no further than this room. You are not to discuss it with anyone, not to speak to anyone but your wife concerning it. Is that understood?"

Alastair nodded.

"Your word, man!" said Nathan Rothschild.

"My word, sir, as a gentleman, a member of the House of Lords, and an officer—"

"Yes, yes. Well, you see, Wellington was in much need of gold and specie to pay his troops on the Peninsula. The Treasury attempted to send money to him," said Nathan Rothschild, in a lower tone. "Ships were sunk. Coaches were stopped. The money did not get through. I went to the Treasury and offered my services and that of the House of Rothschild. For a small percentage, I would guarantee—guarantee! —that the gold would get through to General Wellington."

Alastair felt more and more cold as the calm detached voice continued. His wife, his Sonia, to be involved in this scheme! This horribly dangerous scheme!

"I have devised various methods of getting the gold through. I shall not divulge them to you, of course. You need only know that I had planned with Jacob Goldfine to go with his good wife on a coach through France to Spain, and then to Portugal. Mrs. Goldfine had recently borne a child, and she was not strong. It might have killed her if she had gone. The trip was rugged and dangerous. Also, I had met Lady

Fairley—she had the necessary quick intelligence, and the knowledge of French, Spanish, and Portuguese. When she was asked to go, she did not hesitate—though she risked her life—and her marriage. You see, she does love her adopted country very much," and the tone was ironic.

"She went on that—very—dangerous—adventure?" Alastair felt light-headed, as though in a fever, but his hands were clammy cold. Sonia, in such danger . . . And when she returned, she had been so thin, so ill . . .

"She went. They took one of my ships by night and landed in northwestern France, to take a coach loaded with gold and specie down through France into Spain. They were met, and helped, but of course, it was dangerous, and full of hardships. They did get to their destination. They met Wellington and delivered the gold and specie. The British soldiers were paid, and soon after, they defeated the French in the Battle of Bussaco. Mr. Goldfine and Lady Fairley then proceeded to Lisbon, with the aid of some Portuguese guerrillas—among them Paulo de Mondego. I would appreciate it if you did not repeat his name. We still use his aid in getting the money through." The dry voice finished, and he was still, contemplating Alastair's face.

"How could you—how could you—use my wife—in such a manner? It was intensely dangerous for her—"

"She agreed of her will," said Mr. Rothschild.

"She will never go again!" flashed Alastair.

"No, of course not, she might be recognized," said the financier, with an ironic smile, pressing a bell. "You may go now. I will not forget that you have promised to keep silent about all of this!"

Alastair went to his home, to lock himself in the study for hours. He paced the floor, he wiped his wet forehead. That Sonia had done this—and kept loyal silence—no matter how he taunted and attacked her! That she had dared—that she had performed such a courageous brilliant act. . . . He balanced pride in her against fury with the men who had involved her in the scheme.

When he left the room, he felt himself to be a changed man. Edwina eyed him apprehensively as he went quietly about the house, scarcely speaking. Henrietta was frankly worried, it was so unlike him. Maurice thought he had a fever, and should be bled.

Only Meyer Goldfine seemed to understand. Alastair could not bear the bright chatter and frivolity of society that month. He often went in the afternoon to talk with Meyer Goldfine about Sonia's youth, her early childhood, and from there to the history of the Jewish people, philosophy, and religion. From there they drifted to talk of events in politics, of the Regency Act which had been passed in early February, to the amazing hold that the Prince Regent had on the loyalty of his subjects, and the good he could do for the Jews in Europe.

Alastair began to appreciate Meyer's intelligence and humane qualities, his ambitions for his people, even the use he had made of Alastair and of Sonia in marrying them. In turn, Meyer realized that the young man had grown up, that he could do the Jews active good in Parliament and in society, and that his feelings for Sonia were deep and true. He thanked God every night for that, and added a hope that Sonia would return soon.

March roared out, and April came in, and the weeks went on. The flowers bloomed in the gardens of London, the sellers of lavender thrust their scented bouquets in Alastair's face as he strode briskly through the streets to the home of Meyer which was Sonia's townhouse. He always hoped for news, and was always disappointed.

For April came and went, and still no word came from Sonia.

Chapter
20

ALASTAIR'S mood continued grave. He devoted more time to his duties in Parliament, giving two speeches which were well-received in the House of Lords. Edwina continued to be his hostess, though her plans for marriage to Ralph Hastings were going ahead. They planned to marry in mid-summer.

Society held little appeal anymore for Alastair. He was rarely seen at fashionable gatherings, rarely at balls. He sent Maurice to escort his sisters. Only Lady Barnstable was able to get him with any regularity to attend her dinners. *She* had liked and appreciated Sonia; he could talk to Henrietta's godmother about Sonia frankly.

Sir Philip Ryan had tired of Daphne Porter's demands on him. She was now under some other gentleman's protection. She was cut by many in society, for they considered her coarse, and her affairs occasioned gossip.

Alastair returned early one day to his townhouse to find a messenger waiting for him. He took the brief note from the man and read, *I pray you, come to me, my dear lord. It is urgent. Meyer Goldfine*

As the scrawl was shaken and uncertain, Alastair feared the man had become gravely ill. Without delay, he told Edwina, and set out in his carriage which had not yet been put in the stables.

At Sonia's townhouse he went inside, and was shocked at the pallor of Meyer Goldfine and the shaking of his limbs. He was crumpled into a deep armchair, the black of his garments setting off the fragility of his white hands.

He begged the old man not to rise, and sat down near to him.

"Forgive me for sending for you so abruptly, and for not going to you myself," quavered Meyer.

"No, no, it is my pleasure to come to you. We have not talked for a week," said Alastair, wondering if it would not be amiss to send for a doctor.

"It is this letter—you must read it—" The old man started to hand it to Alastair, then held it back. "No, I forget. It is in Yiddish, you will not comprehend. I must read it to you."

Alastair contained his patience. He was learning patience the hard way. It was difficult for him, like an unfamiliar yoke which must be endured in this life. Matters did not always go the way he wished—events would not proceed on order—people did not act predictably—one must wait, watch, and be patient. He leaned back with a sigh, sitting up sharply as Meyer continued.

"The letter is from a woman named Rosa Bartel. She was the nurse of my dearest Sonia. When she became older, Sonia bought a cottage for her on the coast of Cornwall, near the village of—let me see—" He peered at the letter and read out the name slowly. "The cottage is just beyond the village. You take the turn to the right lane. She has lived there long enough—you will not have difficulty in finding it."

"Is Sonia there?" asked Alastair sharply.

Meyer nodded, and began to read.

My dear Mr. Goldfine:
  I write to you in distress. Sonia begged me to keep silence, and I did for a time. But now I fear for her life, and for that of her unborn child.
  My dear little Sonia is so ill and despondent. She was

ill much of the winter. Our weather was bad, and she did but sit at the fire and weep. If there is aught you can do, I pray you to do it. Does her husband not care about her? I beg your advice. She is too weak to be moved, or I would bring her to London to the physicians.

I beg pardon for disturbing you, but if you can offer some advice, I shall be most grateful.

Your faithful,
Rosa Bartel

Meyer set down the letter, and removed his narrow-framed glasses to peer at Alastair, who had risen to walk about in agitation. "Will you go to her?" he asked wistfully.

Alastair went over to the desk, rummaged for paper and pen. "What is the name of the woman again? And the village and directions?"

Meyer told him, and Alastair wrote it down. "I will go at once," he said resolutely.

As he went toward the door, Meyer said, "I beg you, Alastair, be gentle with her! She is a proud woman, she has been most hurt. It is my fault, I know, that I encouraged the marriage—"

Alastair came back to take the frail fingers and press them gratefully. "Do not fear. I love her, and will take care of her. That does not mean I shall not scold her for leaving me!" Laughing, he raced out of the house.

Alastair went home to pack trunks of his clothes and blankets. He ordered the heavy carriage be made ready. He had been thinking rapidly: he would take Sonia to Fairley. It was not far from Rosa's, and the doctor there was as good as any in London.

Edwina followed him about anxiously. "Have you discovered Sonia? What are you doing? I beg you, Alastair—tell me!"

He kissed her cheek and said gaily, "She is discovered! And I shall take her to Fairley. Tell Maurice that I shall expect him to look after you all, and I will write when we are settled again."

She looked much relieved, and said, "Give Sonia our love. Tell her we wish her well, and hope to see her soon."

It was evening when he set out, but the spring night was bright and cloudless. They traveled much of the night, then stopped to change horses and eat at an inn.

On the morning of the third day, they arrived at the Cornish village, and went through it. It was charming—with young roses clambering the stone walls and the scent of the salt sea in his nostrils. The waves were blue, the sun golden-yellow. It looked like a bright new world to Alastair. He was humming as he rode along, and broke out in song from time to time in his off-key, happy way. The coachman gave the valet a nudge and nodded wisely.

As it passed through the village, the fisherfolk gazed curiously at the barouche as it lumbered along the cobblestoned streets, up hill and to the country lane outside. He noted the women with their laundry baskets under their arms. Out at sea the bright sails of the ship sparkled as the men cast their nets for the daily task of fishing.

He had the coachman turn into the country lane, and discovered at once the huge barouche gathering dust in the grassy yard behind the small cottage. He nodded in satisfaction. Sonia must be here!

He sprang down, forgetting the weariness of the long ride, eager as a boy to see her. Someone came from the cottage— an older woman with white hair and rosy cheeks, peering at him.

"Mrs. Bartel? Where is Sonia!" he demanded.

She stared, then began to smile, glanced at the crested panels on his carriage, and curtsied with her white apron fluttering. "Oh, my lord, you came! I am so happy!"

He remembered his manners enough to introduce himself, then asked again, "Where is Sonia?" He glanced beyond her to the small rose-covered stone cottage, the prettily small-paned windows, and the curtains that blew in the breeze at the two open windows.

"She went down to the sea this morning, with Mrs. Stein. They often walk along the sands, now that the weather has turned fine," said Mrs. Bartel simply. "I told her that she must get out into the air and gain her strength. But she does not eat much, not enough for herself and the child. You will encourage her, my lord?"

"Yes, yes, I will go look for her." He gave orders to the coachman to unload one of his valises and take the rest to the village. They could wait for him there in an inn where they might get lodging. He thought the tiny house would not hold them.

Then he made his way happily down the cliff path to the beach. Stones, dislodged by his heavy boots, rolled down the path, making a light crackling sound as he walked. Alastair saw the strolling pair before they saw him.

Sonia was wrapped in her Scottish blue-green wool cloak, her arm in that of Leah Stein, as they slowly trudged along the sandy beach. They were gazing out at sea, Leah's free hand lifted to point to a sailboat in the distance. Alastair strode closer, watching eagerly for the expression on Sonia's face when she saw him.

Leah spotted him first, and gave him a great smile of unqualified approval, a rare thing for her to do. "There, now, here is my lord!" she cried happily.

The two women stopped, Sonia's head lifted. Alastair stared at the white face, the darkly shadowed gray eyes. She gazed at him, as though in a dream, not uttering a word.

Leah nudged her forward. Alastair came forward to meet her, but could say nothing. His arms closed about her. He felt the slight bulk of her figure, growing big with the child. He felt suddenly overwhelmed by the fact. She was going to have his child! She was ill because of it, and his behavior . . .

He enfolded her in his arms and rocked her back and forth. "Sonia, Sonia, Sonia," he said.

Leah discreetly retreated up the cliff path, leaving them alone.

"Oh—Alastair," said Sonia, very faintly.

He loosened his grip, to tip back her face and gaze down at her. "My dearest Sonia. How could you leave me? I have fretted this whole time! I have gone mad, storming about London and raging at everyone, but no one could tell me where you were."

She tried to pull back even more, but he would not let her

go. "You—you wish a divorce?" she asked dully. "I will sign any papers—"

"No, you goose!" he said huskily. "I want you, and my child! What a bad-tempered pair we are! Our child will be a demon, I am sure! Oh, my dearest Sonia, I have so much to tell you!"

The wind whipped in off the sea in a sudden chilly burst.

"I will take you back to the cottage presently," said Alastair, and drew the Scottish cloak carefully about her. "Oh, my darling, you are so thin and pale! We shall take great care of you!"

"I cannot come back to you," said Sonia, with an effort.

"Of course you must," said Alastair. Then he relented. "Come, sit down with me. There is a bit of sand here that looks clean. We shall shelter in the lee of the cliffs."

He drew her to him, and they sat down beside a great gray rock, which had been whitewashed and scrubbed clean by the ceaseless tides which swept the coast. He put his arm about her, drawing her close, and put her head on his chest. He was content—he had her at last, he had found her. But there was much to clear up. She would not be happy until he explained.

"First of all, I did not go to—the hunting lodge in Scotland. I was furious, but as the days passed, and the journey took me further from you, I regained my temper. Halfway there, I turned about and came back to London. But you had fled!"

"Mrs. Porter was probably furious," said the cool, haughty voice of his wife.

He smiled over her head. "I don't know, I haven't seen her," he said blithely. "We parted long ago, before my marriage to you, Sonia, and that is the truth of it."

She was silent, but he still felt her slight resistance when he attempted to draw her closer.

"I see I must tell you the whole of it," he said, more quietly. "When I first returned from the service, I was—a bit wild. Mrs. Porter seemed amiable, charming. I did—make her my mistress. I was enchanted by her . . . I could not see her true nature, her greed. Then—I met you, and we married. I swear to you, Sonia, by all I hold dear, that I did not . . . have . . . her again after our marriage. She turned

250

o Sir Philip Ryan to pay her many bills. She has now drifted on to some other poor chap."

"Oh," said Sonia, and unexpectedly added, "that was why you didn't want Edwina to receive him!"

"Exactly," he said, encouraged by her quick understanding. "I thought if he had true regard for Edwina, he would not become enamored of Mrs. Porter. After all, he had met Edwina first, and had the opportunity to come to know and appreciate her sweet nature. If he *then* turned to Mrs. Porter, he was a fool, and I shan't have my sisters marrying fools."

Her body seemed to relax a little against his. Encouraged, he went on.

"It seems to me from the first, my love, we did not trust each other. That has been the cause of much heartache, and our pride was such that we could not speak frankly about this. I hope in the future we shall always deal honestly with each other."

"But—I cannot tell you—about those three months," said Sonia, in a mournful tone.

"No, but I know about it," he said quickly. "You must forgive me, darling, in your generosity. I was so furious, so upset by your leaving, I went to your uncle, and Jacob, and anyone I could think of. Jacob threatened to throw me out, your uncle insisted his lips were sealed. However, your kind uncle finally sent me to Nathan Rothschild."

"You—*know*?" she whispered.

"Yes. He told me the whole story. Oh, Sonia, how could you have consented to such a mad undertaking? Your courage is as strong as your wilfulness! If I had known what you contemplated—" He paused and shuddered. "When I think of that dreadful journey, the dangers you encountered—I have had nightmares about them."

"I had to go, for Beryl could not," said Sonia. "And you —you did not seem to care—about me—"

He caressed her soft thin cheek, pressed back a lock of dark hair that had escaped her lace bonnet. "I understand, my love. But it must never, never, never happen again! There must be truth between us at all times. And I shall never let you risk such a journey again. No matter how worthy the cause," he added grimly.

"I am so glad—that you know. I could not tell you, Alastair," she said, with such wistful sadness that he had to tilt up her face and kiss her lips. He touched them with tenderness and gentleness. She seemed so fragile she might break.

"So—it will all be straightened out between us," he said happily. "I shall take you to Fairley and you shall recover there, and our child will be born there. Will that make you happy, my love?"

"But you do not want—my child," she whispered.

He frowned. "Not want it? What nonsense is this?" he snapped, forgetting his vow to be understanding and calm.

"Because—because—I am—who I am—"

"You are my Sonia," he whispered against her lips, and kissed her passionately. "I love you, I adore you, and you shall not leave me again! We shall have the child, and another, and another—"

Now her cheeks began to turn pink, and the heat burned in them. She glanced once at his blazing blue eyes, and then away, shyly—it could not be true! She had lived so long with the idea that he detested her, distrusted her, hated her. Could he possibly love her?

He was whispering his adoration in her ears, as though they were alone in the world and, in truth, they did seem to be. There was not another soul on the sandy beach. The nearest people were the fishermen casting their nets far out at sea, as the sails glistened in the morning light.

"I love you, I love every bit of you. When you are strong again, I shall show you how much! Oh, my darling Sonia, my lovely girl, I have missed you so much. Tell me, tell me you are willing to be my wife forever, and I shall be in paradise!"

She could not resist his ardent pleas. She put her arms shyly about his neck, although somewhat encumbered by the heavy cloak, and said, "Oh, Alastair, I have loved you so long! I do love you, but I did not dare to hope—"

"How long have you loved me?" he said, against her throat.

"Oh, years," she said dreamily.

"No, seriously, when—"

"When we met," she whispered. "I thought you were—like a prince! Someone in a story, someone I would never meet

gain—and when you danced with me, I thought we were
lone in the room, it was so beautiful—"

"Oh, my love, I adore you."

They whispered, and kissed, and kissed again until she
hivered in the cool breeze off the sea. He started up.

"But I must get you back to the cottage! You are not yet
trong," he said solicitously, lifting her very carefully to her
eet. Her cheeks bloomed with color, her gray eyes were lu-
ainous as he smiled down at her. But she was so thin, the
ark shadows under her eyes caught at his heart.

He put her carefully into the shelter of his arm, with his
ody between her and the wind off the sea. They walked
owly along the beach toward the cliff path.

"The cottage is very small," he said. "I shall find a room
t an inn nearby, and come daily to see you. Then when you
re quite strong again, I shall take you to Fairley. Mrs. Pen-
ennis will coddle you, and make sure you take no chances
ith yourself and the child. Oh—and Edwina sends her love.
hey will come down later in the summer."

"Did they—miss me?" asked Sonia wistfully, as he half-
fted her up the cliff path. His strong arm about her, his ar-
ogant voice softening as he spoke to her. Was she in a
ream?

"Miss you? They weep until I am half mad," he said.
And Lady Barnstable scolds me every time we meet. She is
ighty fond of you, you know. And Henrietta—what a tell-
g-off she gave me! Said my temper was as bad as yours,"
ad he gave a rollicking laugh she had not heard for months.

"And how is dear Maurice?"

"In and out of love, like a butterfly. One day he might be
 fortunate as to find someone like you, my darling," said
lastair. "Then he will be truly caught!"

"Caught!" she protested, in more normal tones. "Really,
lastair! How can you speak about it like that?"

He laughed back at her, his blue eyes shining, and bent to
ss the words from her lips. "Am I not caught?" he whis-
ered. "Caught in a silken web of love and desire? I cannot
ink of any woman but you—no one else can appeal to me.
want no one but you. Life was so gray and dull without
ou. I went often to your Uncle Meyer, we had long talks. I

know much about you now, Sonia! He told me about you
childhood, your youth. It was the one solace I had while yo
were gone."

"You spoke—often with Uncle?" She was in a daze. Sh
could not believe it. That Alastair had returned to her, tha
he loved her, that he had talked long with her uncle, and en
joyed their conversations. . . .

"Yes, and I have a feeling I would also like your cousi
Jacob once we stop threatening to knock each other down
said Alastair sunnily. "He is a very smart man. Did yo
know I gave two speeches in the House this spring? Yes,
did, and both were well-received! The Lords pounded th
benches and someone shouted approval."

"Oh, Alastair, how splendid!" She beamed up at him, hap
pily. His arm was close and warm about her, and she did no
feel the coldness off the sea. They strolled slowly along th
cobblestoned road to the lane, and then up along the grass
verge to the rose-vined stone house. He was telling her eagerl
the words spilling from him, all he had done and thought tha
winter—his talks with her uncle, his ideas about politics an
the Regent's doings, as though he had stored up everythin
to tell her.

"Have you been reading the gazettes? Someone wants
bring Wellington home, but I think it would be a vast mi
take. I think he will have the Frenchies on the run, and w
must support him with all we have. What do you think? W
cannot let Buonaparte have his way with us. He will conque
all Europe, then turn on us, won't he? It is in our interest
support the Portuguese and the poor Spanish devils—"

He went on and on, as they entered the cottage. Rosa Ba
tel had a fire blazing in her little stone fireplace in the fro
parlor. They settled down before it while she brought lu
cheon to them on trays.

Sonia did not feel weary at all. She was so close to Alasta
she could reach out and touch him. She could not be do
with gazing at him, as he munched hungrily on the slice
roast beef and the fresh homemade bread of wheat grain, an
drank the homely wine.

He looked weary, but at peace, his eyes sparkling, h

smile flashing at her. He was making plans. They would go to Fairley soon. They would remain there for the summer.

"When will the child come?" he asked her tenderly, turning to her and taking her hand.

"About the first of September," she said simply.

"Then we shall stay at Fairley for a time after that. I think if Edwina wants to marry her Ralph, she must do so alone, or come to Fairley for it. Eh? How about that? I think she will come to Fairley, for she will wish you to be present, if you are strong enough. He is a nice chap—we can talk for hours without fussing, though he knows his own mind, I'll tell you! We must find someone splendid like him for Henrietta, a good fellow. She is a fine girl, and growing up. Seems more sober and sensible than she did," and he went on and on, her hand clasped securely in his big hand, his thumb caressing her palm.

She was happily settled before the fire, watching the blaze as the wood crackled and flared up. His hand was holding hers, he was making happy plans for their future together. She felt at peace, really at peace, for the first time since their marriage.

He loved her! She could scarcely believe it. Her prince in shining armor loved and adored her. He said so bluntly, looking at her as though he could make love to her right then and there.

Sonia felt as though she could lean against his strength forever, that he would be tender and adoring, watching out for her always. After all the turmoil, the quarreling, the pride, and the anguish of their marriage, they were at peace, and one in their desires.

"I wonder how soon we may go to Fairley," she said dreamily.

"As soon as you can travel safely," he said, leaning to kiss her cheek. He drew her head to his shoulder. They sat on and gazed into the fire. "You will be stronger soon," he told her firmly—and she took that as an order—one she would be happy to obey! She wanted to be strong and well, ready for the child when it came. Ready for the demands of her position as his wife, ready to love and give and help him all she could.

"My dove, my dear," he whispered, and turned her face up to his. His lips came down on hers, so carefully, so tenderly, that she could have wept with happiness. But there was no more need for tears or sorrows. They were together again, and for always.